DYING FOR HER: A COMPANION NOVEL

Book 3

KORY M. SHRUM

Dying for Her (2nd edition)
ISBN 978-1-949577-0-20
Copyright © 2014 Kory M. Shrum
All rights reserved.

DYING FOR HER: A COMPANION NOVEL

AN EXCLUSIVE OFFER FOR YOU

Connecting with my readers is the best part of my job as a writer. One way that I like to connect is by sending 2-3 newsletters a month with a subscribers-only giveaway, free stories from your favorite series, and personal updates (read: pictures of my dog).

When you first sign up for the mailing list, I send you at least three free stories right away.

If giveaways and free stories sound like something you're interested in, please look for the special offer in the back of this book.

Happy reading,

Kory M. Shrum

CHAPTER ONE

$\mathcal{I}$t should be illegal to tell a man when he will die.

"Caldwell kills you himself," Gloria Jackson says.

In her dank basement, she drops this on me. She's pivoted her body away from the long metal table used as her work bench, her sketch papers and pencils spread across its cold, metallic surface. She looks up at me from her chair, shows me the picture she's sketched.

Like any AMP, an analyst of necromagnetic phenomenon, she is only supposed to know the day of my death, not particulars. But this is a detailed fucking sketch if I've ever seen one. In the picture, my Python revolver is pressed to the side of Caldwell's head. In the background, a 1940s farm house is on fire. Other mysterious shapes pool around us like ghostly spectators. People? Animals? Whatever the hell they are, they send a chill up my spine.

My eyes fixate on the gun. This .357 magnum tells me everything. It's my lucky gun. If I were to take that revolver out of the steel box I keep it in, and press it to the side of a man's head, I would do it believing I was as good as dead.

When I lower the drawing, I see Jackson's face. The single yellow bulb swinging overhead makes her cheekbones shine. She waits for me to say something.

"Jim—" She uses the old familiar nickname. I haven't heard it in a while. God, if that doesn't add a sense of severity to the conversation.

"Gloria," I reply. In the ten years I've known her, I've called her by her first name only a few times. The furnace kicks on behind me, rattling awake. The house creaks above us, groaning under the weight of the evening hours.

She looks away first and lets the yellow pencil fall from her fingers and roll across the table top.

"I made a green bean casserole," she says and the metal chair screeches across the concrete as she stands up. "I've also got a six pack of Rogue."

"Thank God for small mercies," I say. I'm relieved she's going to let this lie for now.

Upstairs, I put a turkey leg on top of a heap of casserole and as promised, Jackson hands me a cold beer. Across from her at the squat card table, I turn the slick amber glass in my hand to read the label. A skeleton perches on a barrel, taking a shit for all I know, wearing what could only be described as a party hat made of someone's bones.

I rip at the hot turkey flesh with my teeth and the grease melts on my lips. "Dead Guy Ale," I read aloud and turn the label face out so Jackson can read it. "How fitting."

I burst into a loud laugh and she follows, unable to help herself.

"Death," I say, pointing at the little skeleton man. "Shitting on my beer. How fucking true is that right now?"

We laugh so hard tears rise in our eyes and they blur out Jackson's squash-colored kitchen. Her little table wobbles between us as we roll in our seats until the laughter dies away.

I lift the bottle again and Jackson clinks hers against

mine. "To the second loneliest holiday," I say. It is the best toast we have. We are soldiers and have been for a long time. There is no room for a family in this kind of life.

"It's been a wild ride," I say between gulps. Then I set the empty bottle on the table.

"It sure has been that," she agrees, inspecting the bones of her devoured bird with dark fingers.

"I thought I would see it to the end. Sorry I won't." It surprises me that I really am sorry about it. I didn't realize how sorry until I apologized to the one person who's been in this with me since the beginning and is probably just as exhausted as I am.

Jackson shakes her head. "Don't say that."

"All right." I shrug. "I won't say it, but I'm really sorry to leave you with this shit. The good guys were already in short supply."

She looks up then. I think, *no need to be a dick to her now.* Giving me the news couldn't be any easier than receiving it. I sigh. "I won't say it for a third time then."

I don't. In fact, neither of us manage another word for the rest of the night.

CHAPTER TWO

I stand in the dark outside Jackson's house and scheme. On one hand, I am surprised I've lasted this long. I've been stabbed, shot, tortured. Just about anything that can happen to a man in war, it's happened to this body. It is a miracle I even open my eyes in the morning. On the other hand, I can't believe it. Murdered? *Really?*

October 3.

Forty-five weeks from now, I'll be dead. The old survivor in me searches for the loophole, the clause, and the fine print. He is a weathered bastard and has been damn good at dragging me out of the trenches for the last 56 years. Old habits die hard I guess—just like old dogs.

Get the kid to replace you, the survivor says as callous as anyone willing to step on the head of a drowning man, if it means getting to the surface faster himself.

I sink onto the sagging stoop. My worn out boots—a great pair of Bates 922s—crunch dried leaves into powder, while Jackson's words play on a loop in my head.

"Caldwell kills you himself."

I fish pieces of fat out from between my teeth with a

toothpick and consider this while Jackson sleeps in an old, stained armchair in the living room, the blue TV light and game show voices as good as any lullaby. I'm not such a bastard that I'll wake her to talk about this. The tryptophan is the only reason she'll get a few decent hours of sleep tonight. Her relationship with the Sandman is about as shaky as my own, so my questions will have to wait.

What could I ask anyway? I saw it for myself, my gun pressed to Caldwell's head.

That is the clincher really.

If I can get that close, actually put the old Python to Caldwell's temple at long last, it would be the closest I'd managed in the ten years I've hunted him.

Ten years. Ten years since Memphis walked into my office and started all this.

I tilt my head back and look up at the sky. It is clear and I see a few of the brightest stars. My breath comes out hot, rising in white puffs.

Hell of a night, Thanksgiving, the day to be grateful. *And what are you grateful for, you old bastard?*

This beer. I pick up the beer and take another swig.

That the kid is still alive.

That I've still got 45 weeks, which is better than 45 days.

And I've a chance to finish what I started.

I pull my leather jacket tighter around me but I am unable to shake the cold. I lean my head way back and finish the beer. Then I go inside and put the empty bottle on the kitchen table beside the three I've already drained. I try not to make much noise as I do up the dishes with the pink sponge left by the sink, warming my icy hands in the hot tap.

When I decide that it is time to hit the road for the night, I peek into the living room one last time.

Jackson is still asleep in the chair. Her dark face calmer than I've ever seen it awake. I pulled the rainbow afghan off the back of the couch and drape it over her. Then, just before the television show fades to credits, I slip out the front door.

Sitting at the Harding Place and Danby red light, I send a text to Sullivan.

Happy Thanksgiving, kid.

Back at ya, boss. Nearby? Ally made ALL THE FOOD.

Maybe next time kid, already knowing this Thanksgiving will be my last.

Even dead guys need to eat, she quips. The little shit. But what she means as a joke rings heavy.

I am dead, by most accounts. It's been nearly two months since I faked my death. I needed the freedom to go deeper into my hunt and end Caldwell. I just didn't realize I had a deadline.

I park the Impala on the topmost hill at Mt. Olivet's cemetery. It is hidden enough by the large weeping willow above it to protect me from view. No cops checking the grounds with search beams, looking for punk kids, will see me standing over my own grave.

James T. Brinkley. Veteran and friend.

I stand there until I can't feel my face anymore, the icy wind pulling tears from my eyes, my hands cold and stiff again, even in my pockets.

Where would they bury me the second time, I wonder.

After all, this grave is full.

CHAPTER THREE

Friday, March 21, 2003

My head throbbed with a hangover. I'd already taken six aspirins and my gut was so full of rot I was starting to think the liver bleeding warnings on the label weren't for shits and giggles.

When you walk into the St. Louis FBRD office on Figaro Ave, you'll immediately see two long rows of desks—some immaculate, without a stray paperclip to be found, others looking more like the floorboard of my car. My own desk was somewhere in between the two extremes.

While most of the family men in our department were at church functions and family gatherings, heaping food onto paper plates, I spent my Good Friday at my desk, sorting through the case files I planned to follow-up that weekend.

I had two in particular. The missing girl had a depressingly thin file with only a picture, a few statements, interviews, and no leads. Then I had another file on Rachel Wright, also missing, twenty-four years old with a couple of interesting petty crimes to her credit. She stole a car when she was sixteen, a boat when she was eighteen, and was picked up for indecent exposure at twenty-two. The sooner I found both of these girls, the better.

If I had simply walked in, grabbed my folders and walked out, my life might have played out differently. If the aspirin bottle had come open on the first try, maybe I never would have met Jesse Sullivan at all—anything to take me away from my desk at that one pivotal moment.

"This is Mr. Memphis," Charlie said. He took the bottle from me, opened it with a single twist, and tapped two white pills into my shaking palm.

Charlie's eyes were puffy with dark rings beneath them and his chin shaggy with overgrowth. His beard was growing in white, adding to his Nordic appearance: bright blond hair, piercing blue, bird-like eyes, and pale skin that only made those dark circles more noticeable.

His expression wasn't friendly, but I wasn't entirely sure if it was about the hangover or something else. When Charlie heard that I left the service, he begged me to come help him build the FBRD, the Federal Bureau of Regenerative Death. *With your MP background you'll be perfect*, he said.

But when I took the job he'd probably expected me to stay sober.

"Just Memphis," the big guy beside Charlie said and extended his hand. I saw the deep line of a farmer's tan cut across his bicep, the skin beneath almost as white as the shirt. It was strange to see a tan like that in March. We shook. He wore a plain white T-shirt and jeans, the shirt clean with just a hint of yellow in the pits.

I cracked the aspirin between my teeth. "Brinkley. What can I do for you?"

"He wants to file a missing persons report," Charlie said.

They all want to file missing persons reports, I thought. I worked a couple of years overseas, then came back, and it seemed like everyone and their goddamn mother was missing.

Charlie walked away without saying another word and I watched him leave with the sense that he still wanted to talk to me, but hadn't decided what he wanted to say yet.

"It's my buddy, Eric," Memphis said and sat in the empty chair across from me. Memphis didn't fit so well and was forced to perch at the edge of his seat due to his immense size. He swept his sun bleached hair back with a beefy hand. "He never contacted me when he got out of the camp. He swore he would."

"All right. When did you last see him?"

"January 1, 1998. The day they released me from Jerome."

When people started to die, but didn't have the decency to stay dead, the public panicked. Riots, outrage and chaos ensued. So the government rounded up all the Necronites—those who were believed to be time-bombs—either sleeper cells or the result of some kind of deadly biological warfare—and sent them to detainment camps.

It wasn't until science caught up that we realized it was just a neurological disorder, NRD, where brain tissue sends a pulse throughout the body, reactivating its systems and healing itself.

Most of the missing person cases that crossed my desk were Necronites who'd been sent to the camp but never returned home—the missing girl, Maisie and the young woman, Rachel, were exceptions. Necronites yes, but too young to end up in the camps themselves because the camps closed five years ago. My fear was something worse than a detainment camp had happened to them.

"Maybe he got home, got busy, and forgot to call," I offered.

"No," Memphis said. His thick brows were overgrown, jutting down toward dark eyes. "That place was hell. He would've made sure I was OK."

"Maybe he decided he didn't give a shit about you," I said.

It was a bastard thing to say, but every booming word out of this farmhand's mouth tore my skull in half.

Memphis's jaw tensed. He had an Eddie Thomas kind of face, a sort of smashed-in-with-fists look, and I could tell he was trying to control himself. I had a feeling he didn't usually hold back.

"Eric is a man of his word," he said, his gaze steady and jaw finally unclenching. "He promised to check up on me and I promised the same. Something must have happened to make him break that promise."

"Why didn't you file a report sooner?" I asked. "You've been released over five years."

"I've been looking myself."

I snorted. "You a cop?"

"No." He clasped his hands together. "Just good at finding things."

"A search dog then."

The giant stood. "If you don't want to help me, just say so."

I nearly broke my neck trying to look up at him. "Relax. I'll find your guy." And when he looked unconvinced, I added. "Always do."

"That's what Lieutenant Swanson said." Memphis sat back down and placed a saucer-sized hand on each of his scuffed knees. "What do you need from me? What can I tell you?"

I'd heard enough stories about the camps to know it wasn't the Ritz, complete with room service. "Just tell me whatever you think I need to know about the guy and where he might've been going. If I have more questions, I'll ask. All right?"

The man rubbed the back of his head. "His name is Eric Sullivan. We were detained at the Jerome center. That's in Arkansas."

"I know it." I did. Mostly from its WWII history. When

they'd moved out the Japanese-Americans, they moved in the German POWs. But it closed in '44 before reopening in '80 during the NRD scare, almost twenty years after they put Hoover in the ground.

My mind wandered away from the history as I realized Memphis was still talking.

"—picked up in 1996, about a year before Eric. I wasn't adjusting well. I like to be outside. Been that way my whole life. On the day that Eric came, I hadn't see the sky for 412 days. You know what he said to me? "

My headache had edged away from my eyes a bit. I humored him. "What?"

"It's been raining for 413 days. You haven't missed anything." Memphis grinned a big good ol' boy grin. "A man is going through the worst time of his life and just arrived at the gates of Hell and here he was trying to cheer *me* up. But that's Eric for you."

I must not have looked enthusiastic enough because he added. "It was the first time I'd laughed since I'd got to Jerome. I don't know, maybe you had to be there to understand."

"How'd you die?" I asked.

"What?" The man's face colored as if I'd asked him if he wore boxers or tighty-whities.

"If you went to the camp, it means you died, then woke up and some asshole turned you in to the feds. So how did you die?"

"A tractor rollover," he said.

Of course you did, I thought but didn't say it. The aspirin must've kicked in.

"When did Eric get to the camp?"

"March 1997," he said.

"So you were only friends for a few months before you were released."

"About ten months. It was New Year's Day when they released me. But Eric wasn't with me."

"Why not?"

"When they closed all the camps, they let us go in batches," he said and laced his fingers.

It would have been impossible to release all the detainees at once. They'd be owed transportation at the very least. Compensation and a big fat fucking apology at best. They'd only be able to carry so many at a time, and for the sake of order they would let them go in groups. How'd you like to be the last bastard out of that shit hole?

I fumbled for a pen and found one. I tried to scrawl out the few details he'd given me so far, but the pen wouldn't write. "If you were separated, how did you know to plan to contact each other on the outside?"

Memphis clasped his hands together, then shrugged. "Everyone knew for months we were getting out. They told us at the end of October when the election stuff was in full swing. But they kept pushing back the actual release date. First we heard it'd be November. Then it was December."

"So you had time to kill. And he was released after you, but you didn't hear from him like you were supposed to."

"Yes, sir," he said. The sir hackled me. "So I tracked down his wife and kid but they haven't heard from him either."

I lifted up the folders for the missing girls and found a blue pen that actually worked. "He's got a wife and kid?"

"Not anymore. She remarried and popped out another. But they haven't heard from him. Cute though."

"Excuse me?" With a thick blue smear along the inside of my right thumb, I threw the leaky pen in the trash and resumed searching.

"His kid. Looks just like him. She'll be fifteen this year."

"A little young for you, don't you think?"

"Christ," he said. His jaw fell open and his brow furrowed.

"It's not like that. She was twelve or thirteen when I saw her. I was just saying she looks like him."

"Mmhmm." With a fresh black pen I scrawled just the essentials: the dates of their release and imprisonment, the location of the camp, and names.

"What are you writing?" he asked.

"What you've told me," I said. "You don't want me to forget, do you?"

"Well, no." He frowned. "What else do you need to know?"

"That should do it," I said. "But I need a way to get ahold of you in case I have more questions."

"OK," he said. He gave me a local number.

My head cleared just enough to ask a final question. "Before you go, I've got one more."

"Yeah?"

"The wife and kid. What can you tell me there?"

CHAPTER FOUR

44 Weeks

here isn't a night I don't dream about him.

Sometimes he will die in my arms, sometimes in the dirt. But however he dies, it is always some variation of this truth:

In the winter of 2002, I'd been asked to come to Afghanistan. Car bombs were going off every day and the higher-ups were looking for long-range solutions that would keep the casualties low. They liked one or two bodies to roll through the media every once in a while. It kept up the American spirit and fueled the anger and purpose for us being in that god forsaken place to begin with, but if our body counts got too high, well, that was bad for business.

So they'd called in snipers like me to sit in the hillsides which were more like mountainous mounds of dirt than any hills I'd seen back home, or anywhere else really, and shoot at anything that went where it wasn't supposed to.

Look out for women and children, they told us, even dogs. Insurgents had been favoring them lately. Understanding a threat in your head is different than seeing it on the ground, less black and white. When I saw Aziz, a 13-year-old boy for the first time, it was a whole area of gray.

I was above the western gate of a military base on the north side of town. It was mostly an epicenter for supplies near Pakistan, which was easier to travel through than Afghanistan. Convoys would go in and out at all hours of the day, while I lay crouched on the mountain above with my scope trained on the entrance. You can imagine how much time I spent laying there, in the dirt, hiding behind large rocks with my scope sweeping the desert.

When it got really boring, I would imagine all the ways in which I would likely have to use the rifle. I'd practiced the scenarios in my head the way a politician might rehearse his speech before the big day. Running through my strategies over and over again would keep me ready, prepared, I thought. What a joke.

When Aziz died, it was late in the evening. The sun had just reached that unbearable position in the sky where it shined into my eyes for about an hour before finally lowering itself enough that I could see again. The sun had just dipped enough to clear my scope when I saw him. The boy.

He was small for his age, which I learned later, and the second youngest son of a herder who lived in Kunar. Small and thin-limbed, not like our beefy hams back home, fattened on fast food and soda. Just a scrawny thing walking toward the entrance of the base.

At first I assumed he was lost. Why else was there a kid wandering around in the desert? Not just wandering. He swooped and staggered on those thin legs. I found out later it was the weight of the vest that made him walk that way. How far had he walked with it on his chest? We'd seen a few cars try pulling up to various American bases, before shoving women and children out their doors. They realized shoving people from vehicles put us on alert, and had switched to subtler approaches. Now they made them walk across the desert, arriving half-dead and delirious at our doorsteps.

"Hostile," someone yelled into my earpiece. I had a direct line to the guard below.

It startled me. I'd been watching the boy stagger the way a man might watch a snake dance.

"Hostile," a voice said again. "We can see a vest."

I lifted the scope to my face and felt the hot rim of metal brush my brow. I focused on the boy, and saw him and the vest for myself. But there was something wrong about it. I wasn't quite sure what it was that put me off, or what I saw that gave me pause, but I pressed the earpiece and said. "Are you sure it's active?"

"I see a flashing red light, goddamnit," the voice came clear and urgent. "Are you going to wait until he gets to the fucking door?"

I lifted the rifle again and found the boy in the scope, my crosshairs dissecting his skull. I was sure I couldn't do it. It didn't feel right. He was a kid. As I crouched there, watching the boy stagger, I gradually became aware of the growing chaos in my earpiece. Someone was yelling, barking an order. Voices grew and collided with one another.

The boy fell. He hit the dirt hard. No longer fighting against the vest, it brought him down. He wasn't moving. Not a muscle twitched and the smallest echo of the shot rang off the mountain.

I didn't realize I was the one who'd shot him until I eased my finger off the trigger.

CHAPTER FIVE

Saturday, March 22, 2003

I parked my '67 Impala outside a squat one-story house. The white wood had mud-scuffs along the side walls, and the windows were in need of a good clean after an assault of spring showers. A woman emerged from the house with a towel over one shoulder and a bottle of window cleaner in the other hand. I had one of those weird moments when you realize—*I was just thinking that*. Her chestnut hair was pulled up away from her face and her denim shirt was rolled up to the elbows.

"Mrs. Sullivan?" I asked and stepped away from the Impala. I extended my hand. "James Brinkley. We spoke on the phone. I'm real sorry to bother you, ma'am."

Expecting resistance, I laid it on thick. "I've only got a couple of questions. I won't take up much of your time."

"I told you today wasn't a good day." She didn't remove the rubber gloves to shake my hand, nor did she lower the spray bottle pointed at my eyes. I learned long ago not to underestimate a woman, however frail she might seem, so I thought it best to keep a safe distance.

"I know and I apologize, Mrs. Sullivan." I did my best to

look up at her with downturned eyes, but it was hard when I was a good head and shoulders above her. If that didn't work I could try to charm her another way, but I had a feeling it would backfire with Mrs. Sullivan. She had the look of a beautiful woman who was damn tired of being looked at like she was beautiful.

"Phelps," she said and turned away from me toward the first window.

"Ma'am?"

"Phelps," she said again. "I've remarried."

"Right." I put my hands in my pockets. "Mrs. Phelps, I have someone looking for your hus—first husband, Eric. Do you have any information about where he might be? I just want to talk to him. He isn't in any kind of trouble."

She laughed. "Of course he isn't."

I noticed the tension in her shoulders, the way they crept up toward her ears.

"Do you know for a fact he isn't in any kind of trouble?"

Her fist hovered over the glass, rag gripped tightly. "No. I do not know where Eric is." She squirted glass cleaner against the first window pane and handed me the bottle to hold. I remember the way she said his name.

Eric. With sarcasm and resentment sure, but a hint of something softer there on the end. The 'c' not quite as hard as it could've been.

When I didn't move or speak, she continued. "It's been six years since he died. *Un*died—whatever they are calling it."

"You were married for almost nine, correct?" I asked. I wanted to keep her talking because even if she didn't know where he was, she might know where to point me. So I tried to give the impression that I knew more than I really did because the public records surrounding Eric and Danica were few and far between. "How long had you known him?"

She stopped wiping the glass and turned those bright

green eyes on me. Those few stray hairs falling down around her face drew the eye to her jaw and neck. "My whole life. We both grew up around here and got all the way through high school in the same class, most years. We'd been just friends, good friends, until the summer of '87. He was married before, at 18 to his high school sweetheart, Shannon Flick. But they divorced a couple of years later."

"Is she still around?" I asked. Because this was the first time I'd heard of her.

"No, she moved to California or something like that."

"Any kids or anything to tie him to her?"

"Not that I know of," she said. "He let her go and stayed in town to work at his father's garage, another mechanic from a family of wrench-turners, that sort of thing. I was still working at Mabel's Grocer. Neither of us were really the college types. I thought about going to get my teaching degree, but I pretty much let that idea go when I got pregnant with Jesse."

"Eric's daughter?"

She nodded. Her voice had changed at the mention of Jesse. There was more to that, but I was making good progress on Eric, gathering up my next leads. I'd have to come back to the girl.

"She had a real hard time when he died," Danica said. "She hasn't really been the same actually."

"It's hard to lose a father," I said. I handed her the bottle again so she could spray the next pane. I let her make whatever assumptions she liked about me. She must have made some sort of assumption, because when she took the bottle from me she smiled.

"She had nightmares about him for the longest time after he died," she said, scrubbing at the glass. "She would wake up screaming, and we saw doctors about it, tried sedatives, but it didn't work. Then one night she woke me up and climbed into bed with me. She told me Eric was here, that he'd come home."

"Had he?" I asked.

Danica looked at her reflection in the dirty glass before speaking. "I know he's—not dead—but no, I didn't see him."

A strange sensation traced my spine as I listened to Danica. I recognized this feeling from cases in the past. I was hearing something important—even if I didn't know what the hell to do with this information yet, it meant something.

"I asked her if she'd seen him, thinking, 'Oh god, he's finally come back.'"

"Would that have been a problem?" I asked.

"I'd just had Daniel," she said, wiping at a smudge of dirt on her face. "Another man was sleeping in the house. What do you think?"

"Did you know he'd return?" I pressed.

"We got a notice that he would be released New Year's Day. I was at my mother's with the kids for Christmas, you know, so I wasn't sure if he'd come home or not. I don't know if you know, but I am the one who called and—reported —him."

I didn't say anything.

"It's not like I wanted them to come and take my husband away," she said, her voice rising. "They told me these people were sick and needed help. People were panicking about what it meant and everything was just—I didn't *want* him to be taken away, but I have a child, you know."

"But he was taken away."

"And I knew he might be angry at me for that, so I wasn't sure if he'd come home. But I wanted him to. I really did."

"Sure," I said and wondered if she was lying to herself as well as to me. "Is your daughter home now?"

"No." Danica's shoulders tensed again. "She's with her friend Alice, at the Methodist egg hunt. They're bound at the hip those two. But Alice is a sweet girl—and it gets her out of the house."

"Does she know he's alive?"

"No. I don't want her to know," she said, firm. "I told her he was dead."

As I looked at the back of her denim shirt, I realized the door to this conversation was closed and trying to pry it open wouldn't get me anywhere. So I handed Danica my card. "I've taken up enough of your time, Mrs. Phelps. I won't take up anymore. But if you think of something, anything else about Eric that might help me find him, I'd appreciate it if you gave this number a call."

"Is he in trouble?" she asked. She laughed. "Would you tell me if he was?"

"Like I said, a friend just wants to find him."

"What friend?" she asked. "I knew all his friends."

"Maybe you did," I said and turned toward the Impala. "But that was another life."

CHAPTER SIX

Saturday, March 22, 2003

I found the county morgue empty on the Saturday before Easter. The examiner agreed to meet with me, despite the holiday. I sure as hell wasn't going to complain about that, even though the spring air was freezing my balls by the time the skeleton decided to show up and let me in.

A balding, crooked man climbed out of his hearse and shuffled toward me. His face was gaunt with the pallor of a vampire and he looked like he would fall over any second. Someone needed to feed grandpa a good steak dinner.

"Brinkley," I said, forgetting again for the thousandth time to refer to myself as *Agent Brinkley* or even *Sergeant Brinkley*.

"Oscar Sampson, at your service."

"Nice to meet you, Mr. Sampson." I pointed at the hearse. "Are you a funeral director as well?"

"Funeral director, mortician, county examiner, all of the above. In small towns it is more profitable to be a jack of all trades, if you get what I am saying."

"I do, sir, and I'm real sorry to pull you away from your family on Easter weekend."

The old man croaked and cawed and I realized he was laughing. "Purely my pleasure, my dear boy."

"Why's that?" I asked and waited behind him as he turned the key in the lock, and when the door stuck, bumped it open with his bony hip.

"Easter is an excuse for the whole family to come home," he said.

"Isn't that a good thing, sir?" I stepped into the cramped dark room after him. A wave of dusty, stagnant air welcomed me. Cabinets full of medical textbooks and artifacts. A few jars, probably responsible for the rancid chemical smell, rested on shelves. A half-eaten sandwich lay forgotten on a desktop overflowing with papers. In the middle of the room were two large metal slabs for what I imagined to be bodies. That day, they were clean and bare.

As crowded and claustrophobic as the room might've been, at least it was warm.

"I had six children with my late wife, God love her," he said. "But all six of them are no better than shit on my shoe."

I clenched my teeth together rather than laugh aloud.

"The first two—my two eldest sons, John and Jack, fight about everything. This morning, they had a two hour diatribe about butter. Butter. 'It's good for you. No, bad for you. Margarine is worse. Is life worth living without a bit of cholesterol'—that sort of thing. When you get to be my age, Agent Brinkley, you simply cannot dream of giving up even one hour, let alone an entire precious morning arguing about a condiment."

"I understand, sir."

"My third, my first girl Denise, is a lawyer and is always pestering me about my will and financial assets. 'Are you ready to go?' she asks. 'Is everything prepared?' 'What are your wishes?' These would be splendid questions if she intended to send me on a Mexican cruise, mind you. But since it pertains to my death, it gives the impression that she has nothing better to do than wait for me to die," he said. "And maybe that is true. The fourth and fifth, Peter and Pauline, have launched and destroyed no less than ten business ventures, and neither one has reached their fortieth birthday. If even one makes it to retirement with their head above destitution, I'll be surprised. Not that I'll be alive to see it. If nothing else, I pray they soon discover the willpower not to tell me about the latest *opportunity*."

"Maybe the sixth isn't so bad?" I asked, rubbing a finger over the nearest surface and leaving a long clean line in my wake.

I wanted to know what the hell was causing all the dust. The particles in the air alone made my nose itch and eyes water.

He turned and placed the card I gave him with my name and number on the fridge for safe-keeping, his whole frame shaking in his oversized suit. "My youngest, Dolores—Lori as she likes to be called, has many preferences, let me tell you. She's smart and very kind and probably the most salvageable of all my offspring. But that one shall not be carrying on the Sampson line all the same, as she just brought home her girl-friend this weekend. Her *life partner*, she says. Tells us she prefers the terms *lesbian* and *alternative lifestyle*." He shook his head.

"At least there are no bodies this weekend," I said, searching for ground to settle on.

Sampson looked up at me with large, soulful eyes. "I much prefer the dead myself."

With nothing else to throw at him, I thought it would be best if I simply got to it.

"So, you found Eric Sullivan?" I asked.

"I find everyone, eventually," he said. "I'm the only mortician and medical examiner for this county. And Old George, in the next county over, isn't in the best of health, so I shoulder much of his work these days."

"So it is my understanding that a car collapsed on him over at his parent's garage, correct?"

"Indeed. One of the mechanical arms responsible for lifting the car broke. I'd heard it said that Sullivan Sr. was told to replace the lift arms no less than a hundred times. Look what it got him. Thousands of dollars' worth of repairs, loss of customers, and a dead son."

"How did they react to the news that he had NRD?"

The old man shrugged, and realizing he had pulled down the wrong book, replaced it on the shelf and chose another. "Who is to say? What happens in the home—that kind of thing."

"Are his parents still alive?"

"I'm afraid not," he said. "Sullivan Sr. had a heart attack about three years ago. And his wife contracted cancer later that year. I saw her the next spring."

I opened my mouth to ask another question but he cut me off. "Ah here we are. Sullivan, Eric. Died, March 5, 1997. Cause of death: massive thoracic contusions and internal bleeding." When I didn't appear to understand he added. "His chest was crushed by the car. Lungs and heart, *kah*-put."

"Lucky for him, his head was OK," I said and flipped open the small notepad I carried to take notes.

"Ah, yes, I'd heard that," the old man said. "They can't resurrect if they've injured their gray matter. No, Sullivan was lucky I suppose. Had the car fallen forward a bit more instead of straight down, I suppose he'd not have resurrected at all."

"Did you see anything unusual?" I asked, "When preparing the body?"

"No. That is why we buried him. Do you know that you must insist on embalming now? In the past it was simply par for the course but now, we must leave everyone *au naturel*. Just in case. So if you would like to be sure you are dead, Agent Brinkley, I suggest you request embalmment."

"But Eric didn't?"

"No, like most people, I assume he didn't know he had a choice. He was young enough that he wasn't expecting to die. Frankly, I am quite ready to go."

"So you're saying he was buried and then—?"

"Yes," he said. "Mr. Young is the one who heard the bell ringing, late one night up at Remmington's Cemetery. You know, because we've started running strings to the boxes again, safety coffins they're called, like in the old days, just in case." I nodded, having seen the air tubes and bell strings myself. "To hear Young tell it, it was a dark, cold night, and all he could hear was this frantic ringing—said it was the most haunting sound of his life. He still wakes up hearing that bell, or so says Mrs. Young. It was one of our firsts, you understand. When the dead start doing things they aren't supposed to, it stays with you, if you know what I mean."

A headache was starting to build behind my eyes and I knew that if I didn't take more aspirin or even better, have a drink, I wouldn't get much further.

"Anyone else I could talk to about Eric in the area? Any siblings?" I asked but had a feeling that Eric Sullivan didn't have much left to this old life that could lead me to his new one.

"He had an older brother, Dyson, who died in a motorcycle accident when Eric was almost out of high school."

"So no one?"

"Just the two wives and little girl that I know of," he said. "But it is hard to tell these days. I just read in *The Post* that a man had two entire families. Two wives, two sets of kids, two lives. And not one after the other, but both concurrently, for nearly 35 years. Can you believe it?"

"Sounds like a lot of work," I said.

The old man sighed and closed his book. "Yes, but maybe I would've had better luck with the second lot."

CHAPTER SEVEN

Saturday, March 22, 2003

*I*t was almost 11 P.M. when I got a call from Charlie. I'd driven back across the river into St. Louis after scraping the edges of Eric's hometown. I knew I wouldn't find out much more about Sullivan until I had the right questions to ask. But I had enough to get started.

I'd just unwrapped a Hearty Man meal and punched two minutes on the microwave when the phone rang.

"Brinkley," I answered, knowing it was the station, but not sure who was on the other end.

"I have a lead on your flasher," Charlie said.

First my mind went to a case I got during my brief stint as an MP twelve years ago—working cases while I healed a busted shoulder. A veteran used to go into the barracks naked and sing the pledge of allegiance. The mind is strange that way, in how it jumps back and forth through time without reason. It took me a moment to realize he was talking about one of my girls, my current case, Rachel.

"I'm listening," I said.

"Her mother says she came home a week ago to get her birth certificate and a few of her other important papers, like her passport. The girl told her mother that she needed them for a job. So I checked the system for any places who'd requested background checks on her. An insurance company in Jeff City had a hit. She also applied to a printing factory in the same area. Both turned her down, of course."

"What's wrong with hiring an attractive young woman who just happens to detest clothing?" I was trying to make a joke. Not to demean the girl, but because it was Easter night and here my friend was doing the grunt work for a case far below his pay grade.

I didn't need any more proof he was miserable.

He snorted. "I think it's the stealing they're worried about."

"Ah well, to each their own, I suppose."

"What is that sound?" he asked.

"My dinner. The little round table keeps catching, sorry."

"She's only hitting up jobs she isn't qualified for. So I compiled a list of places in the area that are hiring. Figured you could check them out and try to catch her going in or out."

"Brilliant work," I said, sticking a fork into my meal and finding the center frozen. Swearing, I stuffed it back into the radiation box. "Not sure why you even hired me."

There was a long pause before he spoke again.

"How about an O'Malley's bacon burger and a beer?" he asked.

Even if he wasn't one of my oldest friends and my superior, I knew I couldn't turn him down.

"No such thing as too much beef or beer," I said and stopped the microwave. "I'll meet you there."

CHAPTER EIGHT

Sunday, March 23, 2003

O'Malley's was surprisingly full. A large group of men dominated one end of the bar, a few singing loudly in heavily accented English. They were probably Irish. Clearly, the idea of getting drunk on Easter Sunday was a tradition for some. I wondered if it was a tradition they brought with them when the Irish came to build the railroads. Enough of the group had bright red hair to make me wonder.

Charlie sat at the bar, one hand open and waiting as the barman refilled his mug from the tap. When the beer was handed over, foam sloshed against the rim and Charlie bent his head to suck up the mess.

"Hey," I said and slapped his back before I climbed onto the stool beside him.

"Hey."

"So how long have we got? What's your bedtime?"

Charlie harrumphed. "It's hard to tell when I am supposed to be up or down these days."

"I'll buy your drinks then," I said and waved to the barman. "If we get enough in you, you should sleep just fine."

The barman responded to my wave and came back. He wore a white dress shirt under a black vest and white apron. Classy shit. He looked more like a maître d' than a guy in a pub pulling the tap.

I ordered a McSorely's Black and a bacon cheddar burger. If the barman judged me for not drinking a Harp, which seemed to be the beer of choice for much of O'Malley's clientele, at least he didn't give me shit for it.

I slapped the bar top a couple of times, rhythmically, in tune to the music seeping from the jukebox across the way, barely heard over the ruckus from the group at the other end of the bar and the loud TV over their heads. I felt good for the first time that day.

But Charlie's mood was dark—his face turned toward his beer as if he were looking for something in the bottom of that glass.

"What's going on, man?" I asked.

Charlie lifted his beer and took a long drink. Then he licked the foam off his lips. "Why didn't you tell me?"

I went still beside him. I wouldn't lie to him, but I also wasn't sure what he wanted me to say.

After giving me a once-over and not finding what he wanted, he looked down at the beer in his hands again. "I spoke to Lieutenant Brant today."

Here it comes, I thought.

"I know what he said," he began. "But I want to hear you tell it."

"What did he say?" I asked, looking up at the mirror behind the bar. My shoulders were slumped, my face dark. All the excitement I'd just relished over having the first beer of the evening was gone.

"That you shot a kid in a bomber vest and then totally lost your shit."

"Those were his exact words?" I asked. "*Totally lost my shit?*"

Charlie sighed. "No. He said you kept the body. That you refused to let anyone take it away from you and that instead, you wrapped it up like a goddamn Christmas present and hauled it off into the desert. Then you resigned the next day."

"His name was Aziz," I said. "Not *it*, or the *body*, or even *him*. Aziz."

Charlie looked horrified. "How do you know?"

"Because I took him home. I put him in his mother's arms and I put a gun in his father's hands and pressed the barrel to the side of my head and begged him to do the right thing."

I killed your boy. I'm sorry. I'm so fucking sorry. Blow my brains out, please. I beg you.

Charlie stopped drinking his beer. The burgers came, but neither of us moved to touch the hot food. The barkeep asked us something, probably about ketchup, but we didn't answer so he went away.

"Why would you do that?" he asked, quietly, so quietly I almost couldn't hear him over the TV and the cheering.

"There was no bomb. I knew by looking at the vest there was no bomb, but the MP said he saw a light and I pulled the trigger. The light was a fucking keychain, some touristy piece of shit that flashed and blinked. Aziz was a decoy, and I killed him."

"You can't be blamed for that," he said. "If it had been a bomb—"

"There was no bomb." I screamed and slammed my fist against the bar top.

Charlie picked at a fry in his basket and put it back down, rubbing salt behind between his fingers. "You should've told me. You shouldn't be working."

"I have to work," I said. "I *have* to. Sitting at home by myself with nothing better to do than to think is the worst thing that could happen to me right now. I'll blow my fucking brains out."

Charlie considered this. He poked at his fries, contemplated his beer and then finally spoke again. "You need help."

"I need to work. I need to find the girls, and I'll find Sullivan too. But I need to work through this." My desperation was real and powerful. My hands were shaking. I could feel my heart hammering in my chest.

I was asking my oldest friend not to kill me.

"I should take the Michaelson case and give—"

"No," I stopped him. "I'll find her. I need to find her."

"Finding her isn't going to bring hi—*Aziz*—back."

"It's a start," I said.

After a long time, Charlie nodded. "OK. I'll sign off on this, but if anything gets to you, if you start to feel unsteady or—"

"I'll tell you," I told him. "I swear to God, I'll tell you."

CHAPTER NINE

41 Weeks

In dreams, sometimes he dies in my arms. The impossibility of it doesn't matter. The twenty minute hike from the mountain to the base becomes a step or two, and then I'm lifting him from the ground into my arms. The shot that killed him instantly, going clear through one side of his head and out the other, becomes a misfire, clipping his heart or shoulder or gut, and so he is still bleeding when I pull him into my lap and hold him. His white teeth and the whites of his eyes are exaggerated against his dark skin. The teeth chatter as I cry over him. The eyes roll up into his head as I scream at the sky.

In real life, I stayed with his body. I left my post and demanded they find the boy's family. When they told me where to go, I wrapped the boy in a green military blanket and took him home. Even the nights I don't see his face, or watch him die, I can still hear his mother wailing and his father beating his chest, while the goats scream through the night.

CHAPTER TEN

Monday, March 24, 2003

With Easter weekend behind me and almost no news on my desk come Monday morning, I turned my attention to the missing kid, Maisie Michaelson. It had been almost a week since Maisie went missing, so we were outside the 48-hour window where most kids showed up —if they were going to. We had bulletins and missing child alerts everywhere, but that hadn't generated shit, nothing credible anyway. Too often people lied when a reward was involved, desperate for the money, with no regard for the missing child's safety.

I drove out to the house where Maisie lived with her parents.

It was a small house, a Cape Cod with its sloped roof and pointed ridges, at the end of a quiet street. There were two large windows in front, framed by black shutters against the burnt orange brick exterior. To the right of the house, a cul-de-sac was claimed by a few large trees crowded with under-brush and long grasses, but this was separated by a large privacy fence enclosing all sides.

A dog began barking once I closed the door to the

Impala. I'd seen the Saint Bernard once before, through the slits in the fence as it paced back and forth, trying to get a better look at me.

Mrs. Michaelson opened the front door before I even made it up the walk. Her eyes were wide, glassy. Her hands trembled and I could tell that she wasn't sure if she wanted to let me in or tell me to go away. I wish I knew why I had that effect on some women.

"No news yet," I said immediately, shoving my hands in my black bomber jacket. I didn't want her to think I'd come to tell her that her daughter was dead. "I have a few more questions."

Something changed in the woman. Her expectant gaze, part-hope part-terror, hardened. Her back straightened as she opened the door for me.

I stepped into the warm living room and saw that not much had changed. The place was still spotless but that wasn't uncommon. It could go either way—their home could fall into disrepair as they longed for their kid's return, or they could clean constantly, hoping to keep it nice for her. It told me that Mrs. Michaelson was hopeful, hanging on to the dream of Maisie's return more than anything else.

"Have you heard anything, Mrs. Michaelson?" I asked.

"No." She sat on the stiff sofa. "You told us to call if we heard demands, but there's been nothing. Not a word." She rested her hands in her lap, trying out a couple of different places, but seemed unhappy with each option.

"I just wanted to ask," I said and sat in the chair opposite her instead of on the couch at her side. I kept a respectful distance. "I know that sometimes it is hard to remember minor details like that."

"Hearing from my daughter would not be a minor detail, Mr. Brinkley," she said.

"Of course not." The large window behind her let in a lot

of white, cold light, blurring out her face. But I could tell by her tone she was defensive, angry.

"Ask your questions."

"Sure," I said. "I apologize if they appear repetitive. I just want to make sure I have everything right."

She said nothing.

"You dropped Maisie off at school at 8:30."

"Yes. Then I got the call at 11:30 saying she was missing."

"And where were you in between?"

"I'm not a bad mother," she screamed, her voice exploding in the small room around us. "Plenty of mothers leave their kids places for a couple of hours—the pool, the library, the backyard. What was I supposed to do? Not send my child to school? Maisie loved—"

Mrs. Michaelson froze. When she spoke again her voice was much quieter and controlled. "Maisie *loves* school. She started early just because of how smart and mature she is. This is because of the accident, isn't it? I wish one of you would just have the nerve to admit it."

The accident, yes—Last year Maisie wandered into the street and was hit by a car. She died, but woke up and was returned to the Michaelson's. For all I could tell, that had been an accident, and the Michaelson's seemed thrilled they'd gotten their daughter back.

"I don't believe you are a bad mother," I said calmly. Mrs. Michaelson cried at this, as if my words were simply too hard for her to hear. "Accidents happen."

She nodded. "We wanted Maisie so badly. Why would we let her get hurt?"

"I know," I said. The Michaelsons had adopted Maisie after failing to conceive. I didn't think they'd go through all that trouble just to change their minds about having her. Everyone I'd talked to—teachers, neighbors, friends—said Maisie was a sweet and bright kid. As lovable as they came. It was clear Maisie adored her parents and clear they adored her.

"It's like when we first got her," she said quietly, looking up and beyond me, at something I couldn't see. "There is always a danger that the mother will change her mind, you know? That someone will appear and take the baby back. So there are these days where you are just waiting and waiting to find out if you're going to lose her."

"I'm sorry," I said again because I wasn't sure what else to say. When the silence stretched on and I realized that Mrs. Michaelson was in no shape to talk, I decided to try something else. "Mrs. Michaelson, can I take another look through Maisie's room?"

"You've been up there a hundred times," she said.

"Actually, I've only peeked in once, briefly. It was mostly the tech crew that inspected the room."

"What are you looking for?" she said, stiffening on the couch. "Her body?"

"Is it up there?" I asked and regretted it as soon as I spoke. The woman's shoulders began shaking violently with her tears. "I'm sorry. I didn't mean that. It's been a long weekend."

The woman said nothing, just cried into her palms. I watched her for a moment longer trying to consider what to do. Finally I said, "Do you mind if I just go up?"

Still shielding her face with one of her hands, she waved me on with the other.

I climbed the stairs one at a time, noting the family pictures on the wall. Mr. and Mrs. Michaelson with their dark hair and eyes. Maisie with her bright blond locks and big blue eyes. A few had just Maisie and that beast of a Saint Bernard.

Maisie's bedroom was on the left at the top of the stairs. It was pulled closed, probably because the Michaelsons simply didn't want to walk by it and be reminded again and again that their daughter was not home. I was damn sure a closed door still did the same.

I wrapped a fist around the handle and it was warm. I wondered how often one or either of them came up and wrapped a hand around it but couldn't bring themselves to open it. How hard must parents cling to this place between the possibility that they could open the door and find her there on the other side, or open the door and know she is truly gone.

I pushed the door open and was confronted by a barrage of pink. The walls were pink and white-striped satin and the comforter was bubblegum fluff. The room was tidy and I could see lines in the carpet from a recent vacuuming. I stepped into the room.

The sloped ceiling forced me to stoop or risk bashing my head. I picked up a few age-appropriate toys. Pulled back the bed sheets and replaced them, opened the closet and closed it. But I saw nothing out of the ordinary. Nothing spoke to me.

I went downstairs, prepared to give Mrs. Michaelson a polite goodbye before heading over to the school, but I didn't find her in the living room. I called her name, but heard no answer. I resisted the urge to pull my gun, given the fact that I was in someone's home. A child's home.

Then I saw her outside on the opposite side of the glass door. She stood in her backyard, fussing over one of those ornamental trees. With a pair of clippers, she hacked at it ruthlessly, the little green twigs falling away to the deck beneath her. The Saint Bernard tried to lick her face once or twice before she succeeded in shooing it away.

Before I could reach her, something caught my eye. On the fridge was a kid's drawing. For six years old, it was no masterpiece, but Maisie had some skill. Enough that I could tell it was her and a man, holding hands. I would have assumed it was her father, Mr. Michaelson, if not for one exception. This man had light hair, scribbled in by a yellow crayon. But Mr. Michaelson, like his wife, had black hair.

I removed the picture from the fridge and opened the back door. Mrs. Michaelson paused, her blades held open in one hand, the bonsai hanging in the other. The Saint Bernard, whose name I suddenly remembered as Max, galloped by chasing a squirrel.

I held up the picture. "Did Maisie draw this?"

"Yes, why?"

"When?" I asked. I squatted down beside her so she didn't have to crane her neck up to look at me.

"I don't know. It had to be in the last month. I probably wrote the date on the back."

I turned it over and saw there was in fact a date, just a few days before Maisie's disappearance. "Did she tell you who the man was?"

"The tooth fairy, *why*?" The blades in her hand began to look more threatening.

"Did the tooth fairy visit her often?"

She was about to refuse my suggestion. I could see it in her face. Then her irritation softened with a question. "She told us that he visited her all the time, even before she began to lose her teeth."

"Was there anything strange about these visits?"

"They weren't real," she insisted. "They were just a dream."

"Humor me," I said. "Tell me about this tooth fairy."

"Maisie has only lost three baby teeth. We told her to put them under her pillow each time, and then John or I would sneak in to put money under her pillow, except we could never find the teeth and there would already be money under the pillow. The first time I thought my husband did it. The second time he thought I did it and the third time we asked each other and realized neither of us had taken the teeth or given her the money.”

“Could a real man be coming into your house and stealing your child’s teeth?” I asked.

She scoffed. “That’s absurd. The house was locked tight. The alarm was set. I even checked her window every morning and night to make sure it was locked. There’s no way to climb up to it either. A man simply could not have gotten into this house.”

I knew from experience this wasn’t true. “Did Maisie tell you what the tooth fairy wanted or why he was visiting her?”

She looked at the mangled plant in her hands. “Once she told me that he had come and used a *cutie tip* on her.”

“Excuse me?” I said.

“It’s just the way she used to say Q-tip. Cutie tip. She was three at the time.”

“Right.”

“Oh god, no. No,” she repeated. “It was just a dream. No one in their right mind would believe the tooth fairy is real.”

No, I thought, but a man sneaking into a house and lying to a child so she wouldn’t be scared of him, that was a very real possibility.

“What about the money and the teeth?” I asked. “I think John is just trying to trick me. He’s a bit of a joker.”

“If I ask your husband, do you think he’ll tell me the truth?”

“Of course,” she said as the Saint Bernard galloped by again.

*I*t was coming up on six o'clock and the last bit of the city's congestion was starting to clear off I-270. A bright headache was blooming behind my eyes and I knew it was too early to grab a drink. Instead, I grabbed a burger from the first drive-thru I saw and replayed the last several hours in my head.

The husband had denied taking the teeth, even as a joke, but admitted that it sounded like something he would do. The interviews at Maisie's school hadn't turned up much. One teacher thought she might have seen a man matching the description of Maisie's tooth fairy, but couldn't be sure. Another insisted that she'd never seen anyone like that. They both maintained the stance that Maisie went to the little girl's bathroom and never came back, but that there was no way a man could have snatched her. The bathroom was locked, inside their classroom, with the teacher standing outside. There were no windows and no other doors.

She was washing her hands and singing. She loved to sing the young teacher had said. *Then she yelped as if surprised and sort of giggled and I asked her what she was laughing at, but she never answered me. When I opened the door, she was gone.*

Someone was lying.

I had half of my daily burger down when Charlie called to tell me that the flasher was spotted going into a laundromat in South Grove. I thanked him and whipped the Impala back onto the highway.

I pulled up in front of the laundromat to see an old woman heaping baskets into one of those pushcarts. A boy sat behind the counter with a large Big Gulp soda in one fist and the remote to the TV in the other. Would it kill him to be an attendant and actually attend to the elderly woman? Punk.

Then I saw her.

She walked up to the desk with the kid behind it and handed him a sheet of paper and a pen. She bent over the table in a way that drew the kid's eyes down the front of her shirt and made him go all red in the face.

I opened the door for the old lady, who thanked me, and I came up behind the girl working the kid.

"Rachel Wright?" I asked.

The girl turned slowly. Her black bob hanging in frizzy ringlets. My face was doubled and clown-like in the dark glass of her large sunglasses. I reached up and tore off the wig and glasses, realizing immediately that I had a problem.

"Hey, ow. You're hurting me," she squealed.

It wasn't Rachel Wright.

The kid chose this moment to get all chivalrous. "Hey man, she's just applying for a job, get off her back."

"A job, huh? With false information maybe?" I snatched up the application and sure enough, it was Rachel's information printed in the little fill-in-the-blank boxes.

"Why are you applying for a job under a false name?"

She went all doe-eyed and soft in my grip. Then I saw the tears brimming. "Christ, don't *cry*. Just answer me."

"I was unaware of the false information, sir." The kid wised up. Nice tits or not, the rats will always abandon a sinking ship.

I ignored him and remained focused on the girl. "How did you come by Rachel's information?"

The girl was bawling now and I knew I wouldn't get any further with her until she calmed down. I steered her to the Impala by her elbow. Then I cuffed one of her wrists to the oh-shit handle.

"Please don't get the bright idea to jump out of a moving car. She doesn't brake as quickly as she used to. I'd hate to have to drag a sack of meat along until the Impala decides she'd like to stop."

I went to the driver's side door and climbed in. Then I backed out of the laundromat parking lot to the sound of the girl sobbing.

When she seemed tired of crying, I tried again. "You about done?"

"I don't want to go to prison," she said.

"That's why we have it," I replied. "If everyone wanted to go, it wouldn't be much of a punishment, now would it?"

"Please," she begged. She yanked at the cuff and whimpered. It hurt like hell banging your wrist bones on that metal. I knew from personal experience. When she finally realized it would only hurt more, she had the good sense to go still. Or as still as she could, given the uncontrollable shaking of her hands. "Please. I'll do anything."

"Anything?" I asked. "Like buy me a drink?" Just the mention of booze made my mouth water. I counted up the hours. Too long. No wonder my mind had gone fuzzy around the edges.

"Yes, please, anything." She began to cry again. I swore.

"If you'll do anything, start by telling me what the hell you're doing applying for a job with someone else's name."

She cried harder. "I can't tell you."

"Let me guess," I said and turned on the heat. It didn't work great, but I hoped it would help her shaking. "Someone will kill you."

She whimpered and gave me the quivering lip for show.

"Of course," I said and changed lanes, heading back toward the FBRD station.

"And this is the part where I tell you it will only get worse for you if you withhold information. But if you work with me, I'll work with you. I can make promises about witness protection and all that shit and so on. So can we skip to the part where you tell me why you did it?"

She turned toward the window and then looked into the backseat as if looking for a way out.

"Assuming you don't go underneath the car and I break both of your legs by running them over."

Her response to this was to yank at the cuffs again as if she would rather break her wrist and be free than tell me anything useful.

"OK," I said. I scratched my head and searched for some patience. I didn't have much, especially not with the pressure building behind my eyes. "I'll give you some time to calm down and then maybe you'll feel chatty."

When I parked the Impala outside the large brick building—an old post office that was claimed and renovated for the FBRD's cause—her resolve melted.

"OK, OK. Let's just talk, OK? Don't take me in yet."

"Sure," I said. If the little shit who'd cried for the last five miles wanted to talk now, I'd take it. I'd rather use her fear of custody against her than take her inside and hear the *where is my lawyer and phone call* bullshit.

Besides, I couldn't keep her here long. We could detain

and interrogate suspects of crimes related to our cases, sure. But I'd have to send her over to the jail sooner or later, once I filed official identity theft charges.

"I know a guy—"

"Let me stop you there," I said. "A *guy* is pretty damn vague. So why not tell me how you know him and it will save us both a lot of time and energy. Do you get what I'm saying? Speak in complete thoughts."

She blinked.

"For example, you might want to say his name, followed by his relationship to you."

"OK," she said. Her mascara had smeared, giving her dark rings beneath each eye. Not flattering, but neither was the snot coming out of her nose. "Jason, my dealer—like that?"

"Perfect. Don't stop now."

She wiped snot across the back of her hand. "I owe my dealer a bunch of money and I can't pay him. He gave me these papers and told me that if I went around to these businesses and applied for jobs, I wouldn't owe nothing. He told me to start with the high-class shit, places I knew wouldn't take me. Then I should apply for everything else."

I tried not to look as surprised as I was. Cop face isn't always as easy to pull off as you might think. "How much did you owe?"

"A thousand dollars. Sometimes he just let me fuck him for it, but then he wasn't interested anymore. He said I got too skinny."

I glanced at the bony wrist hanging in the cuff. "What's your poison?"

"What?" she asked. Sitting up as if I'd prodded her.

"Your drug. What are you getting from him?"

"X," she said. "I get a little coke sometimes, but I don't like the way it makes my heart race. But I love X. It's the only time I'm happy."

I'd seen her cry enough to believe it.

"There are worse drugs," I said. "So you agreed to file these applications so you could pay off your debt and get more X. And what about Jason? He got a last name?"

She didn't answer.

So I put the car in reverse and backed away from the building. Charlie stood in full view of the glass and watched me go. I flashed him a one minute finger before looking over my shoulder to check my blind spot. When I turned back around to straighten out the car, he was still there, hand on his hip. I motioned for his patience one more time before speeding away.

"Where are we going?" the girl asked. Her voice was high and hopeful through the thick snot coating it.

"I'm gonna treat you to a meal. Your choice. Then maybe you'll remember this dealer's last name and where I can find him. So tell me what you like to eat, sweetheart."

"You're going to let me go?"

"Did I say that?" I just wanted more information on Jason and why he wanted someone applying for jobs in Wright's name.

The girl sobbed again. "Please just let me go. Please?"

"Ah, don't cry," I said. "How about if you stop crying right now, I'll throw in dessert."

CHAPTER TWELVE

Monday, March 24, 2003

'd left the girl in the interrogation room with a couple slices of pizza and a soda. I wanted to finish what I'd started with her, but Charlie wasn't looking so good.

He was pissed and I wanted to know why.

I knocked before entering his office. "Sir?"

"What's with the girl?" he said.

"She's Rachel's dummy. She's been going around putting applications in to make it look like Wright is job hunting. She was also given a ticket to Cabo, dated two weeks from now.

"Why would she do that?"

"Because her drug dealer told her to. I'm hoping to find out why."

The phone rang and after looking at the number, he huffed. He didn't answer. When his cell went off next and he still didn't answer, I put my hands on the back of the chair and arched an eyebrow. "What's going on?"

"How are you coming on the Sullivan case?" he asked, finally looking up from the yellow legal pad in front of him where he was tapping a blue ink pen furiously.

"The wife and kid were a dead-end. Either he was pissed

that she turned him in or he came back and saw she was remarried and split. Either way, it seems no one in his hometown has heard from him and he didn't have much to go back to. He probably started another life somewhere else."

"I want you to prioritize the case," he said. "Find where the hell Sullivan is now."

I stopped shifting my weight from one thigh to the other. "With all due respect, Maisie—"

"Maisie Michaelson is probably dead with her little panties shoved in her mouth," he snarled. "Keep your eyes on Sullivan."

We both went very still. The pen stopped thumping against the paper and I gripped the maroon fabric of the chair a little tighter.

"Sure, Charlie," I said. I used the old name hoping it would soften the irritation in my voice. "I'm on it."

"I don't like busting your balls, but someone wants answers," he said.

"What right does Memphis have to—"

"This isn't about the friend. Just get me what I need, all right?"

"Answers."

"Yes, some fucking answers," he agreed and his shoulders relaxed, inching down away from his earlobes.

"Permission to talk freely, sir," I said.

"I'm not your commanding officer, Jim."

"Can you think of any uses a tooth fairy might have for a Q-tip?"

Charlie's brow furrowed. "Is this a joke?"

"Humor me," he said.

"He wants to make sure there are no teeth hiding in your ears?"

"Maybe," I said. "But I doubt it. What else?"

"I don't have fucking time for this," he said, falling back against his chair.

I threw him a bone. "We are brainstorming a case. Work with me."

Charlie exhaled. "I don't know. He's going to buccal swab your ass."

"Why a buccal swab?" I asked. Buccal swabs, those Q-tips taken to the inside of the cheeks to match DNA to crimes, were a strange association.

"To make sure the DNA matches your teeth. There was a punk in my old school. Hank Hills. He used to beat up the littler kids and put their teeth under his pillow so his parents would give him more money, until they caught on, of course. Little prick."

"To make sure the teeth were yours," I said aloud, trying the idea out.

Could a man, pretending to be the tooth fairy, come into the Michaelsons' house late one night and use a buccal swab on Maisie? If so, why check the girl's genetic history? It wouldn't point to the Michaelsons. They were her adoptive parents. They'd adopted her just after her birth, and it was not a secret to anyone. So who the hell would want to know where the child came from?

Charlie gripped the edge of his desk, stood and unbuttoned his suit jacket. "I told you to focus on the Sullivan case. Forget about the kid."

"Sure, sure," I said, humoring him. I didn't want him to think I was obsessing. He would take me off the case and stick my ass in counseling if he thought it best. "I'll find Sullivan first."

I thought I was lying at the time.

I am at my desk in my apartment in Nashville. I've favored apartments most of my adult life. There is no yard to cut and no responsibility for repairs. You can get one as big or as small as you like, and if you insist on the top floor, preferably a corner unit, it stays pretty quiet. It is also easier to move if all you have to do is break a lease on a furnished apartment. Selling a house full of your shit is something else entirely. All my belongings can be packed into the trunk of my Impala. I do have one storage unit in Atlanta, but even that is on the bare side.

This particular apartment, probably my last, is a nice one-bedroom loft. It has a huge window along the western wall, overlooking the city skyline. I leave my desk and go to the window, watching the sunlight bleed out, expecting full dark to overtake the city at any moment.

I feel Caldwell behind me. I know he's there before I even turn around. It isn't just my soldier senses as I like to call them, the knack for knowing when someone has come up behind me because of some imperceptible sound they've made or simply their body heat alone. I know Caldwell by the buzz in my head.

The pressure between my ears intensifies as if I've stood up too quickly. It isn't my own pulse I hear thrumming in my ears though. It is him, scurrying around in there.

"I wondered when you'd show up," I say, without taking my eyes off the beautiful lights ahead of me. The lights make me think of the parking lot carnivals I loved as a kid, the smell of cotton candy and kettle corn and rides that will take you up and sling you around for a ticket. "What took you so fucking long?"

He laughs then, a low chuckle so unlike the laugh I'd heard ten years ago, the first time I'd met him in the bar when Peaches, the barkeep, had made a joke. Or had we laughed about something else? My memory isn't what it used to be.

"I was nervous," Caldwell says.

I turn away from the window then, hands still in my pockets, and look at him. He is in a pressed suit. The gray looks like something soft and vulnerable, a rabbit maybe. The tie is blood red. At least some part of him can still tell the truth.

"You were nervous?" I ask and try to ignore the uncomfortable pressure between my temples.

He's counting the bottle caps I have arranged in two rows on the table. "Yes. You're thinking of the time I met you at Blackberry Hill. You were all sorts of pissy about being called out as a cop—"

"Federal agent," I correct.

The corner of his lip tugs up. "A *federal agent* and when you went to leave I laughed, rather nervously, because I wasn't sure we'd get another chance to talk."

"That's not how I remember it."

He looks up then. One slender white finger, no longer the

hands of a mechanic or laborer, is pressed to the smooth button top of a bottle cap.

"I know how you remember it," he says. "And you don't remember much at all."

That worries me. What if I get it wrong?—*oh I shouldn't be thinking about this.*

"I wouldn't deny a dead man his memoir," Caldwell says. "Don't worry about that."

"Aren't you a sweetheart," I say. "What should I worry about?"

"This," he says and tosses me a folded piece of paper. It's deeply creased, the folds nearly flat. He's had it for a while and opened it many times.

The drawing is similar to Jackson's, with two exceptions. The first, this drawing is sketched out with a felt pen, not with the pencil that Jackson prefers. So the lines are darker, thicker and more chaotic.

The second exception, I stand with the Python at the ready, but instead of having my gun pressed to the side of Caldwell's head, I'm pointing it at nothing. My barrel is aimed at the great darkness that lies before me, a menacing idea rather than an actual man.

Here, Caldwell stands behind me with both hands wrapped around my throat, his grip suggesting he is just a heartbeat away from snapping my neck.

"That's what I wanted to know," he says. "If they were different."

"Either he flatters you," I begin, but I can't finish, not aloud anyway. *Or Jackson didn't have the heart to show me more.*

"Or she didn't have the heart to *see* more," Caldwell suggests. My look must be unfriendly because he holds his hands up in mock surrender, palms out as if asking for forgiveness. "Delaney is a show off, though, yes. You're quite right about that."

"You're quite right about that," I mock. "Where did you learn to talk?"

"Why?" he asks, amusement curling his words. "Thinking of disappearing yourself? Reinventing your own image? I know a few people who are skilled at that kind of thing."

"I don't run away," I say. *Not like you.*

If he hears this, and why wouldn't he, he makes no response. Instead, he picks up the bottle cap he's been pressing down into the tabletop and tosses it into the air. On the next breath he catches it. "I thought you'd quit drinking so much," he says.

"I thought you'd quit murdering people," I say.

"Old habits die hard." Caldwell smiles then. "Like old men."

"Not all of us can age as well as you do," I say, alluding to the fact that he will not age as long as he keeps dying. His NRD, his ability to die and wake up with fresh cells and a smooth face has kept him young. And if he keeps dying, it will be his mind that goes before his body.

He laughs and I find myself comparing the man I met ten years ago to the one I see now. He's gotten his teeth fixed and a bit more cosmetic surgery to hide the scars along his jaw better. He quit dyeing his hair and let it grow in natural. Now it's the same color as Jesse's again, and he has her freckles too.

"How is my daughter?" he asks. "You spend more time with her than I do."

"If she is your daughter, I'm the Holy Ghost."

"That isn't a very nice thing to say." His eyes darken and I reach my hand behind my back and put it on the Glock resting there.

"She quit being your daughter when you tried to kill her," I say.

I raise my gun to put a bullet in his brain. To hell with

waiting for weeks and weeks for the inevitable. We can do this now and we can do it my way.

But Caldwell disappears. One moment he is in front of me, stepping forward. The next moment I feel two cold hands grabbing me. One squeezes the back of my neck, the other locks my arm into place so I can't shoot.

"Is this dress rehearsal?" Caldwell says, laughing into my ear. He presses himself against me and I consider my options. My cheek burns and I realize he's hit me when reaching around. Not a direct hit, but it will bruise.

"Relax, old man," he says. "I didn't come here to kill you. If I'd wanted to kill you I would have done it a long time ago, don't you think? I've had enough opportunities."

"Why haven't you?" I demand an answer. My anger is real, raw and surfacing fast.

"I am what I am because of you," he says, squeezing me tighter.

The pressure in my brain intensifies and I wonder if I will hemorrhage. Maybe he will weaken some vessel and I'll have an aneurysm here and now.

"You led me to Henry Chaplain," he says. "You showed me the path to my true destiny and all the greatness for which I was intended, and Jesse too."

My blood turns cold at the mention of her name.

"Every day you make her more and more into what she is meant to be. I can feel it. You'll make her ready for me. I wouldn't dare disrupt that."

I break his grip and whirl, wide and angry. I shove the Glock under his chin and it raises to accommodate the barrel. But before I can pull the trigger, all the resistance goes out. I stumble forward, almost hitting the dark glass, the bright city beyond.

Caldwell is gone.

CHAPTER FOURTEEN

37 Weeks

"Oh my God," Jesse wails. "Who *does* that?"

She stands over the computer I've dismantled in her garage. We've moved her car out to the driveway and closed the door behind us so that no one can see me. The bright fluorescents make the computer components shine.

"I want you to put it back together," I say. I offer her the small screwdriver. "Just do what I told you."

She throws her hands up. "And what if he has a Mac. This won't work on a Macbook." She flicks her ponytail over her shoulder and crosses her arms. She has a flair for the dramatic that rivals any drag queen.

"He has a Compaq," I say and offer her the screwdriver again. I'm referring to Mr. Lovett, an upcoming target. Jesse will have to go into his home and steal his hard drive for me. I could do it, but I want to teach her something while I still can.

"You put it in all these little pieces," she whines, but she takes the tool from me. "Why is it in so many pieces? And they are so tiny, look at this." She shakes a chip at me.

"Hurry," I tell her. "We still need to work on your locks."

She glances at the corner of the garage by the door leading into the house. A cardboard box brims with locks, old and new. I told her lockpicking and computer knowledge were essential to life as a secret agent, and it is mostly true. Though technology has changed most of this.

"Can we do the locks first and then the computer?"

I grunt. "Nice try." I know she likes the lock picking. TV has made it just cool enough for her to be interested. But if I let her start there, she'll never do the computer.

"And why do I even have to dismantle the computer?" she complains. "Can't I just take a USB and steal all his files or something?"

"What if you can't turn it on?" I ask.

"I'm not technologically challenged."

"I'm not saying you are, but can you imagine *another* reason why the computer might not come on for you?" I press.

That shuts her up and she gives me a wary look, like she is expecting me to call her out on something. I could. This would be the perfect time to do so. I could say, *I know you have problems with electricity. You bust wires and blow fuses. Just like Caldwell, who can step from one place to another far, far away. You have this gift and you'll have to learn how to work with it, or around it.*

But Jesse hasn't officially told me what is going on with her, and I've heard her lie about the number of lightbulbs she's replaced and blame static electricity far too often. She doesn't want to talk about it with me, and I respect that.

"Agents don't whine. Do your computer," I say and lean against the garage wall, waiting.

"I'm not a whiner. I am, like, the toughest person you know."

"I'll tell Jackson you said that," I begin. "If you don't shut up and get to work. I'm not going to stand here all damn day."

"OK, the second toughest," she corrects.

I shove an overturned milk crate toward her so she can sit in front of the dismantled computer. She plops down onto the seat and starts working.

I watch her face furrow in concentration and a weight settles against my chest. I'm trying to teach her something, sure, but I know this is as much for me as it is for her.

I can't get over Caldwell's words. *You're making her ready for me.*

I hope not. But if I am, how? By teaching her? What was the alternative? Let her die unprepared?

She snaps each of the components onto the board, one at a time. She's figuring it out for herself, without my help. Good. It's better this way.

CHAPTER FIFTEEN

Monday, March 24, 2003

 ran dummy Rachel's fingerprints through the system and it came back for a Heidi Tripe, arrested two years ago for a drunk and disorderly, and six months after that for possession for less than an eighth of marijuana. The second case was dropped.

As she sat in the plastic chair opposite mine, I explained the identity theft charges I was laying against her. I had to talk a great deal about fines and jail time before she opened her mouth.

"Henry Chaplain," she finally told me and pressed her shaking hands to her eyes. When her palms came away dark with smeared makeup, she rubbed them together. "His name isn't Jason, it's Henry Chaplain. He has a place over near Beckett Park, on Page Street."

"Write the address down," I told her. She hesitated, rolling the pen between her fingers.

"He's going to know it was me."

"How would he know?"

"He knows shit. He knows everything."

"You're saying this guy is telepathic?"

Her eyes doubled in size. "Maybe. He has a way of getting into your head, you know?"

"I'll keep that in mind," I said. "Now write down the address or I won't be able to say you were fully cooperative."

She began to cry again but at least she picked up the pen and did what I said, which is good, because Charlie walked by the room and saw me with her. I was going to have to get the hell out of this office if I wanted to get any work done. I couldn't do shit with Charlie hovering.

"So let me just be clear. You were applying to jobs as Rachel because Chaplain told you to throw us off her trail. He said he didn't want anyone looking for her. Did I get that right?"

She sniffed and nodded.

"Good. Let's get you over to County," I said.

Mild reluctance became complete resistance. The girl screamed and refused. When I tried to pull her up from her seat, she scooted back, wrenched her arm away and threw the chair. The commotion drew others. Hunter Connolly and Tom Trainer helped me get her out of the room, cuffed, and into the back of the car.

"You've killed me," she said. She screamed so hard her face was red with the effort. "You've *killed* me."

Charlie appeared beside us outside on the curb. Before I could thank and dismiss Hunter and Tom, Charlie barked his own orders.

"Trainer, get her down to County," Charlie said.

Heidi's face was redder than a tomato as she screamed and kicked the seat in front of her. Trainer gave me a reluctant look but I nodded and handed him the keys. "I'll call ahead and tell them you're coming."

Hunter went back inside and Tom got behind the wheel of my car. As he put the Impala in reverse, Charlie turned to me and said, "Don't you have something else to do?"

I did. As soon as Trainer got back, I packed up my shit and went to the bar. The atmosphere and the company would be better if nothing else.

When I walked into Blackberry Hill, Peaches, a heavy-set old guy who owns the place waved heartily, his great arm flopping like a beached fish. Peaches made me think of a biker Santa. His white hair was pulled back in a ponytail at the nape of his neck and matched his great white beard. On his left bicep was a picture of his dog, Roxanne, a Pit-Rottweiler mix.

"B. You here to practice for the tourney?" he called out.

"Not today," I said. "It's a work date."

Peaches frowned. "Where's the darn fun in that?"

I shrugged. "The house pint will have to be fun enough."

Peaches pulled a frosted mug out of the fridge and poured a Blackberry Hill draft with one tug of the silver tap. He used a ruler to slide the foam off before refilling it.

A boy band came on the jukebox and I snorted foam out my nose. Peaches was an AC/DC, Alice Cooper, and Bon Jovi man all the way.

Pinching the bridge of my nose I said, "What the hell is that?" I nodded toward the jukebox.

"It turns out I've discovered why the replacement jukebox was such a good deal."

"You didn't request this song?" I asked.

"God no, the first time it happened, I pulled all the CDs out and reset it. There isn't a Backstreet Boys tape in that thing. But every once in a while, it will play one of their songs anyway."

"That's some scary shit," I said.

"Tell me about it."

I thanked him for the beer and settled into the darkest corner of the room, a circular booth with lots of tabletop space and a view of the door, bar, pool tables, and dartboards, all reflected in the large mirrors running from one end to the other.

The crowd was thin this early in the afternoon, and I was fine with that. I hoped it would be a slow week night. Not dead, not for Peaches' sake anyway, but thin enough that I wouldn't have to pack up my notes until I was good and ready to do so.

I pored over the photographs I had. Eric Sullivan's, circa 1995, courtesy of the DMV. Maisie Michaelson's, courtesy of her mother, and Rachel Wright's charming mug shot for the indecent exposure charge. And a fourth photo, also from the DMV—Henry Chaplain. He had a smarmy pirate look about him, or it could've been the eye patch, more than the olive skin, dark curls, and sharp cheekbones. I wrote notes for each case, asking myself questions to start me down one path or another.

Maisie: What were the circumstances of her adoption? Where are her birth parents? Were there any family members who were not happy with the adoption? I'd be looking for a father of course, a man with blond hair like Maisie's.

Rachel: What's the connection to Henry Chaplain? Is Henry Chaplain protecting Rachel by using his influence to throw someone off her trail? Do they have a bigger crime planned and Holly was simply misdirection?

Chaplain's record was clean with no priors. If I wanted to know who he was and what he was about, I'd have to use other sources. I had an address, but I couldn't walk up and knock on the door. Nothing shuts mouths faster than showing a badge. Even perfectly innocent people clam up when you do that. But at least I had a good suspicion that the way to find Rachel was through Chaplain.

I put Eric's picture beside Maisie's and there was just something about it. Those faces were speaking to me, but I couldn't make out what was being said. I hated that. I hated knowing that I saw something but just didn't make the connection.

I asked Peaches for another house pint in a fresh frosted mug and he obliged. I was halfway through my third pint before my head cleared enough, the throbbing subsiding and my unsteady hands growing still. I turned my full attention to Sullivan.

Charlie wanted him caught, but why? He wasn't a criminal. There were no entries for him in the system. The only entry I found belonged to the FBRD database. It was only a standard entry for those with known NRD. I had his name, basic public information and death day, some of it courtesy of Memphis. But I doubted any of this would help.

I had two choices.

I could request the files from Jerome, or I could follow the money. When Eric got out, he would've needed money. His assets would've gone to his wife and kid, and since it didn't seem like he filed the paperwork to get them back, he must've gone a different route. So who did he get money from? And where did he go with it? Because a man has got to eat.

I lifted the pint and drained the last of it. Before I drank the last drop, I saw a dark shape in the bottom of the glass grow larger. Someone was approaching me. I tuned my ears to the sounds of the bar. I listened for tension, anger, threats. Nothing. I still drew my gun under the table, resting the barrel against my leg.

"Hey man," a voice said.

I lowered the glass enough to see the man speaking, but damned if I was going to let go of the mug. A gun in one hand and a thick glass mug in the other was better than no weapon at all.

"Yeah?"

"Peaches said you won the dart tourney. That true?"

"Yep," I said. I measured the kid. 5'11. Thick, calloused hands. Scruffy face and blue eyes. He had the look of a laborer in his jean jacket. Factory work or construction maybe. Either was possible around St. Louis, or maybe he was from Illinois, across the river where rents were cheaper. Plenty of the blue collar boys came over to drink in the bars, though they couldn't afford a room here.

"You want to play?" he asked.

I leaned forward so that the front of my jacket would hang open enough to make the movement casual and slipped the gun back into place.

"Sure, kid," I said. I could've been a bastard and refused him, but why? I needed to step away from my notes anyway and give the facts a minute to settle in my mind. The words were blurring on the page, and not because I'd had three pints.

"But let's keep it simple. I'm working," I told him. "How about three throws and the one who hits the bullseye most, wins."

He grinned as if he'd already won. "All right."

First, I repacked the folder and handed it to Peaches for safe keeping.

"Don't look at these, or lose them, or I'll have to kill you," I warned him. I winked for show, but his laugh was tight. Good ol' Peaches, he thought I'd actually put a bullet in him. Good. Not that I liked to threaten my friends, but a man was only as good as the threat he could make.

I kept my eyes on him until he tucked the folder under the register and then I turned to the kid. He had six darts in his hand and gave me three, the ones with red tips on their little green flights.

I let him go first. He was pretty good. He hit the inner-most circle each time, two tips touching the outside edge of the red bullseye and one dead center. With all three stuck, he grinned triumphantly and turned to me. His friends clapped. Then he went to remove his darts.

"Leave them," I said.

"They're all on the bullseye. It'll mess up your shot, man."

"I've got plenty of room," I insisted.

Peaches laughed behind me. "Go easy on them, B. It's too early in the week to be breaking hearts. We're still getting over Monday. "

"I'd like to see you do better," the kid scoffed. Shit talk. The biggest difference between young pups and old dogs. At some point, you get your ass handed to you enough that you quit talking shit and simply hand it out if you can.

"Would you?" I asked and smiled at him. "All right."

I threw the first dart and bullseye. I threw the second and thumped against the board right beside the first, knocking it to the right a little so the little flights veered in opposite directions, two of his darts fell off the board.

"Don't hold back, Danger," Peaches said, chuckling.

I winked at the kid and closed my eyes. I visualized the bullseye in my mind and where I wanted the dart to land. Then I exhaled and threw it. I opened my eyes after I heard the thump against the board. My three crowded his dart in the center. It looked threatened and surrounded.

"Damn. I don't believe it," the kid said.

I slapped him on the back. "Practice kid. It's just practice."

"When the hell did you have that much time for practice?" he asked. "Prison?"

"You think they give you sharp objects in prison?" I motioned for two more pints. Peaches nodded and pulled out the mugs. "How did you learn?"

"Pool and darts is a good way to earn cash. I just went around the bars and played the best, learning what I could where I could. You ain't gotta pay taxes on what you get."

"A man has got to eat," I said and put a pint in his hands. "On me."

Cash under the table. He was right. There were plenty of ways for a man to make cash under the table if he was desperate enough. If Sullivan didn't want anyone's help, he didn't have to take it.

It wouldn't make sense to try and trace the money. I'd have to start with Jerome. Though the facility was closed, hopefully, there was still enough there to point me in a direction.

I'd just handed the darts to one of the boy's friends when I got the distinct feeling I was being watched.

A black woman sitting alone at a table across the room wasn't blinking. She had a pint in one hand and an unreadable expression on her face. It wasn't friendly. Certainly not the kind of look a woman gives you across the bar, if you're lucky.

I held her gaze for a moment. I wasn't trying to intimidate her. I was just wary. She looked damn capable of trouble if that was her prerogative. So I let her look, but I had no intention of letting her come closer.

The blue collar boy said something and I turned to respond. When I looked back, the woman with the close cropped hair was gone. Her pint, still full, rested on the vacated table.

CHAPTER SIXTEEN

Tuesday, March 25, 2003

After getting my file from Peaches, I headed home. Only I didn't make it that far. Charlie called me from his cell when I was about two miles from Blackberry Hill.

"I need you to come to Lafayette Square. Down here off of 18th. Do you know the Square Root Brewery?"

"Yeah," I said and hooked a U-turn while the road was clear. Some bastard still honked though he had plenty of room.

"Head that way," he said. "You'll see the lights. Black and whites are all over the fucking place."

Charlie ended the call without saying goodbye and I pressed my foot down on the accelerator. He didn't say *I found your girl*. He would have if it was Maisie or Rachel. But there was definitely a body.

No other reason would have a bunch of cops and agents standing outside the pub.

I was still two blocks away when I first saw the lights. Great blue and red flashes bouncing off the brick buildings lining the Lafayette square district. The district is what I liked to call ghetto chic. This was one of the nicest areas in the city. Even the brick buildings had fancy molding and big picturesque windows. The landscaping helped to give it an upscale look, but the architecture smacked of row houses no matter how you packaged it.

I parked at the edge of the scene and climbed out of the car. Immediately, my breath fogged in front of my face and the ice in the wind chapped my knuckles. The cold air creeping into my jacket and those flashing blue-red-blue lights woke me up a bit, chasing back the edge of my last Blackberry pint that I shared with the Bobby George wannabe.

The wide, empty avenues running along each side gave a sense of foreboding, but dark empty streets always did.

I walked a few yards past the brewery, past the rubber-necking lookie-lous straining against the yellow tape, until I found my first uniformed officer. I flashed my badge so he'd lift the tape for me.

"Thanks. Can you point me toward Agent Swanson?" I asked.

The officer jabbed a stubby finger toward the edge of the park across the street. I saw a thinner crowd, only a few guys standing between a row of park benches. The white magnolia blossoms glowed like ghostly spectators in the flashing darkness above them.

I crossed the road.

"Swanson," I said, loud enough so he could hear me.

Charlie turned and waved me closer. It was him, another FBRD agent, and the CSI guy taking photographs of the body.

Because there was a body.

A girl lay dead on the sidewalk near a park bench. A large dark puddle of blood and brain spreading out from the back of her head. She wore jeans, sneakers, and a nice sweater—or at least it must've been before chunks of her brain hit the sidewalk.

"What happened?" I asked Charlie, who'd finally finished talking to the other FBRD agent.

"Witnesses say the girl is Kaitlyn Green. The girl over there in the white jeans is her cousin. She confirms they came together. They met a couple of guys, were having drinks. Apparently all was fine and dandy until Kaitlyn told her death story."

"Her death story?"

"Yeah, apparently, last year she was out for a jog and got hit by a car."

"Drunk driver?"

"No. The driver had just turned around in her seat to swat her kid. It killed Kaitlyn but she woke up the next day, diagnosed with NRD. She was very proud of her condition, according to the cousin. She liked to tell everyone about it. Do you know there's a website for this shit? People put their death stories out there for the whole world to see." He looked down at his notes. "Heather Fan is the cousin."

"What does that have to do with the guys?"

"Heather thinks the shooter who put the bullet in her cousin's head is one of the guys. Brian Taft. He apparently reacted badly to Kaitlyn's story, said some shit and left early. Then when they were walking to their car hours later, a man in a mask fitting his physical description grabbed Kaitlyn and roughed her up a bit. Kaitlyn fought back, has blood under her nails and all that, for all the good it did her. He still put a bullet in her brain."

Brains on the concrete. That'll do it. The girl wouldn't be waking up again.

"Where was the cousin?" I asked.

"With her until she ran."

I placed my hands on my hips. "So what do you want me to do? Find the—"

"No," Charlie said. He put away the notebook and turned to me. "You're still on Sullivan. No new cases until you wrap that up. I called you here to talk to the press."

"Me?" I snorted.

"You're good with this shit," he said. "Diplomacy."

"If you say so," I said and looked over toward the news vans clustered at the edge of the crime scene. They strained against the yellow tape like ravenous dogs desperate for the girl's bones.

"See," he said. "You're doing it already."

I put my cold hands in the pockets of my jacket, and leaned a thigh against the black iron arm of a park bench. "What do you want me to say? Or *not* say."

"I just don't understand why some of them feel the need to be all loud and proud about this. Zombie pride or whatever the hell you want to call it. Do you know how many people would love to hide how different they are? How many kids go around wishing they were a different race or had both arms or whatever? They aren't helping themselves by being all in-your-face with everyone."

"So you want them to hide who they are? I suppose we can go back to the days when the *coloreds* were lucky if they could pass. Is that what you're saying?"

Charlie sighed. "No, Jesus. Don't put words in my mouth. I'm just saying that I want to tell Necronites to stay indoors. Do not announce themselves to everyone they meet or they'll all end up with their brains blown out by some bigot. But we can't say that."

"It would be a bad idea," I agreed, wiping at my nose turned cold by the wind.

"So just paint a rosy fucking picture, would you? Let them

know they need to be careful, but also that everything is going to be OK."

"Is it going to be OK?" I asked Charlie my friend, not my superior. I knew he understood when he ran his hand over his face.

"I hope so," he said. "Eventually."

I slapped his back a couple times, mentally forgiving him for being a dick earlier, and jogged toward the white news van perched at the far end of the tape where a black reporter and his camera crew waited. I wondered what he'd say if I'd just repeated Charlie's spiel to him.

"Sir." He called as soon as he saw me. "A few questions if you please, sir?"

I opened my mouth to give my military rank and stopped. Old habits.

"Agent Brinkley." I offered my hand.

This caught him off guard, as it always does when you act civil to the press, instead of treating them like scavengers tearing at roadside carcasses. He had to switch his microphone to the other hand in order to shake mine. A petite little thing, compared to the massive camera on her shoulder, was already positioning herself behind the man for filming.

"Agent Brinkley," the reporter said. "I'm Hal Hemsworth with Channel 6 News. What can you tell us about what happened here tonight?"

"We are not sure about the details yet, Mr. Hemsworth, but it appears that a young woman was shot. It will very likely be ruled homicide."

"Gun violence has been nonexistent in the prominent Lafayette Square district. Is this a new trend?"

Gun violence is a problem all over St. Louis, I thought. Rich neighborhoods were no exception.

I flashed a restrained grin. "I'm no real estate expert, Mr.

Hemsworth. Though this looks like a hate crime. Those usually target people, not locations."

The black man's back stiffened. "A hate crime?"

"Yes," I said. "The young woman may have been targeted for her medical condition."

"Was she NRD-positive, sir?"

"That is what we have heard."

The man turned to the camera then as if I wasn't there. "Once a public safety concern, now a medical marvel, NRD-positive refers to a neurological disorder that allows certain individuals to resurrect from death, assuming their brain was not damaged in the death itself."

I disliked the word *resurrect*, which definitely had a horror film ring to it, but I didn't correct him. After all, I wasn't part of the 2% who has this disorder, so who was I to speak for the Necronites? I sure as hell wasn't much of a champion for their cause. Sure, I was trying to find the ones falling through the cracks, but I was no legislator. I was trying to keep them alive and accounted for. That had nothing to do with improving their quality of life.

"So she was shot in the head?" The camera girl asked. The newsman froze.

"It's fine, we can voice over the clip," he said, his showman face dropping away. "So the young woman was shot in the head?" the newsman asked in the same rehearsed voice as if the girl had not even spoken.

"That is correct," I said. I was looking at the girl and wondering what her interest was. The pained look on her face, what was it saying? This petite, pretty little blonde. Did she have NRD? Was she grateful she could pass? Or was she just pissed to be upstaged by a man and talked over.

I gritted my teeth and stepped back from the crew. "Unfortunately, that is all the information I have at this time."

"What a tragedy," the newsman said, but he spoke to the large insectile eye of the camera. Not to me.

Yes, I thought. But more than a tragedy. It tightened my guts. My girls—and I had come to think of Maisie and Rachel as my girls—were not safe. Their conditions were known and public. They could not hide. And the longer they were out there, missing, the slimmer the chance I could bring them back in one piece.

CHAPTER SEVENTEEN

36 Weeks

I'm sitting on the back porch with Jackson, finishing off a case of Rogue and watching the sun go down.

"You need to tell her," she says.

"You need to cut your yard," I say. "Do you even have a lawnmower?"

"If you don't tell Jesse, she'll never forgive you."

I snort. "You act like I deserve forgiveness. We both know that's not true."

"She's going to find out about Maisie and it will go over better if it comes from you," she says and lifts the brown neck of the bottle to her lips again.

"If I'm going to tell her about Maisie," I say and scuff the bottom of my boots against the little stoop. "Then I should tell her about Aziz too. Hell, I should throw in Gideon. And let's not forget her father."

I take another swig of my beer and feel the last of the foam slide down my throat.

"He said I'm making her ready for him," I confess. "That it's my fault she is what she is."

"Jesse is a good kid," Jackson says. "You can take credit for that if you want."

"No, I can't," I say and look up at the sky. "But you can't deny that he's right. It is my fault Caldwell is what he is. I started this."

Jackson interrupts my pity party. "'A true war is never moral. It does not instruct, nor encourage virtue, nor suggest models of proper human behavior, nor restrain men from doing the things men have always done. If a war seems moral, do not believe it. There is no virtue. As a first rule of thumb, you must know a war is what has always been—an absolute and uncompromising allegiance to obscenity and evil.'"

"Did you memorize that whole book?" I ask.

"I read it every night."

"You need a new book," I say.

"If you don't tell her you're dying—"

"If I tell her, she'll try to replace me." I know that kid and her stubbornness. She's about as good at accepting *no* as a stallion accepting the reins.

"Yes," Jackson says, emphatically. "Yes. If not her, then Rachel."

"Now you're asking me to play favorites." I snort and pull my leather jacket tight. I can't imagine being any colder, but there's got to be colder, right? There's death.

"I don't deserve to be saved," I tell her. I sound repetitive even to myself.

Jackson runs a hand over her head. "If you won't let them save you, then you have to prepare."

For what? Heaven? Hell? I wasn't sure either existed. I say, "I've been writing it all down. Does that count as preparation?"

She looks at me then, the white of her eyes reflective in the moonlight. "All of it?"

"Everything I can remember."

Her face pinches as if a sharp pain has run through her. "Even Micah?"

"I can leave him out if you want," I say, a peace offering.

"No." She looks up at the few stars we can see. "Someone should know."

CHAPTER EIGHTEEN

Wednesday, March 26, 2003

The next morning, before I even left my apartment, I put in the request for all the Sullivan files. I specifically wanted whatever was recorded at Jerome, but I kept my request wide, just in case something interesting was churned up. Then I drank a beer. It was early, but I was having one of those mornings where everything was just a little stiffer than usual and beer helped with that.

I was at my desk by ten. Keeping a schedule—whatever the schedule—helped me focus. I'd been in the military too long to just free-fall through a day now.

Maisie's folder was open on my desk when Charlie appeared, a woman in tow. When I first saw her, I did my best to keep my face blank, though I recognized her immediately.

"This is former military officer Gloria Jackson," Charlie said. He'd quit shaving. His stubble was almost a full beard.

Jackson and I shook hands.

"She is a recent release like yourself," he went on.

"Not released," she said. Her face grimaced then. "Not exactly."

"Have a seat," I said. "What can I do for you?"

Charlie leaned forward one hand against my desk. "Captain Jackson is part of the pilot program I was telling you about." When I looked confused, he offered clarification on her role. "She is an AMP."

I remembered then. The pilot program was an attempt to pair remote viewers, with their ability to draw the future, with NRD-positive individuals, to serve as death replacement agents. This way, someone who could die, but not really, would save lives.

The program still had some bugs. Not all deaths were replaceable and people were still trying to figure out how to make money from this. Insurance companies, healthcare professionals, and law enforcement agencies all wanted a piece of the pie. The paperwork was outrageous, but we had won support by maintaining some stable replacement statistics for the last couple of years.

In the beginning the FBRD had two major functions. First, to investigate all crimes connected to Necronites. Mostly that meant cleaning up the mess from The Great Panic and camp detainment. This meant finding people, reintroducing them to society, that sort of thing. Our second biggest task was to make these individuals a commercial asset to the country by introducing as many of them as possible to what we were calling the Death Replacement Industry.

Our hands were full.

"I've asked Captain Jackson to help you find Sullivan," he said. "It's what she does."

"It's what I do," I snapped. I should not have reacted. I respected Charlie as a superior but he was also one of my oldest friends. He should know I always do what I say I'll do, and I said I'd find Sullivan.

Charlie froze and his blue eyes met mine.

This is about Aziz. You think I'm unstable. You think I'm obsessive. You don't trust me.

I said nothing.

The air charged between us and I wondered if he would reprimand me. If he did, I'd take it without complaint.

"I'll leave you to it," he said and walked away.

When I turned, Jackson was sitting in the chair, waiting. She'd politely averted her eyes while Charlie and I squabbled, which won her some points in my book.

"What can I do for you?" I asked again.

"I'm here to assist in your investigations," she said and before I could get pissed about it, she went on. "I know you don't want my help, but this isn't about you or your ego."

I stiffened. "I'm not one of those dicks who walk around with a puffed up chest."

I had a moment of hesitation before cursing in front of her. As a rule, I try not to curse in front of women, even if they talk like sailors themselves, but on her first day of basic training, Captain Jackson would have heard far worse coming from a man's mouth.

"I saw you compete with the boy," she said, being the first to acknowledge the bar the night before. It was her after all, alone at that table, watching me.

The heat crept up the back of my neck. "I saw *you* watching me."

"You are competitive by nature." Her face was still perfectly blank. Damn she was good. I'd never met a woman before who was as good—maybe even better—at hiding emotions as I was. When she didn't speak, I caved.

"I like being good at what I do," I said.

Her face flushed. "I need you to understand that this is very important."

"Of course it is," I said. "We are trying to save lives."

She regarded me then. Her gaze heavy. It was as if she

knew something I didn't, and was trying to figure out if I should be let in on that secret or not.

Jackson sat up straighter. "I specialize in finding missing people. I've had a 100% success rate in the 134 cases I've worked so far. After we find your three targets—"

"Three?" I stopped her. "You're here to help me find Sullivan."

Her lips flattened. "You're my partner. I'll help you with everything."

"Yes, pushing Sullivan off on you while I obsess about the girl would just prove everyone right, wouldn't it?" I ask.

I was still pretty pissed that one of my oldest friends who was well-acquainted with my abilities thought I needed help. But as much as I hated a finger in my pie, I knew better than to tell Jackson to get lost. If I rejected her offer, Charlie had grounds for suspending me. He could call me irrational and obsessive. Worse, Jackson would probably think it was because she was a woman. Or worse, because she was a black woman. The only thing more insulting than being thought of as an incompetent misogynist was being considered an incompetent racist misogynist.

"I'd appreciate your help on all three cases, Captain," I said. "But I've got a question."

Her shoulders, which had relaxed at my acceptance, tightened once again.

"Why were you following me?" I asked. "Last night at the bar."

"I wanted to make sure I could work with you before accepting Agent Swanson's proposal."

"Do you always investigate your partners before working with them?" I asked.

"It is a new policy. I want to start with the child," Jackson added, drawing attention away from herself.

"Don't let Agent Swanson hear you say that," I said. "He

brought you in to find Sullivan. He doesn't want us working on anything else."

"I know," she said. "But I've already started on Sullivan. In the meantime, I think we can make progress with the girl. After all, I think she is more at risk than a grown man, who probably just doesn't want to be found, don't you think?"

I grinned. "I do, but I can't help but wonder what's in it for you?"

She considered me for a moment longer. Her face twitched and her eyes glazed. Then her hands clasped hard onto the chair. It took me a minute to recognize what was happening.

I leapt up and came around the desk just as Jackson began to convulse. I grabbed hold of her and eased her out of the chair and onto the floor as she shook in my arms. I tried to put her head down gently enough and get her rolled onto her side. My knees against her back, I held her there so she couldn't hurt herself. Charlie and a couple other agents came out to see what the hell was going on.

"Call an ambulance," I ordered. One of the guys ran off without question.

Charlie said, "Jackson has a complicated medical history."

I gave him a *don't be a dick* face.

"But confirmation is always best," he said and went back into his office.

Jackson started to slow in her twitching. Her convulsions gave over to deep rasping breaths as she tried to suck air into her lungs.

I patted her back. "You're all right. You're all right."

She went completely still and I worried she'd passed out. I bent over her to find her blinking and trying to sit up. This whole thing took maybe five minutes.

"Hey, easy there," I said and tried to help her.

"I'm fine," she said and pushed me away. For all her talk,

she was just as prideful as I was. But seeing it relaxed me. Maybe I wasn't the only one with something to prove here.

In a sitting position, her head between her knees, she drew slow and steady breaths. There was spit, snot, and blood smeared all over her nose and mouth.

"Shit," I said. "Someone get us a fucking napkin or something?"

Another guy trotted off and returned with those scratchy hand towels from the bathroom. I handed them over to Jackson who cleaned herself up.

"Are you all right?" I asked.

"No," she said. She didn't sugar coat shit.

Two paramedics came through the front door to collect her. When she refused to get on the stretcher, they helped her to her feet, insisting she get checked out with the equipment in the back of the ambulance.

"You need me to come out with you?" I asked.

She gave me a proper *fuck off* look, and I admit I liked her a little more. I saw a blood spot on the carpet where she'd fallen. I pointed at it when Charlie came up to see me.

"That'll have to be burned," Charlie said.

"A bit excessive, don't you think? She isn't contagious."

"I just got off the phone with her boss," he said. "She said Captain Jackson has a history of seizures. She is fit for work, but these *episodes* can be expected. Apparently they are still working out the kinks in her treatment."

"What the hell did they do to her?" I asked. I tried to remember what I had heard about AMPs. They were soldiers who'd volunteered. First they were taught remote viewing, a remnant from the military's ESP research in the 90s. Then, they were subjected to tests and alterations in the hopes that the NRD condition could be recreated successfully. The military thought soldiers who couldn't die as long as they wore good helmets were a hell of an asset.

I watched Jackson through the glass. She sat in the back of the ambulance, her head tilted so a paramedic could shine a light up her nose and poke at her with gloved fingers.

"They messed with her brain," he said. "Her boss called it ferromagnetic material. It's what they injected into the volunteers' brains when they were trying to turn soldiers into Necronites. Find out what crazy fucker came up with that idea and let's uninvite him to dinner, all right?" For just a moment, he was my friend again. My old friend who served in three tours with me. Charlie who used his own knife to dig a bullet out of my ass. Just good ol' Charlie Swanson. "I heard it killed 98% of the volunteers, or so severely retarded them that they wished they were fucking dead. Jackson should count her lucky stars that she isn't pissing through a tube and eating through a straw."

I watched Jackson turn and spit blood onto the concrete. Count her stars indeed.

CHAPTER NINETEEN

Thursday, March 27, 2003

I got a hit on Henry Chaplin. I couldn't let Charlie know, so the moment he stepped out, I slipped from the office and met my contact at the 7-11 near Hamilton.

Fizz was a jittery kid, early twenties, who would roll over for cocaine the way a dog will roll over for a good belly rub. I'd caught him with a gram about a month after I moved to St. Louis, but I knew he was big on the drug circuit and let him go rather than bag him. He was a small fish, and when you're working crime on streets as bad as the ones in St. Louis, it's important to think big.

So my policy was to let the little fish go and see just where they swam back to. Fizz hadn't disappointed me.

I'd taken his picture with my phone, made him hold up the coke and everything. Then I lied and said that the statute of limitations on that was 10 years. If he was a good boy, he'd never see the inside of a jail. If he crossed me, *well*—I let him assume the worst.

When I pulled up to get gas, Fizz was standing outside the pump smoking a cigarette despite the giant *no smoking* sign over his head. He had bright blue hair that looked like one of those Japanese anime characters. I'd seen lots of them with bright hair and shimmery eyes, showcased on posters, billboards, and store signs around Okinawa where I was stationed for two years. Fizz also wore shades that reflected the store, parking lot, and cars around him like twin mirrors or giant fly eyes.

The cigarette glowed brighter with a deep inhale. His fingernails protruding through fingerless motor-cycle gloves were chewed down to the nubs, bloody cuticles dried from an assault hours ago.

"Tony," he said when I put the Impala in park and opened the gas cap to insert the nozzle. It was the fake name I'd given him when I busted his ass. No need for him to know who I really was. Besides, I always thought I looked like a Tony.

"Fizz," I said. "You were quick on this one."

"It's because everyone who knows the difference between shit and a pony knows who the fuck Chaplain is."

"I didn't know," I said and mashed the button marked unleaded. I was turned away from him. It was how most of our conversations went. I pretended to do some bullshit thing, he pretended to ignore me.

"Because you're a cop," he said. "Who'd tell you anything?"

"All right," I said. "So what don't I know about him?"

Fizz flicked his ashes and looked up at the sky. "He's the biggest dog in town. He's got eyes everywhere and if you piss him off, he doesn't make threats. One minute you're breathing and the next you're not."

"Just drugs?" I asked, watching the gas numbers climb up and up on the little pump readout.

"Are you fucking listening, man? No, not just drugs. Everything. He's into everything."

"All right," I said and felt like I was talking down an angry horse. "So what would he want with girls?"

Fizz snorted and flicked his ashes. "Who doesn't want girls?"

"Sex slaves, trafficking, things like that?"

"Sure," Fizz said and shrugged his shoulders.

"What about *special* girls?" I asked. I returned the nozzle to the pump and removed the squeegee from the bucket of washer fluid. "He got any need for special girls?"

Fizz plunged a thumb into his mouth and started gnawing on the flesh.

"Fizz?" I pushed.

In my periphery, I saw bright blood bloom in the rim of his thumbnail and Fizz sucked it hard.

"Come on, Fizz," I started. "Don't make me—"

"Don't make you what?" he snorted. "A few years in prison for drugs is shit compared to what Chaps is gonna do to my ass."

First the girl and now Fizz.

"Is he really that bad?" I asked, hoping he'd clarify why Chaplain had everyone running under the fridge when the light came on.

"You've no idea, man. I heard he made a guy dig out his own fucking eyeball with a screwdriver."

"Just give me something," I said. "Anything."

Fizz finished his cigarette and threw it on the ground, smashing the butt before crushing it with the tip of his steel-toe boot. I thought he'd just walk away then, but instead he gave me what I wanted.

"I hear he makes movies with girls. The special ones."

"Movies?"

"And Heidi told it to you straight. That's his address, but you're as dead as Heidi if you go there."

"Heidi Tripe?" I asked. "How'd you hear about that?"

Fizz snorted, a half smile crooking beneath the twin mirrors of his shades. "Get a clue."

With his cigarette done and my gas pumped, he turned first. I wanted to call after him and demand the little shit give me the full story. But Fizz was only useful to me alive and free. I let him go.

"Be at his place at 9 P.M. tomorrow," he said when he was halfway across the parking lot. He turned and flipped me the bird, but kept walking backward. "Bring $500 in cash or they won't let you in."

"That's a lot of money," I said and flipped the bird back. "What's it for?"

He didn't offer an explanation. Instead he shrugged. "It's been nice knowin' ya."

CHAPTER TWENTY

32 Weeks

I'm hunting Caldwell to the four corners of the earth. Every paper trail, everybody I am sure he has a connection to, every business deal, *everything*, I take it all in and make a meticulous inventory of his strengths and assets. But I can't find out enough about him. I read excerpts of his biography on the internet, the bestseller:

TIMOTHY CALDWELL, APPOINTED LEADER OF THE UNIFIED Church, is a holy man, connected directly to God. Caldwell, as he is called by his followers, a simple one word name like our beloved Jesus—

Or Madonna or Cher, I think, leaning back in my computer chair and blinking several times to lubricate my eyes.

He has demonstrated his miraculous faith healing to countless followers during his sermons at the Adams Street King of the Holy Angels church. These standing-room-only events are full of the faithful, desperate for salvation or a chance to speak to loved ones once more.

"He knew my grandmother's name, her address, even her cat. He knew everything about her, even what she said to me on my wedding day. I've no doubt this man is connected to God."
(from an interview with Mary Eloise Bethel of Oak Park).

I READ ALL ABOUT HIM AND THIS BULLSHIT PERSONA HE'S fed the world, but it doesn't tell me where to hit him. Can I destroy his financial assets? What is money to a man with his abilities? Can I defame him? Not with his powers of mental manipulation. He would twist that back on his accuser with a vengeance.

So where to hit a man like Caldwell? Where would it hurt most?

I don't know. So in the meantime, I keep myself moving.

I've racked up some favors over the years and I've been calling them in. Even little ones that mean next to nothing —*can I borrow your hunting gear? Just the orange stuff, thanks. Your shovel? Your M40 gas masks*—so on.

I'm calling in the favors, because if word gets out that I am dead to the few people who know otherwise—actually dead this time, I want everyone to feel like their balance is paid in full. Not being able to repay a man can eat at you over the years. I know that firsthand, and I don't want to leave that kind of carnage in my wake. After all, why save the favors? It isn't like they'll accrue interest.

I have two exceptions, two people whose favors are no small matter.

The first is in St. Louis.

It takes me just four hours to get to the St. Louis Psychiatric Rehabilitation Center, because I'm coming from Kansas City following up on some intel that I received from a friend. Horns blare as pissed off people try to vent their frustrations along I-70. Construction that was supposed to be completed in December hasn't been finished and it is nearly March.

Moving this slowly would drive anyone crazy, but I don't mind. I need time to think about what my contact told me and about what I should tell Rachel when I see her.

He's taking people, my contact said. *People who've been replaced and their agents. There's a guy on the inside, an AMP reject who says C's looking for something.*

Apparently, he thinks he can work some kind of voodoo by putting all these people together in a drug-induced trance state.

But what about the kids? I'd asked him and I think of Maisie again. What does he want with the kids?

Kids are 65% of the replacement industry, he said. *Do the math.*

When I arrive at the asylum, I put the Impala in park outside the main entrance. The front is a large sweeping entryway with columns stretching up several stories. The boxy, brick exterior imposes on the landscape around it. It makes me think of a creepy orphanage I saw in a film once, with the exception of the green and gold dome on top, very Moscow-esque. The inside is no more cheerful with its white cinder block walls and the tile floors which makes me think of hospitals.

On the fourth floor I find Gladys behind the desk, a nice woman with shriveled hands and an outdated beehive hairdo.

"Hello, Jimmy." Gladys says, grinning. She is very proud of the fact that despite her age she still has all her teeth. "What a pleasant surprise."

"I was close and wanted to check on our girl."

"Good, good," she says and pushes the sign-in sheet toward me. Then she hands me a black pen so I can scribble my name in the blank. "She's just fine."

I watch the old woman shuffle around the desk and come toward the double doors that lead to the sleeping quarters behind me. I mumble assenting sounds while she blabs about nothing until she stops just in front of Rachel's door.

Rachel is sitting cross legged on her bed with a girl opposite her. A suicide, I guess, by the long jagged marks that climb up each of the girl's pale wrists. The girl's palms are face up in Rachel's hands as Rachel peers into them with an expression of serious contemplation on her face.

Her black bob has fallen forward and hides her eyes, but I can see her lips moving in a hushed whisper.

"Ah-hem," Gladys says and the girls look up. Rachel's face brightens. I can't help but smile back.

"Well, *hello*, stranger," she says to me.

My momentary happiness curls at the edges, drying up as I remember what I've come here to tell her.

"None of that hocus pocus nonsense," Gladys scolds, and the girl with the mop of unruly curls piled on top of her head, yanks her hands back. "Go on to the cafeteria for a while, Jo. Let Rachel have some time with her friend."

Jo, with a red face to match her curls, slides between Gladys and me, then takes off down the hallway toward the cafeteria. Gladys puts an arm on my shoulder and squeezes it. "Take as much time as you need, Jimmy."

"Thank you," I say and step into the room. I take a seat at the end of Rachel's bed, feeling Jo's warmth soaked up by the mattress.

Neither of us speak until we can't hear the clanking of the nurse's keys in the hallway.

Rachel arches an eyebrow. "I think she likes you."

"She's old enough to be my mother."

"No mother would look at her son's ass like that," she says and leans back on her hands to inspect me.

"You're a palmist now?" I ask. "You're going to have a card table in Jackson Square before I know it."

She arches her eyebrow again. "Are we going on vacation?"

My smile falters, or some other way, I give up the game.

She jolts upright, tall and tense, grabbing onto my hands. "Oh my God, what happened? Jesse—"

"She's fine," I say. "Jesse's fine."

"Oh God, then it's you," she says, squeezing my hands tighter. "What is it? Whatever it is, I can protect you. Unless it's cancer. Then you're just fucked."

I grin. "It's not cancer."

She exhales, visibly relieved. "If your health is good, we're good. I can replace anything else."

I look down at her hands in mine. So small and slender in comparison, she could be a child. "It's complicated."

"Jesucristo el dramatismo!" she exclaims.

"Don't pretend to speak Spanish," I tell her. Rachel is Hispanic, her father Puerto Rican and her mother Honduran. But she wasn't raised by them. As a toddler she was found in the desert wandering alone, either dropped by coyotes or her own parents. A white couple in Arizona took her in and raised her when her family couldn't be found.

"I've been reconnecting with my roots," she says in a serious, low tone. "I now understand why I've loved guacamole so much my whole life. It's the tree of my people."

I laugh because that's what she wants. "Be serious. It's hard enough to get through this conversation without you teasing me."

"I'm not," she argues and pretends to pout. "I'm trying to tell you I feel *whole*, as a *person*. Do you think they'll let me have an avocado tree in here?"

I run my hands through my hair and try to think of how to begin.

"Is it that bad?" she asks. The joking has been put aside. Her eyes are wide with worry.

"Jackson did my death reading," I say.

"I said—"

"Let me finish. Please, it is hard enough to think," I beg.

She exhales and folds her arms. "OK. *Continue.*"

"Caldwell is going to kill me," I say, but even as I get the words out of my mouth, I hear the little voice inside me, that old bastard survivor speaking up. *Not if I blast out his brains first.*

"How?" she asks.

I think of the discrepancies in the drawings, one with Caldwell's hands around my neck, and the other with just my gun up and pointed. "It isn't clear," I say. "There are a couple versions of the story."

"Then it can be changed," she says, earnestly.

"Are you going to let me finish?"

"We changed it for Jesse," she says, ignoring me. "She was supposed to die in that basement and so was Ally and everyone else, but I saw it and it was changed. We did that."

"Please let me finish," I beg again, squeezing my temples. "For the love of all that is holy, let me say everything I need to say and then if you want to argue with me or berate me, fine. But just let me finish a fucking thought."

She falls back against her pillows and arches her eyebrow as if to say, *well, go on then. Out with it.*

"I need two things from you," I say. "Consider them last requests."

She opens her mouth and I brace myself but the words never come. Instead, she snaps her mouth shut while her face reddens with the effort.

"First, I need information." The furrow between her eyes deepens.

"I want you to tell me everything about your special abilities."

She blinks as if she hasn't heard me.

"I know you have abilities," I go on. "You and Jesse are like Caldwell. I want to know how it started and what's happened. I need to know exactly what you're capable of and what you think Caldwell has to do with any of it, but let's start with what you can do."

She waits as if expecting me to stop her again. When I don't, she speaks up: "When it started, I didn't know what the hell was going on. It just sort of consumed me, you know?"

"No," I say. "I don't." Because I don't understand. I'm not sure I believe in Heaven or Hell or angels. But I've seen with my own eyes what Caldwell can do, and I know something is happening to Jesse now. I have to understand it if I'm going to stop him and help Jesse. "Make me understand."

Rachel exhales and her cheeks puff up on both sides. "I had delusions for a long time. There was a guy I would see. He'd be in my home or on the street. No one else saw him and sometimes people would walk right through him. So I knew he wasn't real. Because death-replacing damages the brain, I just figured I was shot, you know, like busted. So I didn't tell anyone. But then when I woke up from that last death, I was raw."

"In pain?"

"Yeah, but a very particular kind of pain. I'd say itchy but that's not right. It's kind of like the feeling you get late at night when you can't sleep. You feel like you might need to pee, your legs are restless and all that—that feeling times a gazillion."

I have no idea what she's talking about, so I keep my mouth shut and listen.

"That day you found me all cut and shit," she says, "I was totally overwhelmed by the power. That's really the only word for it I guess. Power. It's a lot like being a walking live wire."

I can picture that day well enough. Jesse and I had come over to check on her after a replacement. The girls feel pretty rough after a job, and so when Jesse wanted to take Rachel some jellybeans, I was on board. But when we got there, Rachel was in her living room, naked and bloody. She'd cut herself up pretty bad and had smeared the blood all over her naked skin and the floor around her.

Rachel came at us with the knife she'd used on herself, but I stopped her. I sent Jesse back to the car for her own protection and I held onto Rachel, trying to calm her down.

But I remember what I saw clearly.

When I'd pushed her down, trying to pin her and take the knife away, the whole house started to shake. Pictures fell from the walls. Chairs overturned. Drapes and curtain rods tumbled from the windows. "Do you remember what you said to me?" I asked her. "When I was trying to calm you down, you said some things to me about Caldwell."

"I told you he was Jesse's father," she says, her cheeks red with embarrassment. "I said she was going to destroy all of us."

"But I'd never told you he was her father," I say. "So how did you know?"

"Because Uriel told me. He's the guy I saw. See. But he isn't just a guy," she replies. "He's an angel. He's the one I'm channeling when I do whatever it is I do. He's the one that's told me everything about Caldwell, Jesse, and what the hell is going on."

"So what does he say?" I ask.

Her eyes well up with tears. "You think I'm crazy."

"It doesn't matter what I think," I remind her. "But no, I don't think you are crazy."

She takes a minute to breathe, slowing down her exhalations, no doubt a mechanism she learned these past few years in the asylum.

"Uriel says we are special. NRD and death replacement, all of that is just a symptom of what's happening."

"What's happening?" I try to sound encouraging rather than skeptical.

"The world is changing, like it always does." She shrugs. "But because we've developed consciousness as a species, we now have a choice as to what it will change into. We have that power now, to make it whatever we want."

"How is your angel or power supposed to change the world?"

"*I'm* not going to change the world," she blurts. Laughter comes high and nervous from her constricted throat. "I just move stuff."

"Move stuff?"

"I can move things. People, objects, or myself. You know, *stuff*."

"Show me," I say.

"No," she says. "If I use it I'm open and vulnerable."

"Why?"

"Caldwell will know," she says. "I don't want him to know what I can do. I'm not ready to face him."

My heart sinks when I hear this. I really need her to accept the favor I'm about to ask, even if it scares the shit out of her.

"So Caldwell has an angel too, that he can use to change the world?" I ask.

"Yes," she says. "But I don't know which one. I just know that he has been going around stealing other people's powers."

You made me what I am, he'd said. He's right, because I am the reason he discovered how to take power from someone else. My chest constricts around the truth.

"We can talk all damn day if you want, but you said you need two things from me. Two. What's the other favor? Information and—?"

"I want you to promise that you'll take care of Jesse. If I

die, you have to go to her. Caldwell will try to kill you both. You're safer together. You can combine your gifts and keep each other safe."

Her mouth falls open but I say what I need to.

"Jesse still thinks of him as her father. There may be a time when you have to face Caldwell *for* Jesse. Do you understand?"

"We agreed this was the safest place for me," she says.

"I know," I say and squeeze her knees. "I'm asking you to take a big risk. You'll have to break out of here and get to Jesse on your own. You'll have to use your resources."

"You're asking me to kill him for her."

I say nothing.

"If Caldwell even finds out about me—" she begins. "I'll never get the chance to do what you're asking."

He's going to know anyway, I think. *The next time he sees me.* "I know I'm asking a lot."

"You're going to die trying to kill him," she says, tears in her eyes. "And you want me to do the same."

"So if I die, you're going to stay here and leave Jesse unprotected?"

She throws up her hands in frustration. "No, of course not."

"Then tell me you'll do it," I demand. "Promise me that if anything happens to me, that if you don't get a call from me on October 4th, your bags will be packed and you're out of here."

"Promise me you're going to at least *try* not to die," she says. Her jaw works furiously as she clenches and unclenches her teeth. I wonder if she still has the mouth guard I gave her to mitigate all the grinding she does in her sleep.

I exhale. "If it comes to me or Jesse, you know what I'm going to choose."

She looks down at her lap.

"Promise me, Rachel. If I'm gone, you two have to stick together. I want my girls to survive. That's my last request. I want you both to live long and happy lives."

When she looks up again the collected tears are spilling over. "Okay, fine," she spits. "I promise. I promise, you asshole."

A giant weight is lifted from my chest. *They can do this*, I think. *They can do this without me—if it comes to that.* "Thank you."

She smacks my arm. "You're a moron. Just stop talking already. I can't bear to listen to any more of this martyr nonsense."

"I'll stop talking," I say and stand from the bed. I cross to the door and close it, giving us a bit of privacy. "If you'll show me what you can do."

*J*ackson is sitting in the dark of her living room when I come in and she has a gun in her hand.

I drop my bag on the floor and pull my own gun. In situations like this, it is suicide to ask *what's going on? What's going on* could be a bullet to your brain.

"He's not here anymore," Jackson says and sits forward, resting each of her elbows on a knee. The gun hangs loosely between her legs.

"Caldwell?" I ask.

"He had a message for me, from Micah."

I step out of the small living room and go into the kitchen. I don't turn on any lights, but I do take a moment between opening and closing the fridge to listen for that buzz in my head, that telltale sign that Caldwell is here, lurking, even if I can't see the bastard.

I hear nothing.

I go back to where Jackson waits on the couch and offer her the beer in my hand. When she shakes her head no, I pop the cap off with my keychain bottle opener, put it in my front pocket with the plan to add it to my growing tabletop collection. Then I sit down beside her.

I wait. If she doesn't want me to know the message, she doesn't have to tell me. When I am pretty sure she isn't going to say anything, I start. "Are you going to tell Jesse he's your brother?"

"No," she says. "Why should I?"

I shrug. "You're right. Why would she need to know that? I guess I'm wrapped up in my confessional. Writing down all of your sins, all the things you blame yourself for, it just gets into your head, you know?"

"How's Rachel?" she asks.

"Good," I say. "Tough as nails, and still just as much of a smart ass as Jesse. God only knows how they ever got along."

"I believe they appreciate each other's humor."

"Yeah, that's probably it. Anyway, she's good. She seems healthy and in control of herself."

"Does she still see angels?" Jackson asks as she thumbs the safety back on and rests the gun against her knee.

"One, named Uriel apparently," I say. "But it's more than that. She can move shit around. Like Carrie White or something, but hopefully it won't end in a bloodbath."

"Unless it's Caldwell's blood," she says.

"That would simplify things. Was he able to get in?" I tap the side of my skull.

She shakes her head no. "I've been expecting him for a while. It's why I've been sitting and sleeping on the couch. There's only one way in and out." She points to the living room in front of her.

Her sofa has an uninterrupted view of the room. Unless Caldwell developed the ability to hang through walls, he couldn't creep up behind her here. "If he can't bounce around me like a goddamn lemur, he's got just the mind games."

"But that doesn't work with you, right?" It was true a long

time ago, but I've learned never to assume that because your ass got lucky once you could play that card until the end of time. Most luck has an expiration date.

"No," she says. "He couldn't get into my head. But he can still play with my emotions."

"You don't have emotions," I say, faking cheerfulness. "You're a warrior."

She grunts. "He said my brother asked for the pleasure of killing me himself."

My fingers tighten on the cold glass. "He was lying."

"No," she says and taps the gun against her leg. "I know my baby brother. He never forgave me for what happened."

"You were kids," I say.

"It doesn't matter. Not to him."

I don't say anything to that. If it were me, she'd say the same thing. I think of Aziz, lying motionless in the dirt, blood coming out of the corner of his mouth. *You were only doing your job. How could you know? You are a good soldier, protecting our boys, our home, and democracy. You did the right thing.*

No matter how many times I'd heard this crap, I never believed it.

And I know the other side of the coin too. Charlie. Once we'd been so close I would've died for him. Then he betrayed me.

No, there was nothing I could say to Jackson that she would accept.

So I let the silence grow thick between us. I lay back against the couch and balance the bottle on one of my knees. I try to relax the muscles in my back which are tense from all the miles I've put on the odometer today. I open myself up to the peaceful feeling of exhaustion trying to grab ahold of me. The cushions beside me soften as Jackson sits back herself. Then I feel a hand on my beer, pulling the bottle from my grip.

With my eyes closed, I listen to her gulp it down and wonder just how many moments, dark quiet moments like this one, did I have left with her.

"Do you ever just feel like an old computer?" I ask her, thinking of that clunker I gave Jesse to disassemble. "There are all these tablets and iPhones and apps where you can turn the heat down at home while you're taking a shit at the office."

She laughs.

"That's how I feel with all this dying but waking up, and angels and oh-I-can-climb-in-your-head-and-make-you-think-you're-a-beautiful-pony shit. I miss the days when all I had to worry about was someone with a gun."

My eyes open and I turn to look at her. She's smiling down at the beer as if it's told her a joke.

"What?" I ask.

"They shoved magnetite in my brain to try and make me a better soldier," she says. She twists the neck between two fingers and just smiles at me. "If you think about it, it's like an upgrade. I've been upgraded."

Before I know it we are both laughing, deep and desperate sounds spilling from our throats.

CHAPTER TWENTY-TWO

Friday, March 28, 2003

I spent the morning doing paperwork. I know some guys hate to write up their reports, but I find it soothing. I still do. Something about dotting the 'i's and crossing the 't's gives me a sense of completion and closure that I rarely achieve with a gun in my hand.

It helped that Charlie was out again instead of pacing his office like a caged animal, gnawing at the furniture and breathing down my neck. I felt pretty damn good until Jackson ruined it by slamming a stack of file folders on my desk.

"Jesus, Jackson," I said and erased the spastic nonsense I'd typed into the word document. "God forbid a man enjoy a peaceful morning."

"This is bullshit," she said.

I saved the report I'd been working on and turned away from the computer. "If this is about the fact that Detective Swanson ordered a physical for you, I—"

Her face scrunched up with irritation. "I am often undermined because I am a woman and black, why should I care if I'm also undermined because of my health and disabilities?"

I thought it best to keep my mouth shut.

"I'm talking about the files on Sullivan. Look," she said.

I didn't ask how she got the files before me. I opened the folder she offered from the top of the stack. It was very thin. I'd seen detainee files before from previous missing person cases I'd worked since joining the FBRD. This wasn't even the full four-page admittance form. Basic information like his DOB was present. Other parts of the processing record were deleted.

"What the hell is this?" I asked. "Where's the rest?"

"Exactly," she said. "Did you notice anything?"

I looked down at the first page again, searching for anything out of place. Then I saw it. The processing number was missing. The number I needed to find more information on Sullivan had been removed from the document.

"Where's the PNC?" I asked, unwilling to believe they'd scrub off the very code I needed to continue my investigation.

"Good question," she said.

"It doesn't make sense," I said. "Charlie has been losing his mind over trying to find this guy, but then we're given doctored files? Do they want him found or not?"

"Maybe they want him found," she said, sitting back in her seat and rubbing her forehead. "But they don't want us to know why he must be found."

My guts clenched. It took me a second to realize I was expecting another seizure, like the last time she sat in this chair.

"Don't look at me like that," she said. "I'm fine."

"Are you? I heard they're still trying to figure out what to give you."

She shrugged. "Some drugs work. Others work but cause problems. I'm alive, aren't I?"

I let it go. "You'd know better than I would."

She fell into a pensive silence. When she spoke there was a weight to her gaze. "I've seen something like this before."

I looked up so she knew I was listening.

"He was an operative. Deadly guy. But he went MIA on a mission and they wanted to bring him back, but didn't want anyone to really know why they were looking for him or who he really was."

"So do you think Sullivan works for someone and that someone is unhappy with his job performance?" I'd heard worse theories.

"He has a lot of mechanical knowledge," she said. "And he's hard to kill. He would make a decent operative, especially if they trained him up during the years they had him detained."

Before we could brainstorm this theory longer, my phone rang and I answered.

"Get down here," Charlie said. He gave me an address.

"What's happened?" I stood and pulled my leather jacket off the back of my chair. Jackson did the same.

"I found the Michaelson girl," Charlie said, but his voice wasn't reassuring. Whatever he had for me wasn't good news.

"That bad?" I asked.

"That bad."

CHAPTER TWENTY-THREE
Friday, March 28, 2003

*J*ackson and I pulled up outside the address and found the house still smoking. A fire of this magnitude would burn for a while, smoldering long after the last of the flames were gone. Jackson and I took the Impala, parking it on the curb opposite the house. I crossed the street to find Charlie with his back to the flames. He spoke as soon as he saw me.

"The firefighters recovered three bodies, burnt beyond recognition with only dental fragments available for identification. Just teeth were found for the little girl," Swanson said as the three of us stood outside the smoking house.

I felt like I'd been kicked in the balls. My stomach ached deep inside and it was pretty damn hard to suck air into my lungs.

"How many teeth?" I asked as a memory surfaced.

"Three," he confirmed.

"Why three?" I pressed. "Did they knock the rest out of her head?"

"No head," Swanson said.

"Excuse me?"

Heat rolled off the house and the air smelled like a camp-fire, all that burned wood wafting into the breeze.

"The little girl was decapitated. The coroner thinks it was done post-mortem, probably by her kidnappers."

"So where is the head?"

"We don't know."

"So you identified Maisie Michaelson with no head, just three teeth?"

"It's enough to extract DNA."

I rubbed my brow. "You can extract DNA from a baby tooth but not from the bones of a corpse?"

Charlie raised his voice. "I'm not a forensic fucking scientist. I'm just telling you what I was told. Do you want to know the rest of the story or not?"

I waved him on.

"This house belonged to George and Carolyn Kilns. They recently lost their daughter in an accident. She was about Maisie's age, died from an undiagnosed allergy. Their daughter also went to Maisie's school. We don't know all the details yet, but we suspect they kidnapped the Michaelson girl and tried to keep her for themselves."

Jackson's face said she was just as pissed as I was. "Why would they do that?"

Charlie looked at her as if for the first time. "A child who cannot die sounds like a dream come true to a couple of grieving parents."

"Then why cut off the kid's head?" I asked. "Why dispose of a head?"

"Who fucking knows? Maybe they were insane. Maybe they decided to murder her and kill themselves, but knew they had to fuck up her brain to do it."

"Pretty extreme. Nothing a shot to the head wouldn't have accomplished."

"It doesn't matter," Charlie said and threw his hands up.

"Case closed. The girl is dead. Are you going to lose your shit on this? Carry her headless corpse out into the desert?"

The world warped as if the fire were melting it away. Charlie looked like he might apologize, but closed his mouth and walked toward the uniform officer on the other side of the tape. Jackson took a step closer and I braced myself for her questions about Aziz.

"She isn't dead," she said.

I exhaled the breath I was holding. My gut didn't think the girl was dead either, but I'd been wrong once or twice before, especially when I really didn't want to be wrong.

"Why do you say that?"

"Because I viewed her last night," she said. "She's alive and she isn't here."

I tried to remember what Charlie had said about the remote viewing process. Something about seeing images or hearing sounds in their minds and then sketching down the clues. I could only remember the history. I knew it was a technique developed by the military, to see if ESP espionage was possible. When they failed to replicate NRD—particularly the ability to resurrect—someone got the idea to teach their volunteer soldiers remote-viewing instead. I couldn't remember how they'd made the connection between remote-viewing and the failed NRD experiment.

"Would your 'viewing' show her dead though?" I asked.

"Yes," she said. She sounded pretty damn confident. "She isn't dead."

CHAPTER TWENTY-FOUR

28 Weeks

My eyes shoot open and I grab my neck. My head buzzes from the sudden lack of oxygen and my throat muscles flex as if trying to shake off whatever is crushing my windpipe. I only swipe at the air around me unable to connect with anything. There is no hand, no assailant. I see spots in front of my eyes, those dancing black and white blips that I know are the precursor to passing out. In the dark of my bedroom, I start to wonder if this is a dream.

The sensation disappears. As suddenly as it came, the pressure around my throat vanishes and sweet relief washes over me. I lean forward in my bed and draw in deep lungfuls of air. My head still buzzes, but the blackout dots clear. Caldwell sits by the window in the white armchair placed there by whomever decorated this apartment.

"That felt good," he says, folding his fingers back to inspect his nails. "Was it good for you? I hear asphyxiation to the point of unconsciousness can be euphoric."

I reach for the gun under my pillow. It isn't there. Caldwell lifts it up so I can see it in the pale light coming through the windows. "Too slow. You see, if I pop in while you're sleeping, I can deepen your dream state. I can bring a marching band through here and you'll be none the wiser. It's a fantastic trick, don't you think? I have you to thank for it."

"Stay out of my head," I tell him. My voice is gravelly at best. I'm not sure if it is from being choked or from sleep itself.

"No, you see I didn't choke you," he says and sits forward in his seat still holding my gun. "I just told your mind that you were choking. Then your obedient muscles constricted and the lungs closed."

"You can't control Jackson. And you can't control Jesse."

He looks up. "I'd love to test that theory."

I lean against the headboard and pull up my knee to rest my elbow on it.

"You're right about Jackson though. Her brain damage protects her. If you only had a little magnetite in your brain, you'd be all right. But you are 100% meat up there, so we can have all the fun in the world." He leans back in his chair. "You know you were dreaming about the boy again?"

Aziz's soft face surfaces, still a baby face that wouldn't see a razor for years. The sound of goats crying and his mother's screams rise up from the darkness.

"Stop," I tell him, believing these visions are his doing. "I'm not in the mood."

"That's not me," he says. "You don't need me to torture you. You do a great job of that all on your own."

"To what do I owe this honor?" I say and meet his eyes. "This is the second time you've come over just to play. Do you have it that bad for me?"

He sneers. "Practice makes perfect. Do you know there was a study where basketball players were asked to supplement their drills with visualization? The control group who didn't practice in their heads as well as on the court showed less improvement. So you see, I'm getting better and better at killing you every time I imagine doing it. If I'm going to snap your neck in a couple of months, I might as well get good at it. Otherwise, I might botch the job and you'll have to choke to death on your own blood. Would you like that?"

"Just tell me what you want." I don't like being trapped in my own bed, weaponless.

"I want to kill you and get this over with," he says, pressing an index finger to the side of his skull.

I open my arms. "What's stopping you?"

He laughs. "The fact that if I kill you now, I'll change the future. And right now the future looks pretty good, so why risk it?"

He stands from the chair and comes toward me. My whole body tenses, but instead of launching an assault, he pulls something from his pocket and hands it to me. It is a sheet of paper folded into a small neat square.

I open it, beginning to recognize Micah's artwork by sight.

In the picture, Jesse is in Caldwell's arms. He is carrying her somewhere and she is either dead or unconscious, I can't tell which. I search the picture for clues, anything to tell me where or when this happens.

I try to form questions that will keep him talking. Maybe it is harder to read my mind if he's wrapped up in his own. "If you wanted her, you could just step in and take her at any moment. Why haven't you?"

His eyes darken. "We both know Jesse is different."

"Because she's your kid. Don't tell me something so trivial is going to hold you back from your plan of world domination."

"She's much more than that and you know it."

I think of the angels, of what Rachel has told me and her theories about what else is going on.

"Ah, so Rachel has been called?" Caldwell says, his face lighting up with interest. "That is one less rat to smoke out."

"If you hurt either of them, I'll kill you." My head is hot and the anger warms my arms and chest. It feels good.

"You'll try," he says, dismissing me. "What I don't understand is why you don't tell Jesse more? Why haven't you told her about Maisie? Why haven't you told her about us and what you did for me?"

"What can I tell her about Maisie?" I ask, seeing an opportunity. "Is she alive?"

He doesn't answer me.

I focus on my hands, rough and square on the coverlet. I breathe. I don't let a stray thought seep into my mind. "What did you come here for? Just to show me another picture and gloat?"

"Maybe I was feeling nostalgic," he says. "Like you with that little memoir you're writing. I can't help but think of how this all started and marvel at how we got here."

"Do me a favor," I say, yawning. "If you want to stop by for another late night chat, next time bring some beer, would you? And maybe a burger. I love the Hawaiian Handful from Rudy's, just so you know. They put this—"

My throat slams shut. I gag, reaching up to grab ahold of my neck and claw at it. Caldwell is right in front of me then, his face inches from me. He shoves my gun against my temple. "I'm not an errand boy."

I cough and open then close my mouth like a fish out of water. I suddenly feel like a bastard for all those summers on the lake with my father and his brothers. How many perch, sunfish and catfish had we thrown on the deck to choke out like this?

"Stop investigating me. Stop looking for clues for how to stop me. There is no stopping me." Caldwell spits the words into my face, shoving the barrel harder into the side of my skull. "You have one job. Be the fuckup you are. Make the stupid decisions that you make and if you try anything else, I'll kill the little spic you've got holed up in the hospital. Do you understand?"

He releases me and disappears.

My gun falls through the air and bounces against the coverlet beside me. I breathe, slow my thoughts and adrenaline as best I can. I am alone again.

And once again, I must swallow my questions about Maisie.

CHAPTER TWENTY-FIVE

Friday, March 28, 2003

I made it all the way back to my apartment, even dragged my ass up the stairs to the front door before I decided I couldn't go in. As I stood outside my door, the intensity of the silence weighed on me. I'd been down this road before. Silence at a time like this could drive a guy crazy. I put my fists in my pockets and turned back the way I came.

It took me seven minutes to get to Blackberry Hill. I must've come in with my tail tucked because just one look at me and Peaches harrumphed.

He placed two shot glasses on the bar as I slid onto a stool. "Who died?"

"Maisie Michaelson," I said. "She was 6."

His mouth fell open and his eyes went wide. "Fuck."

I nodded because I had nothing to add. What was there to say? Worst case scenario, the Michaelson girl was dead. Best case scenario, she was alive but there were a slew of insurmountable roadblocks between me and her, stretching the distance farther and farther between us. I had Jackson and her magic eyeballs. Maybe that would be enough. I'd run so many of these operations that I knew killing someone was an easy solo job, but finding something and bringing it back took resources we didn't have.

Peaches sloshed tequila over the rim of each glass and pushed one toward me with a fat finger. "On the house."

I picked it up and threw it back, slamming it unnecessarily against the wood. But the pain felt good in my palm, sobering. He filled it again and I threw it back once more. We went four rounds that way and he matched me shot for shot. It was the third shot before I realized what I'd done, my heart plummeting into my chest. I'd called her the Michaelson girl, not Maisie. I was creating distance in my head. I was giving up.

No, I thought. *Maisie. Maisie. Maisie— I won't give up on you, kid.*

"Oh God, not again." Peaches grimaced and looked over at the jukebox.

"Have you tried reprogramming it?" I asked. I realized the high-pitched whine was not in my head, nor was it an injured cat. It was another boy band song blaring from the jukebox.

His eyes went wide and he slapped the bar top. "Of course, darn it. I've torn the thing apart and there is nothing in there. Just the AC/DC, Johnny Cash, Aerosmith and all that."

I grunted. "One of life's great mysteries."

"OK, we've got to switch to the soft stuff," he said, returning the tequila to the top shelf. "Or I won't be able to count the till."

"If I shoot your jukebox," I added. "Don't take it personally."

I accepted the frothy mug with the house pint fizzing inside and also put a twenty on the bar. Peaches shook his head and scraped a thick nail over the white stubble lining his jaw.

"Put it away, B," he said. "Save it for another day."

He left me to my thoughts then. He played barkeep to his customers while the noise of darts hitting the board sounded behind me and pool balls clacked on a table across the room. The televisions above us broadcasted a soccer game and a Grand Prix race. *Slim pickings* Peaches would say, since he preferred boxing or football himself, neither of which were in season. The best he could hope for was baseball, which wouldn't start up until next month.

I let the sounds of the room, the familiar warmth of these walls, soften me until a man slid onto the stool on my right. My fingers were cold from the frost on the glass and I tried to warm them by rubbing them against my jeans. I stole a glance at the man without being rude. I tried not to be the grumpy bastard who gave everyone the evil eye, but I was too seasoned not to inspect a man who'd come this close.

He had freckles across his nose and hazel-green eyes. His thick brows were a different shade than the shaggy hair framing his face. A dye job maybe. The scars around his jaw and neck were interesting, almost a clean line from ear to the chin. I assumed it went all the way around, but I didn't ask. Maybe his overgrown scruff was meant to hide it, or maybe it was none of my fucking business. It was rude as hell to ask a man what shitty thing had left its mark on him.

"What do you recommend?" he asked.

His voice was low, almost too low to be heard over the din of the bar, as if he wasn't accustomed to talking to others.

"If you don't order the house pint Peaches will take it personally," I said, which was true enough.

"Peaches?" he asked. He measured me with his eyes and I let him. Sometimes, when work went bad, I would rough up the first guy I saw. Some punk like this one would bother me at the wrong time and leave with a bloody mouth for no good reason. To say I was reformed was an understatement.

"What'll it be?" Peaches asked him, placing both hands on the bar and waiting for instruction. His long gray ponytail had fallen forward over his shoulder and was resting on his big paunch of a belly, stretched beneath a black AC/DC shirt.

"The house pint," the man said, almost like a question.

Peaches liked the answer and pulled a frosted mug from the mini cooler behind the bar. "House pint it is."

"What jerk chose this song?" the stranger asked, looking at the jukebox against the far wall.

"I'll give you $100 if you can solve that mystery, man." Peaches washed mugs in the sink and still wet, pushed them into the back of the fridge to freeze.

The guy beside me asked a couple of questions, but I didn't gratify him with an answer. My silence made him nervous I guess, because he laughed. Peaches must've felt sorry for him.

"Don't bother B, here," he said. "He's had a rough night."

"Sorry to hear it," the guy said and gulped his pint. "What kind of work do you do?"

"He's a federal agent," Peaches said.

"Peaches," I said and squared my shoulders. "Come on."

"Drugs?" the guy asked.

Peaches corrected him. "Missing people."

"Seriously?" the guy said and sat up straighter.

I didn't want to talk about work. I sure as hell didn't want to talk about Maisie to the first yahoo who walked through the door.

I left my half-finished drink on the bar top and stood. Then I zipped up my leather jacket and left.

"Aww, B," Peaches called after me. "Don't get pissed, man. I'm just proud of what you do."

I said nothing, choosing instead to step out into the cold city night.

CHAPTER TWENTY-SIX

12 Weeks

Caldwell left me the picture. I spend the rest of the night in front of the big open window in the kitchen overlooking the city, watching the night fade to dawn and then catch fire with daylight. I stare at the image of Jesse in Caldwell's arms and try to decide what to do.

It could be a trap.

Taking this picture to Gloria might very well set us on the path that leads to this. Or doing nothing could be our downfall. I'm not a god. How the hell am I supposed to know which choice is best?

I stuff the folded page into my pocket and go out to the cold Impala. I drive across town to a little squat house overgrown with weeds. The kitchen light is on when I pull into the gravel driveway and I marvel at that for a moment. Jackson has a tendency to walk from dark room to dark room long after sunset.

Then I see the hearse in the driveway.

I creep up to the back of the house and let myself in. I hear Kirk's voice for only a moment before the front door slams shut. I don't have to creep. I could say hello. After all,

Kirk is one of the few to know I am alive. But I'm not in a chitchat mood. I slide through the house toward the kitchen and find Jackson there alone. She reaches up and turns off the light.

"What's going on?"

She grabs a Coke from the fridge and offers me a beer. I turn her down. "He believes someone has been stealing Jesse's clothes from the funeral home. He can't be sure, so he's going to wait awhile. He asked me to check on her."

"So what will you do?" I ask and sit opposite her at the table.

"I'm not a goddamn Magic 8 Ball," she says. "You can't just shake me and find out what will happen."

The picture in my pocket grows heavy. She takes a long drink and then puts the can down to look at me. Her face scrunches.

"Why are you here?"

"I would never take your gifts for granted," I say, realizing I'm completing my internal train of thought rather than answering her actual question.

Her face hardens. "Did he come see you again?"

I pull the folded sheet of sketch paper from my pocket and hand it to her. With a furrowed brow I've seen many times over the last decade, I watch her open it up and smooth it flat with her hand. Her expression punches a hole in my chest.

"Micah drew this," she says, softly. The tenderness is unmistakable. I nod.

She studies it the way someone might study the Mona Lisa or a Van Gogh. Her finger touches some of the lines as if they are butterfly wings. "He's good. See how clearly he draws the shadow and the light. The chiaroscuro—I taught him that."

"I'm sorry," I tell her.

"No," she says. "Thank you. I've always wanted to see his work."

I tell her about Caldwell's visit.

"You're still dreaming about the boy?" she asks.

I snort. "I don't think that's the most important thing I just said to you."

"You have to forgive yourself for that. It was a direct order."

I snort again. "A direct order."

"We've all received an order or ten that we didn't agree with. It doesn't mean we had the power to refuse it."

"Do you think Sullivan would have done it, if she thought it was wrong?"

A smile quirks in the corner of Jackson's mouth. "No."

"No," I agree. "As much as it irks me, I love that about the kid. I could tell her to kill someone and she'd tell me to put my foot up my ass. You'd never get her to do something wrong unless you convinced her it was the right thing to do."

"You believed it was right," Jackson says. "If the bomb had been real, it would've killed a lot more people. You acted on what you believed to be right."

She drinks her Coke and looks down at the sketch lovingly as if it had been drawn for her by her own children—if she'd ever had any.

"How is Jesse's training going?" she asks.

"Slow. She argues more than she listens, but maybe that's a good thing. She's got the lockpicking down. Her aikido is getting better and her Shotokan is pretty good. She gave me a kidney shot the other day that brought tears to my eyes."

"Is she ready for the Lovett job?"

"She'll do all right."

She looks up at me then. "Is she ready for him?"

I see Jesse defenseless in Caldwell's arms. A trick or not, it's there in black-and-white.

"I don't know if she'll ever be ready."

CHAPTER TWENTY-SEVEN

Saturday, March 29, 2003

I showed up at Chaplain's fifteen minutes before 9:00 P.M. to scope out the scene. I considered calling Jackson. She was good with a gun and had an instinct about her. There were worse people to have as backup. Besides, the deeper we went into this, the more I trusted her. She seemed the only one willing to do what was right—whatever the cost.

I decided to go in alone.

For ten minutes, men filed into the large house near Beckett Park. Both sides of Page Street were filled with parked cars, arranged horizontally along the curb. Some cars had a single soul. Others had four or five.

I recognized a few—drug peddlers and pimps—and marveled at what classy company Chaplain kept. But there were plenty of faces I didn't know, and some of the men were far too polished to be anyone's Eastside pimp. And why they were here, filing into the large, dark house on Page Street, I really wanted to find out.

It wasn't until I saw Fizz climb out of a car with two other men, all three of them with unnatural hair colors: pink, orange, and green, that I made my move. First, I watched them approach the front door, then pause on the porch to present what I assumed was the admission fee.

I took a breath and made sure I had a boot knife and my loaded Beretta before I climbed out of the Impala.

I came up behind two men trying to enter the house. I hoped the door men would assume I was with them, grouped together with more familiar faces, I wouldn't look so suspicious. I also watched their actions carefully so I wouldn't fuck up. They handed over the money and then were patted down. I realized then my gun was a mistake even before the large man to the right of me placed a beefy hand on it.

"No guns," he said. He had a big neck, little head. Not the most flattering combination.

"Shit, I forgot," I said. "I'll put it back in the car."

"No," he said. "I'll take it."

I hesitated and saw his feathers ruffle. Fine, I'd give up the gun if I had to. "Sure, hang on to it for me."

$500 lighter, I stepped into the dark house. A soft music seeped in from somewhere I couldn't see.

Speakers might have hung from the ceiling or were tucked into dark corners, but there was simply not enough light in the room for me to tell. Louder than the music was a soft murmur of excitement.

The electricity of anticipation charged the air. I followed the crowd in, and found that seats had been arranged in rows like a small theatre. I took an empty seat at the end of the second row. I wanted a clear shot for the door if I needed to make a break for it, but I also wanted to be close enough to the "stage" to see what the hell was going on. A velvet rope cut the room in half, the kind used in theaters to queue lines.

On this side of the velvet rope, which hung between two brass posts, we had uncomfortable metal folding chairs. They were despicably low to the ground, and my knees bent up comically when I took a seat. The sounds of grit or sand scraped against the wood floor underfoot. On the other side of the velvet rope, a bedroom—or the replica of one—waited.

A fluffy white duvet was thrown over a mattress held up by a brass bed frame, the bed itself empty and waiting. Overhead lights burned down on the scene, the bed, the night tables, the old rug, dusty and neglected beneath the bed. Definitely a set for play.

When I glanced up to identify the source of the light, I saw the speakers and the cameras. But the cameras weren't trained on us. They showed no interested in the men filling the metal chairs on this side of the velvet rope, the shuffling and anxious men. Those black eyes were oblivious to the low, excited voices. The men sat on the edge of their seats, their necks craning stage left, eyes trained on the dark door for the first sign of—what?

What was coming? Whatever it was, that's what the cameras cared about.

The anticipation broke when a girl bounded through the door crying.

Her cheeks were tear-stained and her long white gown the parody of innocence. A man came through the door after her. He was in street clothes. His jeans were faded at the knees and he wore a battered pair of Rugged Blue work boots.

He followed her into the room as she tried to escape, her eyes wide, blue, and wet. But there was nowhere to go. There was only the bed and us beyond the velvet rope. Her blond hair was long, tousled.

"Please," she screamed. She rushed the rope. "Please."

Men in the front rows, who I had not seen until that moment because they blended perfectly with the shadows around them, stepped forward. They pushed her back into the spotlight, into her attacker's arms. Someone—more than one person—laughed.

I grew tense in my seat, having a sick feeling that I knew where this was going and what was I going to do about it.

He lifted her kicking and screaming and threw her onto the bed. She was so light and the force of his strength so great, that she bounced on the mattress, her legs going wide for a moment and her mouth opening in surprise. She tried to roll off the other side, but he grabbed her by the hair and pulled her across the mattress to him.

She screamed.

He hit her hard across the mouth and she stopped struggling. I'd moved to stand without realizing I'd done so until a hand was on me, pulling me back into my seat. The hand gripping my arm tightened and pulled me down without letting go.

"He hasn't even gotten started," Fizz said. His eyes were shiny in the dark. His bright hair muted in the shadows. "You wanted to know what he does with the special girls. Then watch. And you are seriously outnumbered, man."

I didn't mention my lack of backup.

"That isn't your girl anyway," he said.

He was right. Even if they'd dyed her hair blond and added extensions, the girl's heart-shaped face didn't match Rachel's angular one. If I busted open this place now, and Rachel was being held somewhere else, they might kill her, dump her, or sell her to the highest bidder.

"Just watch," Fizz said again.

I didn't want to watch. The man was raping her, right there in front of everyone. The bed squeaked in a terrible sickening rhythm. Regardless of her unconsciousness, I looked away, but couldn't block out the noise. "You can't expect me to watch this and not do anything."

"That's exactly what you'll do," said Fizz. "Unless you want to die. You can't escape here with your life and hers."

My mind raced for the options of how to walk out of here

with the girl. I couldn't leave her here. I also couldn't die and leave Jackson alone with the burden of finding Maisie.

My thoughts were interrupted by a low hissing and boos from the crowd.

"What's happening?" I asked and sat up to see over the heads in front of me.

"They're bored," he said.

I wondered if I looked as horrified and sick as I felt. "Isn't this what they came to see?"

"No," Fizz said. "We can see girls getting fucked anywhere. Porn, hotel rooms. Why pay to see a dude beat his nuts soft while we sit quietly in our seats?"

A man appeared on the side lines wearing dark cargo pants and a black T-shirt. I recognized him immediately.

"Chaplain," I whispered and for a moment I saw his dark eyes turn toward mine as if he heard me over all the commotion caused by the viewers, cramped together in the dark.

When our eyes met, I felt strange. A shiver ran over me and my hands relaxed.

Fizz had also gone very still beside me, but I observed this as if from a great distance. Chaplain broke our locked gaze then and turned to the man who still had hold of the girl, but was no longer thrusting his dick into her. As Chaplain stared at the back of the man's head the man lifted the unconscious girl's long slender arm as if to consider it. He took it in both of his hands almost delicately. Then he snapped the arm.

The girl came awake, screaming. Her eyes wide and bulging. Her scream was that of an animal's as her arm bent back unnaturally at the elbow. The mechanical way in which the man moved, the lack of passion or interest that he'd held for the girl just moments before, I didn't understand it until much later.

He slipped a large, calloused hand, definitely a working

man's hand, under the pillow and when he removed it, a shining blade caught the overhead lights and gleamed.

Gripping the handle tight, he thrust the blade down into the girl's chest—again, and *again*, and again. Every time he pulled out the blade, bright red bursts blossomed on her white gown, the blood pooling and spreading until it sprayed from her mouth in desperate coughs.

She was crying, her face screwed up in pain, but no sound was coming out. I saw all of this, and every time I started to get upset, or react, something in me relaxed. Then the man let go of the knife just long enough to wrap both of his hands around the girl's neck. He choked her, squeezing until her wet, red face, bulging with veins relaxed.

She was dead.

She was *dead*. Something inside snapped awake.

"They come to watch them die," I said. I looked up to the cameras trained on the scene and knew the truth of Chaplain's operation. "The NRD girls are murdered for the films. Snuff films." I'd heard of them. And as long as they don't damage the brain, they have an endless supply of fodder. "Fizz, have you seen a girl with dark features—Fizz?"

People were leaving, but Fizz was frozen in his seat. His eyes forward. I nudged him but he didn't respond.

I felt eyes on me and looked up. Chaplain stared at us from the spotlight until someone came up to ask him a question.

"We will get it in editing," he replied to whatever the concern was.

"Fizz, we need to go," I said because I'd realized we were the last two in the house, with Chaplain staring hard at us if in deep consideration. A man came and collected the girl's body, carrying her back through the dark door as if she'd never been there at all—save the bright blood stain left on the white bed. Another man stripped the sheets to reveal stain on top of stain.

How many girls had died here in this bed? How long had these shows been going on?

"We really need to go," I said again, because I needed to assemble a team. I needed to come back, tonight even, and burn this hellhole to the ground.

Yes, I should go home. Don't worry about the girls. The one I'm looking for isn't even here and the ones that are want to be. Paid actresses. They love dying. Much like the girl who loved to tell her death story, these girls are also proud of their talents. And think of how many innocents who die for such horrible films to fill such horrible needs—they are practically obsolete now. Safe.

No one here is unhappy or hurt. No one.

I stood from my seat and turned toward the door. I felt heavy, on the verge of sleep. I turned back to Fizz one last time but he still sat in his seat, staring silently ahead as if watching a show only he could see.

He'll be fine. Probably doesn't want to be seen leaving with me anyway. Go on. I need lie down. I'm so tired.

I walked out into the night. The March air hit me with just enough force that I came awake, alive again on the steps of the Park Street house. I felt like I'd walked into a room, but had forgotten what I came here for. I looked across the street and saw the Impala waiting. So tired, with a headache blooming behind my eyes, I made my way to my car. Then I got inside and went home, having completely forgotten about my gun.

CHAPTER TWENTY-EIGHT

I woke up the day after the *show* at Chaplain's and still felt off. My mind was foggy as if I'd drank too much. I remembered going to Chaplain's, seeing Fizz and the horrible show, but the whole thing had a haze to it. I had images of the girl smiling and laughing in my head, but I couldn't quite place them in the timeline of the evening.

Had she come out before and said something to the crowd? Greeted us in the doorway? I wasn't sure. But that sense of her comradery was infectious. She knew it was all a game and was happy to play. *She asked for it. She enjoyed it.* Don't let her acting fool you.

I went to the bar early. I'd learned that the best way to counteract a hangover was to simply start drinking again. When I walked into Blackberry Hill, Peaches wasn't behind the bar. An open doorway cast cold gray light across the bartop, making it shine. I stood there, looking around the place, at a loss as to what to do with myself. Then the door was darkened by a plump figure and Peaches appeared, carrying a case of beer. Behind him, a man with a dolly pushed in more cases stacked high.

"Just unloading the truck," Peaches called when he saw me. "You can help yourself if you like, or give me five."

I decided to wait. It wasn't that I didn't know how to pour myself a drink. But it felt wrong stepping behind the man's bar. This was Peaches' place.

Peaches grinned when he saw me and I didn't have a drink in hand. "Sorry for the wait, B. You're here early."

"I was dreaming about your beer," I said. "It couldn't wait. Besides, anything with the word blackberry in it is suitable for breakfast, right?"

He pulled a mug from the cooler and opened the tap. "Darn right."

I spent the next two hours sipping beer and trying to clear my head. I ordered a basket of French fries from the kitchen and watched the baseball preseason stuff on the large TV overhead.

I was dragging the last of the fries through a mound of ketchup when a man sat down beside me, the same man from the night before. "Shit."

"Don't run off just yet," he said.

I didn't bother to tell him that I didn't have it in me to run anywhere. Again, I wondered about the scars on his face and jawline. A car wreck maybe? With all that glass cutting up his face? Or was he a boxer or something like that?

"I'm sorry if I pissed you off last night," he said. "I meant no disrespect. I have nothing but admiration for guys like you."

"Guys like me?" I grunted and washed down the salty fries with the last two inches of my beer.

"Peaches said you find people. That you've been looking for the ones who were swept up by The Great Panic and were never seen again."

"Peaches needs to keep his mouth shut," I said, just as the

barkeep appeared to refill my beer. Peaches gave me a nervous, lopsided grin.

"I'm trying to say thank you," the other man interjected.

"For what?"

"I was in the camps," he said. "And let me tell you, no one was looking for us then."

I stopped trying to get away from the guy and faced him. His eyes were soft. Sincere. He wasn't lying to me for some kind of attention. There was no bravado there. No *ah, man, the shit I've been through* just beneath the surface, waiting for an invitation to wallow.

"I'm sorry to hear that," I said because what the hell can you say when someone admits something terrible like that. "How long were you in?"

"About three years," he said.

"That's long enough to change a man," Peaches chimed in. He'd been smart to keep quiet until now, giving me long enough to forgive him. But he'd made it clear that I would definitely have to be more careful as to what I shared with him.

Peaches went on. "I was locked up for just 18 months and believe me, I wasn't the same when I came out as I was when I went in. And I was just in normal prison, you know? Not like the camps." I'd heard Peaches' incarceration story before. I didn't care to hear it again. A petty drug charge and cost him almost two years of his life—and darkened his record just enough to make good employment hard to come by.

"When did you die?" I asked the other.

"1997," he said.

I let my confusion show. "But the camps closed in 1997. How did you spend three years locked up?"

He scoffed. "Because the government always does exactly what it says it will?"

"You're saying the camps stayed open?" My mind whirled. I thought back to the thin file folder on Sullivan. On the idea that Memphis was put on a bus and sent home but he didn't hear from Eric—maybe because Sullivan wasn't released?

"How many did they keep?" I asked.

"As many as they could," the other man said and pushed his empty pint toward Peaches who filled it with a solemn face. "At first I thought they'd kept me because I didn't have anyone waiting for me. But Peaches says your desk is packed with missing person cases. Maybe they kept whoever they could, regardless of the consequences. After all, whose door would they be able to bang on for answers? We were moved once the camps officially "disbanded" and it wasn't like they left a trail for us to be found. Some buses went home, others didn't."

"Where did they send you?" I asked.

"I don't know," he said. "Do you think they told us where we were going?"

"Landscape?" I asked.

"Desert," he said.

Arizona maybe, I thought. My mind swam with this information. The camps didn't close. What if they still weren't closed? It would certainly explain the pressure Charlie was getting from his higher-ups, but it wouldn't explain the desperation to find Sullivan so quickly. And there was Maisie —I wasn't over Maisie. Until I had a plan though, I might as well keep myself busy.

"Are they closed now?" I asked.

He paused. "You want my best guess? No."

"So how did you get out?" I asked.

"They got tired of me."

It was a lie and I knew it. But why? People lie for a lot of reasons. It could be something as simple as the fact he didn't really know me, or trust me. Or it could be so much more than that.

I should've known it was so much more than that.

CHAPTER TWENTY-NINE

10 Weeks

I drive to the cemetery again. As I pull through the gates, I see Kirk, tall, black, and bald, stepping out of the funeral home in his solemn suit, standing proud before the plantation-esque building. It rings sourly of darker times, when Kirk would've been little more than a butler for some arrogant white prick. He lifts his hand in a hello and I raise mine in return. I should talk to him. I'm sure Jackson will take my body here, and we should talk about that—as if the after is any of my business.

As the Impala chugs up the steep hill, an old and familiar dread twists my guts.

I've been avoiding my grave, I realize. As if in coming too close to this piece of earth with my name on it, the ground will split open and swallow me. As if by walking on my own grave I am asking for it, but it is more than that.

I park beneath the willow tree again and climb out. Long knotty tendrils swing in the welcome breeze as I cross the grass to the marker ahead. From my vantage point, I see Kirk's hearse slide down the hill and out the iron gates, turning right onto the main road before disappearing.

I sink to my knees in front of the grave. The July heat is unbearable even this late in the day. The sun burns the back of my neck and a weak breeze pushes through my hair. Already I can feel the sweat trail over the skin trapped beneath my leather jacket.

Like armor, I won't take it off.

I reach out and place a hand on the rough headstone. "Fuck, Charlie."

I imagine the corpse in the box below—both corpses—entangled in each others' limbs, where I so unceremoniously dumped them.

"Why did you do it?" I asked him. "Why would you ever help him?"

About ten months ago, Caldwell made his first strategic move against Jesse. A small cell of his killers, led by a man named Martin, used local prostitutes to set up fake death replacements. Jesse, believing she was doing her job and saving someone's life, was tricked and attacked. Her head was almost fully decapitated while I was detained and questioned.

Realizing we were in trouble and in a shitty situation, I disappeared. But unless killing is the order of the day, I couldn't work alone. So I asked two friends, two guys I trusted, to help me with my investigation.

What's going on, Charlie? I'd asked. *Is the FBRD corrupt? Is it someone else? We have to find out the truth.*

Of course, Jim. I'll help you. You know that.

I look up at the sky and feel the heat on my face, the back of my neck itching with sweat. My hands feel warm and swollen as I rock back on my heels.

I can still hear the way Charlie laughed, like he was out of his mind. He must've been to hand me over to Martin and Caldwell like that.

"Why Charlie?" I ask again and touched the granite. "I

could never give Jesse or any of them up. How could you do it to me?"

I wipe sweat off my face with the back of my hand and sigh. I get up, brush the fresh cut grass off my knees and head back to the car.

I'm grateful I never told Charlie about the second boy in the desert.

CHAPTER THIRTY

Winter 2002

I took Aziz home. His family had reported him missing two months earlier. They said he was walking the goats too close to the border in Kunar, the province of their home. When he did not return, an elder from his village went to collect the boy, but only found the goats.

I wrapped Aziz in a green military blanket and put him in the backseat of the car, sitting up like a swaddled baby.

I paid the driver 3000 Afghan Afghani, crisp red bills. "I'll give you three more if you bring me back. Alive."

I wore a uniform and held my assault rifle in plain sight. I did not want to scare him, but I did not want him to think he could screw me over and leave me on some hillside with the body of a dead kid either.

"I understand," he said with enough conviction that I believed he did.

We drove away from the base out to the hills. You would imagine desert, I'm sure, but these hills were green. The road was narrow and steep, but the car got us to the village where Aziz lived.

"Wait here," I told him. His black eyes regarded me warily as I climbed out and retrieved Aziz from the backseat.

I carried the swaddled boy into the village, toward a group of young kids wearing sky blue tunics, kicking a ball between them. I didn't want them to see Aziz, so when I saw an elderly man propped against the building, one hand clutching a staff as he watched the children play, I went to this man instead.

Without showing him the stiff child in my arms I said, "Aziz Yusufzai." I didn't know much Arabic and really hoped I was pronouncing the name right.

The man used the staff to pull himself up to his full height which was still a good head and shoulders beneath my own. He reached out and placed a shaking hand on the scratchy army blanket.

When his hand cupped the boy's head, his face crumpled and a low wail came from his throat.

Immediately, faces appeared in every door and window. The children stopped playing and turned. Women came toward us from the houses.

The man with the staff tried to pull Aziz from my arms and I had to lower him to the ground so that he wouldn't be dropped.

A woman fell on Aziz, tearing at the blanket with such a ferocity that I was forced back by the growing crowd. More and more hands were on his little body, unwrapping him with a wild desperation.

When his face was finally uncovered, the noise became unbearable. Women screamed as if being gutted alive. Children began to cry and several men beat their chests in fury.

Someone grabbed onto me. The man with the staff, I realized, pulled me through a dark door deep into a house. We went through room after room until arriving at last in a shadowed inner chamber. He motioned for me to wait.

When I kneeled on the dirt, my hands resigned to my knees, he seemed satisfied.

I was left alone with the gray shadows stretching along the terracotta.

I don't know how long I waited. The room only grew darker as the cries outside died away. I imagined Aziz being carried away to another room and laid lovingly on a floor where his father and mother would place their hands on his cold body.

I had been crying when someone finally came back. It was three men. The man with the staff was among them, an elder maybe, as all these tribes seemed to have them. The other two men were much younger, perhaps sons, one tall and the other short.

"I speak for my brother," the smallest of the three said. His accent was thick but I'd heard worse. "What has happened to his son? How did you find us?"

I looked at the man in front of me. His eyes were red and his hair disheveled in a way that looked as if he'd been tearing it out. Looking into his eyes, I told him in English, of the first time I saw Aziz, wandering toward the base with the dummy vest strapped to his chest. I left no detail out, not even the fact that the vest was unarmed and his son died for nothing. The brother translated everything in Arabic spoken softly over my own, the music of the language almost hypnotic.

When I finished, I pulled my assault rifle from my back where it had been resting.

All three men stepped back, but I turned the rifle around and offered it to the father.

"Please," I told him, looking up at him from where I kneeled. "For Aziz."

He didn't move to take the gun.

"Come on." I screamed and shook the gun. "I killed your boy. Do it."

The shorter and perhaps younger brother spoke over me again. He said so many words that the translation couldn't have been direct.

When the father refused to take the gun a second time, I laid it on the floor at his feet and waited. I began to cry and did not hear them leave.

I waited there through most of the night until the sun came again. Someone had brought a plate of food but I didn't eat it. I probably added insult to injury on that one, but I just didn't have it in me to take anything from this family.

Hours passed and they didn't return.

They didn't want my life, but I had nothing else to give. So I left. I pulled myself up, stiff from kneeling all that time and headed back to the car. When I stepped out of the house, I saw no one. I heard a low, mournful hymn coming from somewhere and I saw firelight through one of the windows, but no faces.

I was surprised to find the driver was still there on the hill where I'd left him.

I immediately gave him several more crisp red bills from the pockets of my fatigues. "How long have I been here?"

"Eight hours," he said and accepted the money.

"Why did you wait?"

"They pay me to wait," he said. I climbed into the car but he didn't drive.

"Let's go," I told him, thinking he was confused about my intentions.

"They pay me to wait," he said again, pointing over the dashboard into the road ahead. At first I didn't see anyone, but then two shapes, and a smaller third, emerged from the shadows.

I climbed out of the car, recognizing the smaller brother and the elder, probably their father. But I had not recognized this boy, maybe a year or two younger than Aziz.

"You must take him," the brother said.

"Excuse me?" I stepped back as if he'd swung at me.

"His name is Aaquel and he is a good and smart boy. Take him with you."

Anger rose fast and hot from my chest. "Are you fucking kidding me? Do you really think you should trust me with another one of your children?"

The man with the staff asked something and the brother rapidly translated. Nodding, the old man replied in Arabic.

"He will be safe with you," the brother translated. "You must take him."

"No," I said. "I can't do that."

Again the brother translated to the elder who replied.

"You would give your life, but not your protection?" the brother said.

"It isn't a matter of protection. I don't know what you're thinking. It's no better out there." I jabbed a finger at the road stretching out behind the car. "The whole world is shit."

Again the fevered Arabic translation was exchanged. The old man leaning on his staff gripped it more tightly. I turned to leave and he grabbed onto me.

His eyes met mine and I saw in the rising sunlight the blue ring of blindness eating at his vision. He spoke in soft, tremulous Arabic.

The brother translated. "The Taliban they come to our villages and they take our children. They feed false promises and anger to their hearts. They lead our boys away and make them soldiers. Soldiers like you."

He released me but he kept talking.

"If the boys do not come willingly, they are taken. One year, maybe two and they will take Aaquel and we will only pray another good man will bring his body home."

"Maybe the war will be over by then," I said.

The old man smiled, a patient and sad smile, like the one you'd give a child who can't comprehend something.

"The war never ends," translated the brother. "A soldier should know that."

I looked down at the boy for the first time. He was fairer than Aziz, pretty like a little girl, his hair curling by his ears and his eyelashes thick and dark. He had the pout of a starlet, those brown eyes as black as the tunic he wore.

"I don't know what you want me to do," I said. "I don't know how to help you."

And I realized it was a sad fucking truth. I could kill their children and I could pay for that mistake with my life—but anything else—I had no clue.

"Get him out of the country. Educate him. He needs English and an occupation. See that he lives to be a man."

I looked out over the horizon and saw the first fiery strip of sun there. I stared at the boy. He did not look any happier about this proposal than I did.

"Please take him," the brother said again, as the old man's hand shook against my arm.

"Get your things," I said. I looked at the boy again. "I'll be in the car."

The men gave the boy rushed instructions in Arabic and touched his head in turn as if blessing him. He already had his things I realized, when he hefted a sack up onto his shoulders and then climbed into the backseat of the car.

"Thank you," the brother translated and the elder touched his forehead.

"This is a mistake," I said and I climbed into the car. The driver finally started to obey me again, reversing the subcompact and churning up dust around us. Both men stayed in the road and watched us go.

We travelled to the border in silence. The driver was blessedly quiet the entire ride, though I know he must have heard and understood more of that bizarre conversation than I did. If he had questions, he knew better than to ask them. Maybe he thought his silence would be rewarded with more crisp red bills.

The boy did not speak either. I watched him in the little mirror on the back of the visor as he rolled his window up and down. The wind blew back his curls and when dust swirled into the car, he rolled it up again.

The driver stopped in Khost as I instructed. I paid him more money than his time was worth and he took it.

We watched the driver disappear into the clotted streets before I headed toward the hotel. Call me a paranoid bastard, but the driver didn't need to know where we were heading.

I told Aaquel to wait outside as I went into a hotel and got a room. I also asked to make a phone call, doing so with one eye on the boy with a pack slung over his shoulder.

Once I put the boy in the room, I told him to lock it behind me and open it for no one. I twisted the lock a few times, stepping in and out, hoping he understood. Then I went back out into the throngs of people and found a market where I could buy enough food and snacks to hold us until my contact came through.

Even after I returned with food, Aaquel wouldn't talk to me.

"How old are you?"

"Do you want to watch TV?"

"Does your mother know that your grandfather gave you away?"

All my questions received no reply.

He fell asleep sitting upright, still wearing his tunic, with his little sack clutched to his chest as if I might steal it. I stayed awake through the night until a rough knock came at the door the next morning. I checked the window before opening.

"Brinkley," Rakesh called out, his boisterous laugh followed him into the room. He wore a white shirt and pants, sunglasses hiding his eyes. "It has been a long time, my friend. When you called, I was so surprised."

The boy in the bed sat up, watching us.

"Oh he is pretty," Rakesh exclaimed, grinning at the boy. "It is good that you give him to me. If we close our eyes one minute, he will be a bacha bazi the next."

I pulled my wallet from my pocket and handed the remaining cash over to Rakesh.

"No need, my friend," the man said, pushing the dollars away.

"Just take it," I told him. "In case he wants or needs something. Hell, in case you have to pay to keep someone's mouth shut. I'll give you more when we meet in New Delhi."

Rakesh grumbled but took the cash as I knew he would. I may have saved his life in Marrakesh, but he liked money as much as the next man.

"OK," Rakesh said and waved to the boy. "Let's hit the road. We have a long way to go."

When the boy didn't respond, Rakesh spoke again in Arabic. The next thing I knew, little fists pummeled my back and side.

"Hey, hey," I said, trying to snatch the hands furiously pounding me. "What the hell?"

"You sell me," he said. "You lie and you sell me."

"Oh he does speak," Rakesh said, laughing.

I grabbed ahold of his hands and forced him to stop hitting me. "Stop. Stop."

He tried to wrench away but I held him tight. "You lie and you sell me."

"Do you understand English?" I asked him. When he didn't reply I tried again, "Rakesh, can you translate?"

"Sure thing, boss," he said, amused. "But in my country,

we just whop these upside the head and move on with it." Rakesh loved American movies and did not always use the expressions he learned from them correctly.

"Humor me," I told him, then I turned to the boy. "I am not selling you. I know it looks that way because there's money and he is taking you away, but that isn't what's happening. He is my friend. I trust him to take care of you. Do you know the word trust?"

The boy's wrists relaxed in my hands. He spoke before Rakesh finished translating. "I understand you."

"My friend is going to take you to an orphanage about 300km from New Delhi. I know the man who runs this orphanage. He is drawing up papers now, so I can adopt you. You aren't going to be there long, but it is a safe place where we can hide you until I have some documentation, OK? I can't take you out of Afghanistan without papers and I can't get papers here, so we have to sneak you into India. I will meet you at the orphanage. Just wait for me there. I'm not sure what we will do next, but I've got a couple of friends that might be able to help us. Do you understand what I'm saying?"

"You have many friends," the boy said.

Rakesh snorted.

"Not enough, kid," I said to him. "Do you understand what I'm saying about the papers?"

"We cannot leave without papers," he said, the last bit of tension gone from his voice. I released him.

"Yes, or they will take you away from me and might not even return you to your family, which would be bad."

"It would be bad," he repeated.

"So you go with Rakesh and you do what he says, OK? I will see you soon."

"How long?" the kid asked and I could see Aziz in his face.

"A month," I told him. "I'll get there sooner if I can. But until I do, just think about what you want to learn when I send you to school."

"English," he said.

I grinned. "You're doing all right. What else?"

"I want to be the most powerful man in the world."

Rakesh laughed big and boisterous, one hand on his jiggling belly. "Do not we all."

"What'll your new name be?" I asked him. "For the papers?"

He looked down for a moment and then grinned. "Gideon Bale."

Rakesh and I were both taken aback.

"Gideon?" I asked. "Where did you hear that name?"

"He is a smuggler," the boy said, with an excitement I hadn't seen yet. "He is the most powerful man in the world."

"Never heard of him," Rakesh said.

"It is in a story," the boy replied.

I should have known then I was in trouble, but at the time I just smiled. "Gideon Bale it is."

Caldwell left me a note folded into a little tent, and sitting on top of the notebook I'd been using to write down my memories.

I thought you knew about Charlie. When I was finished I put him back the way he was. You really didn't know?

I grab my coat and I drive to the cemetery. The Impala chugs up the hill past the funeral home and hearse and I yank up the parking brake once I pull her into the shade of the willow tree.

I jump out of the car and go to the grave.

"Is it true?" I ask as if Charlie can sit up and answer me. "Oh my God, is it true?"

I feel sick. I turn and heave into the grass beside the grave.

"God, I'm so sorry, Charlie. I didn't know. You shouldn't be down there," I say, a little self-conscious of the sound of my own voice. The sour taste of vomit burns the back of my nose and throat. "I'll rebury you."

Again I see Charlie's face the moment he betrayed me.

The eyes were glazed, unfocused, but not with hatred I realize. It was because someone was wearing him like a glove, the way Chaplain used to do it.

"I'd forgotten what it was like, when he gets in your head and fucks it all up."

God, how it had fucking hurt to hear Charlie laugh while Caldwell's men tore me up. Martin, the worst of the bastards got what he'd deserved. There were still traces of his burnt corpse in Kirk's crematorium, I'd wager.

But Charlie and Smith, the Boston detective I'd also asked for help—I should've handled that better. *Especially you Charlie.*

"He had you," I say, feeling the uncomfortable ache in my knees build. "And I didn't fucking know."

Jim, he'd said with a smile. *Am I glad to see you—*

I cringe at the memory: Charlie in his living room, rising from his chair, his face bright with relief until I put a bullet through his forehead.

Of course Caldwell wiped him clean. Why wouldn't he? How better to hide his tracks than to leave no memory of the crime? When I walked into Charlie's house and raised my gun, he had no idea why.

"I'm so fucking sorry, Charlie," I tell him. "God, you must've thought—"

We all make mistakes, he said, sitting in his FBRD office ten years ago, listening to me recount the story of Aziz for the fifth or sixth time. *You couldn't have known.*

"I only make it worse. Everything I touch is shit," I tell him, rubbing my fingers along the etched granite of my name. It should be me down there.

You always do the best you can, I hear my friend say. *You're the one who shows up even when he doesn't have to.*

God, I'm so sorry. I should've known. I shouldn't have acted out of anger. I should've—

"What if he does that to me?" I ask. "What if he makes me hurt Jesse or Rachel? Jackson?"

What's stopping him?

I wipe the sweat off my brow and slide my palm against my damp jeans. "Gideon Bale is a comic book hero," I tell Charlie's body, throwing the last spade of dirt into the new grave. "I had to look it up."

The crickets saw at their own legs, filling the night around me. I see the hearse coming up the road, headlights bouncing off the trees and grave markers around us.

"So you see, not only did I lie to you about why I left the army and why I came home," I tell him. "I killed one brother and ruined the other."

Kirk parks the hearse behind the Impala and gets out. In his hand is a large gray urn. Once he is close enough, he offers it to me. "Detective Smith."

"Thanks," I tell him and switch the shovel to my other hand so I can accept the container of ashes. "I'll send this to his wife in Baltimore. Anonymously, of course."

Kirk looks down at the grave. The smooth marker with a dove on each side of Charlie's name, freshly chiseled. "It looks good."

Charles Roebuck Swanson

Hero and Friend

April 10, 1952-October 15, 2012

My throat is tight but I manage some gratitude. "Thanks for ordering this and giving me the plot."

"Not to be grim, but your grave is available again." It sounds like a question.

"Not for long," I say. He nods as if he knows this. Maybe Jackson told him already. "Have you gotten any closer to taking him out?"

"I've tried putting a bullet in his brain 23 times in the last six months alone," I admit. How many rooftops and hotel rooms had I scouted? I couldn't tell you. "Long range sniping mostly. The problem however is his AMP. I haven't figured out how to kill a man who knows I'm coming."

"By that logic, you would think you could save yourself," he says, placing a hand in each of his suit pockets.

"Maybe," I tell him because he is right. "Maybe I will."

CHAPTER THIRTY-THREE

Monday, March 31, 2003

"We got him," Charlie said. He slipped into the chair opposite my desk and grinned.

"Sullivan?" I asked.

Charlie snorted. "I fucking wish. No, we got Brian Taft. The guy who killed the girl outside the bar last week. Tuesday, remember?"

A sickening image of a skull peeled open like a blood orange came back to me. "Yeah the hate crime in Lafayette. Kaitlyn Green."

"Exactly. He confessed and everything. Saves me an assload of precious time. Speaking of Sullivan, how goes it?"

"I'm following a new lead," I admitted and then I thought of a way to say what needed to be said.

Charlie waved his hand. "And?"

"What if the reclamation detainment camps weren't closed?" I asked. I watched his face, measured his response. When he didn't look surprised, I added: "Have you heard of any camps that are still open?"

"No," he said. "The last closed last year."

"But that is five years after they said they were closed," I replied. Charlie looked up with dark eyes.

"What is going on?" I asked him. "What the hell kind of case is this? Why are you riding my ass so hard about it?"

I thought he would dismiss me, maybe tell me to mind my own business and do as I was told. It sure as hell wouldn't have been the first time I'd received such a command. But instead, his eyes went all soft around the edges and the air in his chest came out in a sudden whoosh.

"I don't know everything because I'm not cleared to, but I've heard things. Everyone hears things. They kept the camps open—a few of them anyway. They saw the opportunity for scientific discovery, warfare development, all that. They kept people, dissected them, tried to understand the biology behind the condition and see if it could be replicated. Some of it failed —which is how we have freaks like Jackson walking around."

I stiffened at his derogatory remark about Jackson, but I didn't interrupt.

"Eric Sullivan *could* have been one of the ones who were kept behind. He *could* have been the most promising subject available to them. One scientist called him *highly compatible* with their research, another *an invaluable asset.*"

"So where is he?"

"He escaped," Swanson said. He exhaled the word escaped as if he'd held it inside himself for too long. "I was told that he broke out of the facility where he was held and that he began attacking the other facilities. Bombing them, destroying them and killing the people inside. Some pretty ruthless shit."

I frowned. "How does one man have the means to do all that?"

"Apparently, he was in possession of many state secrets. The way they tell it, Sullivan was there of his own accord.

They were paying him well, treating him like a king in exchange for his help."

"If that was true," I said, but I had doubts that a man locked up in a detainment camp would suddenly decide to help his captors. "Then what changed?"

"Who fucking knows? All I know is that they want him found and returned to their custody immediately. Dead or alive. Or some fucking state in-between."

"If this is so important, why am I on the case?" I asked.

"You're not the only one. They've got their own people looking too, I'm sure," Charlie said. "But you're the only one I trust."

I let the compliment settle in before I asked. "Who are they?"

Charlie slipped out of the chair with a snort. "When your clearance is that high, you don't have a name anymore."

I wanted to press my luck and push for more information, but Charlie turned and frowned at me then. "Where's your Beretta?"

I looked down at the shoulder holster nestled against my ribs to see the backup SIG Sauer resting there instead. "I misplaced it."

"A Beretta is a hell of a thing to misplace," he said.

I made a dismissive gesture but his comment nagged at me. In fact, since I woke up that morning and reached for the Beretta, expecting to find it on the nightstand. When I found nothing a strange feeling flicked through my mind. The fog that clouded my thoughts made me wonder if I should stop drinking so damn much. Or at least I should cut back.

CHAPTER THIRTY-FOUR

Tuesday, April 1, 2003

I'd just opened a beer when a furious pounding rattled my apartment door. I pulled the SIG without a second thought and called out from the kitchen. I was sure to position myself just inside the room first. If some lunatic blew a hole through my front door, at least I'd have cover.

"It's Jackson," she said. "I'm not here to kill you."

I snorted at that. It was her delivery mostly. She wasn't being funny, and that made it funny. She said it as if attempted murder was a serious consideration for people like us, and I guess it was.

I opened the door. She was clutching a newspaper and looked as if she'd slept as well as I had. Lucky for her, the dark circles under her eyes weren't as visible as my own.

"What's up, Jackson?"

"You drink too much."

"And you can only walk upright if you take about fifteen pills," I said. "What's your point?"

She considered that for a moment then let it go. To her credit, she never mentioned my drinking again.

She thrust the paper at me which I accepted with my free hand. It was folded back on itself to frame an article: *Dead Child Stolen* was the headline, with a handful of paragraphs outlining the crime. Someone broke into the city morgue and stole a child's corpse. The incident occurred two days ago and the parents of the dead child could not be reached.

"That's some sick shit," I said.

"I don't think it's for molestation," Jackson said as if reading my mind. "I think it is a cover up."

I saw where she was going. "Why would someone cut the head off a corpse and dump the body in a house fire?"

"To make us stop looking for the child," she said. She spoke as if I was an idiot and trying to get through to me was a pain in her ass.

"Maisie," I said.

"Yes."

"Say her name," I said.

"Why?"

"Because I just realized that you never refer to her by name."

"Why do I need to say her name?"

"Why are you so against saying her name?" I pressed. I had feeling I knew why, but I wanted to see if she'd admit it.

She stared at me stubbornly then said. "I found Rachel."

Ah a name, I thought, but not the one I wanted her to say. She showed me the address and I recognized it immediately.

"No," I said. "She's not there."

Jackson frowned at the address she'd written on the top of the article then looked back at me. "Yes, she is. That's correct."

Something in my mind churned. Memories came back but blurry and for no particular reason I shouted. "She's not there."

Jackson took a step back. "Why are you angry?"

I didn't answer. The heat in my face added to the confusion. "I know that place and she isn't there. She isn't in any of the houses on Park Street. In fact, you can scratch off all the houses near Beckett Park."

"You're being irrational," she said. "I know she is in this house. What do you know about the place?"

"I'm irrational. Says the person who can't even say a child's name because naming her makes it harder. It's harder to find a dead child with a name."

Her face went smooth, but if I didn't know better, I would have sworn she looked triumphant. "Have you ever been there?"

"No," I said, but as I said it a strange feeling washed over me. Confusion again. I thought I was telling the truth but it didn't feel right.

Her brow pinched. "Are you sure?"

"Yes, Goddamnit."

She didn't believe me. I could tell just by looking at her.

"Fine," she said. "Just get in the car."

CHAPTER THIRTY-FIVE

Tuesday, April 1, 2003

We parked the Impala on the curb outside a small house at the end of a cul-de-sac. The house looked nice and in good condition: two stories, black shutters against the white, ridges of wood. The numbers 567 to the right of the red door were curly and fantastical. I would have thought the house was dark and abandoned if not for the smoke rising from the brick chimney.

The only problem with the smoke was the *for sale* sign in the front yard. The padlocked front door, protected by a key code, didn't look like anyone had been to see it in a while, officially anyway. And it was no surprise that the house hadn't sold.

It was in one of those lower-middle class neighborhoods of St. Louis where there were more *for sale* signs cropping up every day and fewer moving trucks rolling in. Considering the grass was a bit too long, clearly neglected the preceding summer, I'd have guessed the house was on the market for at least a year.

I turned to the passenger seat where Jackson sat watching me. "You think someone has Maisie in there?"

"Yes," she said, reaffirming what she told me on the way over.

"Then why did you come at me with all that Rachel shit?" I asked. "Why didn't we come straight here?"

"You're not ready," she said, measuring me with her eyes again.

I felt my face grow hot, which was always the first sign that I was about to bite into someone and shake them like a dog toy. Jackson didn't give me the chance. She pushed open the Impala's heavy door and stepped out onto the adjacent curb. She was already around the front of the car before I got out.

I was curious how she planned to get in with the front door padlocked. She went to a window on the ground floor and pressed up against the glass. The pane slid open silently. Brilliant, of course, because if someone was in there toasting marshmallows by the fire or whatever the hell, we didn't want to make a sound. But also, I wondered how she knew to check this window. She came right to it. She could have checked any of the windows or all of them and found them locked. But she knew.

She had the window open and was already pulling herself up into the ledge before I could offer her a boost. She was in good shape. I had to admire that. She was hard as a rock through her arms and up through her back and chest. She could move her body with slow, deliberate movements, sliding through the window without the smallest sound of fabric brushing the ledge. I admit I had an impure thought when I considered placing one or both hands on her ass just before she pulled her legs through.

Back on her feet, she crept into the dark room toward the door without offering me a boost up. *Thanks a lot*, I thought, but let the animosity go when I realized her hands were full. She had her gun out, pointing forward as she crept from the room. She checked left and right outside the doorway. Then swinging left into the hall, she disappeared. I had both hands on the ledge when Jackson called out.

"Brinkley, the front."

I let go of the window ledge and dropped back down. Then I ran toward the front of the house. As I cut the corner, the street and other houses coming into sharp view, I saw Jackson hanging out the front window, the one closest to the chimney. "He went that way."

She jabbed a finger right and I ran across the front of the house and hooked a corner. Just before the corner cut itself, I saw the man. He wore faded jeans and a jean jacket, work boots, and his hair, almost shoulder length, was a light brown. I also saw Maisie, swaddled in a pink princess blanket. Her eyes were wide in concern, but otherwise she looked unharmed. Her blond curls were pulled up into a single ponytail on the top of her head.

When her kidnapper cut the corner again, the child dropped something and immediately the wailing began. "Frederick. *Frederick.*"

As I whipped around the corner there was no one. Thinking he'd simply sped up, I ran faster, only to collide with Jackson. She hit me hard in the shoulder.

"Where did he go?" I demanded.

"He didn't come this way," she said, out of breath herself.

"I saw him cut that corner," I said.

"He wasn't on that side. I swear."

I looked around her and saw only the next house. I didn't believe the man could have dived into one of those windows holding a child, not in the half a second between Jackson and myself. For the same reason I didn't believe he could have slipped through the ground level windows into the basement. First of all, they looked too small for a grown man. If he'd shoved Maisie in alone he'd run the risk of seriously injuring her on the fall to the floor.

I turned and looked at the great wide field behind us. Nothing. If he'd run out into the field, we would have definitely seen him. So where the hell was he?

"People don't just disappear," I said.

"Or fly," she added.

We searched the area. Basement to attic, house and field. Nothing. The living room was full of little girlie things and too much pink, but there were no clues. No trail. There was no electricity in the house, which explained why the fire was needed. The big house would've been too drafty for the little girl otherwise. Finally, I retraced my steps and found what the girl had dropped. A black and white teddy bear that looked more like a dairy cow than a bear, with its large black eyes, clutching a red heart that said, "I love you."

"I heard her call out the name Frederick," Jackson said. "Maybe that is the guy's name."

I shook the bear at her. "Or this is Freddy, the teddy. She didn't start screaming until she dropped it."

She thumbed the safety on her gun. "She is alive and she was here."

"Good job," I said. It was automatic and maybe a bit condescending. "I'm sorry I doubted you."

She ran a palm over her head, flattening the inch of hair there. "How big is this?"

I stared out at land stretching before us. "Pretty big. But you're not talking about the field, are you?"

She ignored me. "Why give us a missing child, then fake a child's death, and take us off the case? It doesn't make any sense."

"None of it makes sense. Why has a kidnapper been sitting in a house with a little girl? He has to eat, shit, sleep. He has to leave the fucking house to steal bodies from morgues. What happens to Maisie then? Is he working alone? Or with someone? There are too many questions."

Jackson shoved her gun into her holster and started walking back toward the car.

"He won't come back here. He's not stupid."

"You're probably right," I said and followed her, still holding Freddy. "He didn't get this far by being stupid."

She waited for me to reach inside and unlock her door. Then she climbed through. "Just take me back to my car. We won't find anything else today and I have to go back to the drawing board. I'll have to find her all over again. With the Wright case—"

My windshield shattered. It took me a second to realize what happened. I still hadn't processed why my windshield exploded when Jackson grabbed my arm and yelled. "Drive."

A bright burst of blood was blooming on her left shoulder.

"Shit." I started the Impala as more bullets came through the windshield, shattering the back window next. "Motherfuckers. Stop shooting my car."

I threw the Impala in reverse and punched the gas without lifting my head. Jackson too had slumped down and covered herself with her good arm. The bullet must have ripped through the tendons, if her arm had gone dead on her, lying limp at her side as it was. I'd been there once and it was hell to recoup.

I berated myself for going soft, getting slow. If we'd been in a combat zone, I'd be dead right now. Stupid.

I was well down the street before I raised my head again. I saw a man who looked vaguely familiar standing in the middle of the cul-de-sac, gun raised. He shot several bullets, probably emptying the clip but none of them hit us.

I made it out of the neighborhood and onto the main road without picking up a tail.

"That was too easy," I said to Jackson, giving her the clear to get up from her seat, but she didn't.

"It's clear," I said again, but still no answer. I leaned over, taking my eyes off the road just long enough to get a good look at her. She was unconscious, slumped in the seat, the blood seeping steadily from the wound. "Shit."

The last thing I saw was her eyes rolling up in her head as she started to seize.

"Shit. Shit. Shit." I shoved the pedal to the floor. "Hang on, Jackson. Stay with me."

CHAPTER THIRTY-SIX

Tuesday, April 1, 2003

I got Jackson to the hospital and made sure they could get the bullet out, start the transfusion, and give me an update on her condition before I called Charlie. The nurse had just told me that the transfusion was a success and the bullet was removed OK—all good signs. I thanked her.

Then standing in the waiting room, watching the nurse walk away, I dialed Charlie's office number. He answered on the second ring.

"Where the fuck have you been?" he asked.

"Jackson got shot," I said. Before he could overwhelm me with questions I told him the story, most of it anyway. Jackson had a lead in that way of hers, we checked it out, saw the girl alive, but lost them. As we were leaving, some asshole shot at us and Jackson took a bullet. He listened to all of this without objection and when I finished, I was greeted with only silence on the other end of the phone.

"The girl is alive? You saw her?"

"Either Maisie Michaelson has a twin, or it was her. Also,

the guy had sandy blond hair, like the blond from the picture she drew. You know, the one I got from the fridge."

"Why the fuck do I care about that?"

"I thought you'd want to know."

"Sandy blond hair? Do you know how many bleached assholes prance around St. Louis?" he quipped. "What the hell am I supposed to do with that?"

"Jackson is going to be OK," I said, trying to cool my own temper. "When she wakes up, maybe she'll even have a picture of Maisie's kidnapper."

"As if we could get that lucky," he said.

I considered my next words. "So you believe me?"

"Of course I believe you. Why the hell wouldn't I?"

"You were quick to pull us from the Michaelson case and accept the girl was dead."

"Oh so this is a big conspiracy now?" he asked.

I didn't answer. I considered my friend's tone. Considered our history. "You wouldn't cover something like this up, would you Charlie?" It was half-question, half-statement. "If you were involved in a cover up, I'd be willing to believe it was for a good reason. Just tell me this is important and I'll believe you."

His voice softened.

"Jesus, Jim, you think I lied about the girl?" he asked. "I was told she was dead, that there was evidence she was dead. If I went around questioning everyone, I'd never get anything done."

It was true, I was a dissenter when compared to Charlie. It was why I'd always worked better alone. Scout and snipe missions were perfect for a guy like me. I didn't have to believe anyone but myself.

"If you say you don't know what's going on, I believe you. But do you think this is 'big'?" I asked.

"Quit going all *Beautiful Mind* on me and get your ass back to work. I want a formal report, in writing and on my desk, before someone crawls up my ass looking for it."

"Yes, sir," I said and tried not to sound like a disgruntled bastard when I said it.

"And the bullet. Get it to ballistics."

"That's the best idea you've had all day," I said and hung up. The nurse was walking toward me again and I took a few steps forward to meet her.

"She's awake," she said. "If you'd like to check on her."

"Thank you." I made the formal request for the bullet.

"I'll notify the doctor," she said. Then she was silent as she led me up the elevator to the patient rooms on the fourth floor. When the door opened, she held it but didn't get off with me. "Room 413."

I thanked her and stepped off the elevator. It was easy enough to find Jackson's room, after looking through a few dark doorways. I was reminded that I never liked hospitals. I thought it was the smell that made me uncomfortable. Or the solemn way in which everyone walked around. I didn't like all that doom and gloom. But mostly, it's the smell.

Jackson's bed was folded up, holding her in the sitting position. Her left shoulder was bandaged tightly with fresh gauze and the color had returned to her cheeks.

"You could've died," I said. "We got lucky."

"April Fool's," she said.

"Do *not* tell me you hired someone to shoot you as an April fool's joke."

"No," she said. "I was trying to be funny."

"Ah." I spared her a smile. "We will have to work on that."

"Yes." Her dark eyes were so serious that I couldn't help but laugh. She was growing on me.

"I'll try to top your joke next year," I said. "I'll need that long to prepare. A gunshot wound is a hell of an act to follow, you know."

"Did you call Lieutenant Swanson?" she asked.

"Yes. I don't think he knows what is going on."

"*Think?*"

"I *hope*," I said.

She nodded as if she understood. "I need my pictures and things from my place. They aren't going to let me out of here any time soon, and I need them now."

"I'll pick them up for you," I said.

She hesitated.

"Do you have another errand boy on call?" I quipped.

"No," she said. "I'll give you my keys. Just go pick them up and bring them back, please."

"Sure," I said and fished the keys out of her jacket pocket per her instructions. I made a mental note to bring her some other things as well, whatever I thought she might like to have at a time like this.

I was almost out the door when she called me back.

"Brinkley," she said.

"Yeah?"

"Keep both eyes open."

CHAPTER THIRTY-SEVEN

Tuesday, April 1, 2003

I stood in the dank hallway of the apartment complex where Jackson lived. I double-checked the address, and sure enough, this was it. I didn't know what I was expecting as I turned the key in the lock and pushed open the front door.

Flowery shit, maybe. All the women I'd spent time with had that way about them. Their homes were clean and bright and smelled the way the women themselves did. Sometimes like fruity shampoos, or cookies and shit. Other times they smelled like the department store perfumes they wore. Their couches had throw pillows and the rooms had rugs. Scented candles, potpourri, art on the wall, or even curtains to "tie the room together" as my mother would say. But those women had been civilians and Jackson was a soldier. Everything about her apartment said so.

The living room was white and stark. The walls had nothing on them but scuff marks. No curtains, rugs, or even a couch, and this absence gave the impression that Jackson didn't intend to stay here long. Books and research materials lined the walls in piles. If each heap was part of an elaborate organizational system, I couldn't tell.

The apartment was one bedroom, but the bedroom had only an army cot with a sleeping bag rolled over it. No pillow. Beside the bed was a glass of water and a row of pill bottles. I opened a duffle bag that I'd found beneath the bed with clothes, a gun and ammo inside. I threw the pills in too. I also grabbed the paperback off the sleeping bag, stealing a brief glance at the cover. *The Things They Carried* by Tim O'Brien.

It went in the bag too.

When I turned around I found the pictures. All over the wall were drawings. Some of them were very detailed, while others were hurried sketches. I tried to take them down gently, careful not to rip the corners pinned with tape. I rolled them up and taped them closed, but the thick pencil etchings were already beginning to smudge.

I expected to find all the lady cosmetics in the bathroom, but again, I was wrong. A bar of soap was in the shower, no shampoo, but I guess with her short hair she didn't need it. On the sink was just a toothbrush, toothpaste and some hand soap. I took the toothbrush and toothpaste. Then I zipped up the duffle and threw it over one shoulder. The kitchen had only the standard appliances: a range and fridge. The counters were bare. The sink had a few dishes but no evidence that she'd actually ever cooked here. A knife and fork, a water glass. The fridge had some fruit and bread in it. Half a gallon of milk and four 2-liters of Coke. The cabinets held only peanut butter and coffee.

"What the hell do you eat, Jackson?" I asked and hefted the duffle up higher on my shoulder.

"We have to be careful about what we eat or it interferes with our medication," a voice said. A slow, melodic voice. I turned and found a man, shades darker than Jackson, standing in her doorway. One hand was empty but the other was suspiciously edging its way behind his back.

I drew my gun first. "Stop."

When he brought his hand around his back slowly, he wasn't holding a gun. He was holding a bouquet of daisies.

I didn't lower my gun. "You shouldn't have."

"Is she here?" he asked. Then he shook his head. "Of course not. You wouldn't be carrying her stuff in a bag if she were here. Is she OK?"

"What's your name?" I asked.

"What's yours?" he countered. "You see, I come to see my girlfriend and you're holding a gun and carrying off her possessions. I'm just holding some flowers. Who is more suspicious here?"

"Good point," I said and lowered the gun. "I'm her partner. I'm just picking up a few things for her."

He nodded as if he knew this. "Brinkley."

It sounded like a question. "Yep, that's me."

"Well take these too," he said and extended the daisies toward me. "I brought them for her." I had to lower the gun or drop the bag. I dropped the bag and came toward him, gun up but not a kill shot. Here I thought I was slick shit but dropping the bag was what he wanted all along, I just didn't know it.

A clump of daisies smacked my face at the same moment pain shot up my elbow. Before I could react, someone was throwing me. I managed to tuck into a sloppy roll but I still came down too hard on my busted shoulder. When I popped back up, the guy—Jackson's so-called boyfriend—was yanking at the duffle zipper.

As soon as I realized the gun was in the kitchen floor, I dove for him. We hit hard and because I was the bigger guy, not necessarily the more fit, mind you, he rocked back on his heels and hit the wall. He rolled me again and I realized immediately he was trained. Good training. He knew how to move his body and mine, and when it came to hand-to-hand combat, time was of the essence. I knew better than to swap blows with a trained, fit guy at least ten years younger. I didn't make it this far by being stupid. Most of the time. I'd get tired before he did. So I brought my knee up hard and connected with his groin. Nothing fancy, but it did the trick.

I dove for my gun, and this time when I rolled back the safety with a flick of my thumb, I didn't hesitate. I put two bullets in the wall behind him before he darted out the front door and was gone. The duffel bag was busted open on the floor, shit everywhere. He'd even stepped on the toothpaste on his way out, and a thick creamy line of blue gunk was smeared all over the side of the bag.

I checked the hallway and the apartment to make sure I was actually alone again. Then I cleaned up the mess and repacked the bag. It wasn't until I had everything reorganized that I realized what he had taken. The pills were missing. Fucking junkie, I thought.

Shoulder throbbing, gun still at the ready, I lifted the bag and got the hell out of there.

CHAPTER THIRTY-EIGHT

Tuesday, April 1, 2003

"You never told me you had a boyfriend," I said. I tossed the duffle at her feet and watched it bounce once on the hard hospital mattress.

The color drained from her cheeks. "What did he want?"

"Your pills apparently," I said and unzipped the bag. I held it open so she could see inside. "Anything else missing?"

She sifted through the bag with her right hand, the other being wrapped close to her chest. When she mumbled off the name of some narcotic I didn't know, I asked, "Is that bad?"

She ran a hand over her head. "No."

"Were those pills important?" I asked.

"I can refill them. He must be out."

I cradled my throbbing shoulder. "Hasn't he ever heard of a fucking pharmacy?"

"We have to get ours from the VA," she said. "They are very specific drugs."

"So your boyfriend's like you?" I asked.

"He is not my boyfriend," she snapped. "And he isn't like me."

"Right, sorry. He just stole your pills." I wasn't so clueless that I'd push a woman who was clearly telling me something was none of my business. So I sat down in the little seat beside the bed instead.

"Why did he give you those?" I asked. I pointed at the daisies beside the duffle bag. She blushed when she saw them.

"What?" I asked.

"I thought—never mind."

"I'm not the flowers type," I said, trying to be gentle about it. I wasn't trying to humiliate her. I thought he was bad news. "Just for the record, I'd give you a gun. And you'd probably be the first woman to appreciate it."

Her brow furrowed. "You're favoring your shoulder."

"Yeah, your friend twisted it a bit."

"He's not—"

"Yeah yeah."

"He's my brother."

"Well that explains his moves. Did you beat him up as a kid?"

"He's a year younger than I am. Ever since we were little he's had to follow me around, do everything that I do. When I joined the Air Force, he did too. He's one of the few things I remember—from before."

"What are you saying?"

"When they put the magnetite in my brain, it wiped everything clean. I survived, but I don't remember who I was before. I've only a handful of memories. Micah—my brother —is one of them."

"Why would you let your brother do that to himself?" I hadn't meant to be such a bastard about it, but the words left my mouth before I could stop myself.

"They recruited him. They thought something about my genetic makeup is what helped me survive the procedure, so they called Micah in. I told him if he did it I'd never speak to him again. He accused me of trying to keep the glory for myself. " She snorted. "Because this life is so goddamn glorious."

"Was he trained to be an AMP like you?"

"Yes, but he was discharged from the program. He got into a fight with his commanding officer," she said. She licked her dry lips. "Micah's got a temper. He doesn't know when to shut his mouth or take a swing. He blames me."

I snorted. "For his temper?"

"No, for his discharge. When he was court martialed, I was supposed to testify in his defense. I refused. I knew if I did, they'd let him stay and it would only be a matter of time before something worse happened to him. I wanted him out of the service."

"When was this?"

"A few years ago. He's been working odd jobs since. He quit speaking to me of course. But then our aunt died of colon cancer four months ago and he turned up at the funeral. He apologized. Said he wanted to make up. He hoped I would help him get a job as an AMP through the agency. I tried but because of his past they won't take him. I guess they are picky right now, what with trying to produce reliable statistics and all that. When I told him they said no, he tried to steal a bunch of my things and took off. That's pretty much how it's been. He gets angry, takes off, but comes back asking for pills. He needs them like I do, but he's too embarrassed to go to the VA hospital. He's got limited benefits because of his discharge."

"Does he always bring flowers?"

"No," she said. "That was a first."

Something about all of this didn't sit right with me. Then again, I'd never been one to trust junkies. They could be unpredictable and self-serving and generally just made me uneasy. I never denied that I was a paranoid old bastard.

"Do I need to stay here with you?" I asked. "Is he going to

try and show up and punch air bubbles in your IVs or something? Suffocate you when the nurses aren't looking?"

"I should be OK." She didn't convince me of shit.

I leaned forward and grabbed the paperback off the pile of crap she'd pulled from her bag. Then I kicked off my boots and put my socked feet up on the edge of her bed. The page fell open to a spot marked with a Chinese food business card, but I flipped back to the beginning.

"Ah," I said and put the card on the table by the bed. "We might need that later."

She smiled, finally relaxing into her pillows.

I began reading *The Things They Carried*, starting with the passage marked. "First Lieutenant Jimmy Cross carried letters from a girl named Martha, a junior at Mount Sebastian College in New Jersey. They were not love letters, but Lieutenant Cross was hoping, so he kept them folded in plastic at the bottom of his rucksack. In the late afternoon, after a day's march, he would dig his foxhole, wash his hands under a canteen, unwrap the letters, hold them with the tips of his fingers, and spend the last hour of light pretending."

I looked up at Jackson.

"Jesus," I said. "This is going to be sad, isn't it?"

She smiled and that was enough for me to go on.

CHAPTER THIRTY-NINE

I watch over Jesse through the night. It's become a habit. I am worried he will just appear in her bedroom and carry her away like he does in that god awful picture I've got in my pocket.

But I don't see Caldwell or anyone else, and I wonder again why? Why? If he wants her, he can just take her. He did it to Maisie, so why not take what he wants now?

Because it isn't what he wants. This realization only brings another round of *why?*

Conflict avoidance? I doubt it. Is he afraid of her? Maybe. It is one of the few things that makes sense. Or it could be that he wants something more.

If I kill you now, it will change the future—and I like the future just fine.

When another sun rises and Jesse is deemed safe, I get into the car and drive.

I make my way to Atlanta, taking I-24 southeast past the shopping malls of Murfreesboro and then up through the mountains by Sewanee. The Impala slides along the river past that familiar Georgia peach sign. When the skyline erupts into view and the interstate morphs into a six-lane beast, I merge onto 285, heading for Grant Park.

I am looking for a particular 1920s bungalow on Kendrick Ave. When I spot the gray-blue house, elevated from the street by a steep incline, I park. Then I climb the steps toward the white door.

I glance at the porch swing to the left before lifting my fist to knock on the peeling white paint. That is when I notice the door is open a crack.

I draw my gun. Without a word, I ease the door open and step inside. A red carpet runs the length of the room before terminating at a wall, diverting left and right toward rooms unseen. Just as my eyes fall on a large statue of some eastern God, the metal of a barrel presses to the temporal bone behind my ear.

"What kind of gun do I have in my hand?" A smooth voice asks, jovial with a hint of amusement. The accent is crisp, British. I checked the room when I came in but hadn't even seen him.

"A 9MM," I say, measuring the small muzzle against my head.

"Nope," he says, amused. I mistake the humor in his voice for relaxation and make my move. But when I whirl, I'm jabbed in the chest by something.

"Ah, ah, ah," he says with a smile. "It's 5000 volts here."

I look down and see a cattle prod is pressed against my torso, and the gun being eased away from my head was actually a Glock with a slender suppressor on its end.

"You've gutted the prod," I say and holster my gun. I'm not afraid Gideon will zap me or shoot me. He is giving me a show.

He grins. "If you have the prod against their back it is more likely they will not take your gun. You can zap as soon as they try to turn on you. I am a fan of two-handed weapons, as you know. And I modified this."

He pushes a button on the base of his prod and a 5-inch dual blade protrudes from the end, just above the prod's tip.

"In case shit gets serious," he smiles. He twirls the prod around and demonstrates its dexterity. "All assuming hand-to-hand is not the order of the day."

"Very clever," I tell him and he smiles at my praise.

Darting to the wall, he puts down the prod and gun, then picks up a gadget. "I am a big fan of remote detonations and information acquisition these days. This here controls a bug half the size of your fingernail. It can be navigated with a remote to any location. It also has a magnetic USB that will connect to any port on command. You only need to get it close enough and *zhoop*."

I nod because Gideon does this every time I visit. He shows me his latest toy with relish.

"I am expecting a drone on Monday. I can't wait to try it out on the Maradux Outfitters. Are you still going to second me on that?"

I look down. When I manage to meet his eyes again, I take Gideon in. He is taller than I am by at least four inches. His broad shoulders taper down to a slim waist. He might look like a man now with that dark shadow at his jaw and those ridiculous curls, but his face is still the face of the 11-year-old boy I met ten years ago.

"Then the rumors must be true," he says as if I'd just punched him.

"I wondered if you'd heard," I say.

"Of course," he says, with a bitter smile. "I hear everything."

It is not a pompous exaggeration. Gideon has an amazing memory. He retains everything he's ever heard, seen, or read since the time he was three. Couple that with the fact he is a fast talker, highly adaptive, and a survivor, Gideon has quite the skill-set. His love of Iranian comic books romanticizing the smuggler's life should have been my first warning sign that he would take to this life too easily.

"So what are you here for?" he asks, not even trying to hide his disappointment or pain. "Is there still a chance for a final Brinkley and Bale adventure?"

I rub the overgrowth on my chin. "You may have to do this one without me. Consider it a last request and we will be even for the boat incident in Morocco."

"And the brothel in Singapore?"

"Sure," I say and glance around, eyes falling on what looks like an imperial crown. Then I do a double-take on what I think is a ruby the size of an egg.

Gideon is intrigued by my offer. "And you'll forgive me for the drug lord's daughter in Mexico City, or the shrine theft in Kyoto, or—"

"For all of it," I say, because I can't really be mad at this kid for anything. "It is a big favor."

His joviality falters at the edges. "You aren't just going to die, are you?"

"It looks like it."

"You have the girl." His cheeks burn red. "Use her."

"It's not really me he wants," I tell him, and he knows I'm talking about Caldwell. "If she tries to save me, she's just going to make herself more vulnerable. I can't let that happen." I think again of the picture in my pocket. Jesse dead in Caldwell's arms. That could be her, trying to save me.

"Then use the other one," Gideon says, the anger spreading to his ears and neck. "You cannot just die."

"I'll do whatever I have to do."

His hands hang limp at his sides. He opens and closes them as if they are numb. "I can't believe it."

"Soldiers die. You know that better than most people."

"You can't just give up." Gideon shouts. "What about my training? What about—"

"You don't need me," I say and it is true. Whether or not he realizes it, Gideon outgrew me a long time ago. "You're smarter and more capable than I ever was. And wars aren't being fought the way they used to be."

After a moment he says, "I do not want you to die."

"That's a sweet thing to say," I tell him. "But I don't know what to tell you."

"Did you only come here to say goodbye?" he asks, slapping the side of his leg softly.

"No," I admit. "Like I said, I need your help."

"Do you really?" he asks. "Or is it some petty request to make me feel useful?"

He knows me too well.

"It's a real request," I tell him. "This is important, Gid. I need to know that you cannot be bought. The man who wants to kill Jesse has access to a lot of money."

His face stiffens again. "You know I don't care about the money."

"If you won't take his money, he may try to give you information," I go on. "He will try to buy you somehow. He'll offer you whatever you want most and if that doesn't work, he will try to kill you."

"I like him already."

I rub my head.

"Is that all?" he asks. "You come to tell me not to work for a bad man?"

"No," I say.

"Of course not."

When I give him a look, much like the look I would give him in the courtyard at St. Anthony's when I learned he broke this or that petty rule, he softens.

"What else do you need?"

"I want to know how to take him down," I say. "What is his weakness?"

"Shoot him."

I laugh. "I've tried. He has an AMP who is always five steps ahead of me."

Gideon shrugs. "Shoot the AMP and then shoot him."

"I've tried that too," I tell him. "It hasn't worked."

I remember the first time I put a gun in Gideon's hand. He was fourteen and had begged me for two years before I finally caved and taught him to shoot.

"Are you sure you will forgive me for the brothel?" he asks, with the smallest of smiles. He's trying. That's all I can ask. "You were *very* angry with me."

"Yes. I forgive you. Just find out what you can." Even as I ask him, the guilt washes over me. I see him standing there, this young man who should be in school. His memory retention, his talent for espionage, and his desire for power and wealth—I should have never encouraged him, no matter how much he begged. Loneliness is a dangerous flaw.

"So will you help me?" I ask.

Gideon pulls a gold coin from his pocket and fingers its rough edge. Finally, he meets my eyes. "As you wish."

CHAPTER FORTY

Wednesday, April 2, 2003

took one step inside the door and Charlie yanked me into his office. "How the fuck did a bullet from your Beretta end up in Captain Jackson's shoulder?"

I froze. The room began to spread out in front of me, elongating, and Charlie himself warping out of proportion.

"What?" I asked.

Charlie heaved a sigh of relief. "Oh thank God. I didn't think you'd be so stupid, but I wanted to be sure."

"*What?*" I demanded again.

"The bullet dug out of Jackson's shoulder is a match for your Beretta. Well, *a* Beretta. I don't think you shot her but—"

"I *shot* her," I repeated.

Charlie waved his arms. "Keep your voice down. I'm saying I don't think you shot her, but the bullet is a match. Pair that with the fact that both of you claim you saw a girl who is supposed to be dead, and the wound was nonfatal, it is starting to look suspicious. And don't get me started about your service record."

I considered his words. I'd asked him if he was part of

something big, and believed him when he said otherwise. Here he was doing the same for me. "What do you want me to do?"

"First of all, find your fucking gun. We don't need someone running around shooting people with your firearm, do we?"

"No, sir," I said.

He cut his eyes up to me as if to warn me not to be cute.

"Secondly, find Sullivan. We will all breathe better if you do. The crows will stop pecking at my eyeballs and I can quit pissing on your head."

"The girl," I began but Charlie was prepared for me.

"The girl," he countered, "is probably safe. For now at least. If she really is pink-cheeked, fed, and swaddled in princess blankets with teddy bear companions, then no one is using her little skull for a jerk-off tool. We on the other hand are being fucked three ways 'til Sunday. You need to find your gun, find Sullivan, and then find me a drink. The girl can wait."

She can't, I thought. But I wasn't dumb enough to start that conversation up again. Charlie's desk phone rang and he frowned at the number on the screen before answering it.

"Swanson. Yeah. Uh-huh. Yeah I think I know him. Really? He's right here." Charlie lowered the receiver. "It's for you."

I reached out and accepted it.

"Hello, sir. Agent Benjamin here. We have a body down at the riverfront. We'd like you to come down and ID it."

"I'm no coroner," I said. I switched the receiver to my other ear. Charlie's eyes never left mine. "What can I do for the body?"

"Yes, it is unorthodox sir, but we feel like you may be connected to the crime."

"Why is that?" I asked.

"Because the body we dug out of the river, sir, it has your name carved on its chest."

CHAPTER FORTY-ONE

Wednesday, April 2, 2003

I parked on the street near the St. Louis riverfront. An engraved granite stone sat between two concrete pillars. The pillars stood like guards. Chains from each side were locked to the granite sign and meant to create a barrier.

I stepped over the chains and descended to the walkway below, heading left. With my back to the bridge, I moved toward the swarm of uniforms in the distance.

When I got close enough for someone to stop me, I held up my FBRD badge and was allowed to pass beneath the tape that roped off that segment of beach. It wasn't a beach exactly, not the kind I knew growing up in North Carolina anyway. It was a sandy bank beside a body of water though, and I stopped before I even got to the bloated body.

It was the smell. The stench of dead bodies was never something I'd gotten used to, no matter how many years I'd been in this business, but I particularly hated the stench of bodies pulled from water, or left out in the heat to fester and rot. In the case of water bodies, something about the fishy odor of the river mixed with the corpse was particularly unpleasant.

I smeared the menthol offered by the tech under my nose and didn't feel embarrassed by it. I know some guys who'd insist it's a sign of weakness to accept the *help*. I found it more embarrassing to puke on the corpse.

The body was naked, mostly unidentifiable because of the bloat and bizarre bluish color. The genitalia had been mutilated, rather savagely. My name was carved on his chest all right, and not artistically. The *B*, *r*, *n* and *e*, were jagged scrawls rather than soft, round letters. I accepted a pair of gloves offered by one of the techs.

"Whatever he used," I said, fingering the edge of the wound with my gloved hand. "It wasn't sharp enough."

"Do you know him?" the man who escorted me to the body asked.

Instead of replying, I went on. "The blood under his fingernails could be his attackers."

I remembered what Fizz said about Chaplain then, about his ability to make a man shove a screwdriver into his own eye.

"Or he could have been forced to mutilate himself," I offered. "It would explain the jaggedness and uneven approach. He wouldn't have been able to be precise through the pain."

"I know it might be hard to identify him," the man said.

I turned then. I looked up and measured him for the first time. His face blanched and he took a step back.

"I know him," I said. "But I don't know you or why you deserve the pertinent details for this case."

"I'm Detective Smith, from Boston," he said.

That explained the attitude and the accent.

"I've been tracking a killer for a long time and believe he's taken up in St. Louis. It's been a decade since I started this task force. Most guys last three years. I've been riding this for ten years," Smith said.

I arched an eyebrow. "Why are you telling me?"

"I want you to understand that I'm dedicated to this. I want to close it, and here I have a body with your name carved on it, and the body fits my killer's M.O. perfectly. Throw me a bone here, Agent Brinkley. Please."

I nodded. I knew what it meant to go hard on a case for that long.

In retrospect, I know even better now than I did then.

"His name is Harry Fitzgerald," I said. "I busted him with narcotics, an insignificant amount, and let him go in exchange for his collaboration."

"He was your informant."

"Fizz, as I liked to call him, was good. He gave me what I needed, and clearly someone found out."

"What were you working on now?"

I looked up at the other man. While I disregarded him at first, a work habit unfortunately, I took him in more fully now. He was maybe 5'10", chestnut brown hair and a pointy jaw. His hook nose was crooked and the acne pock marks on the side of his face weren't as bad as they could've been.

"Who was he following? Who was he narking on?" he pressed.

My mind blurred and warped. I looked for the answer and couldn't find it. A strange, feverish chill slid down my back. "I can't remember."

"What?" he said.

I stood up. I hoped I didn't look as incompetent as I felt. "I can't fucking remember."

"That's real convenient."

I pointed at the blue hair, wet and sticking to the unrecognizable face. "I ID'd your man and I told you what I know. Call me if you need anything else."

Smith yelled after me but I did not turn back. I kept walking at a slow and steady clip to the Impala.

CHAPTER FORTY-TWO

Wednesday, April 2, 2003

Since Jackson was still out of commission at least another day, I hit the bar. I admit I was hoping to run into the guy again, the man who seemed to know something about the internment camps. But I showed up real early. I played darts with the young Bobby George wannabe until I grew bored. Then I challenged his friends to pool.

I had a considerable buzz by the time someone slid onto the bar stool beside mine.

"Just the man I was looking for," I blurted, not entirely on top of my game. I was just this side of drunk, which was dangerous.

"Really?" he said and smiled.

"What's your name?" I asked. "I never got a name."

He turned and considered me for a moment. Then as if realizing just how far gone I was, he grinned. "Aaron Reeves," he said. "But you can call me Reeves. That is what agents, cops, and all those types do right? Last name only?"

I thought about Charlie. "Reeves it is."

"Are we celebrating something?" Reeves asked and accepted the pint that Peaches readily put in his hand.

"My partner was shot and my best nark was found in the river with his balls cut off," I said. I lifted my glass. "Cheers."

Reeves looked horrified and so did Peaches.

"Water for you," Peaches said. "A dead body in my bar isn't good for business."

Reeves had forgotten about his beer. "Someone is trying to kill you."

I shrugged. "Someone is always trying to kill me."

Reeves stared harder as if he was unsure how to proceed. After a long pause he finally said. "Someone is actively hunting you. Why else shoot your partner and kill your informant?"

I shrugged and the stool slid from beneath me. Reeves reached out and caught me by the arm.

"Uneven floor," I muttered.

"Earthquakes," Peaches offered with a grunt.

"This isn't San Fran," I said, aware that he was making fun of me.

"You pissed someone off," Reeves said again.

"I'm always pissing someone off," I slurred. Peaches laughed companionably. "What else is new?"

Reeves was perturbed. More perturbed by the news that I was on someone's hit list than I was—at least after all the booze I'd put in me.

"You need to be careful," he said. His cheeks were red even in the low light. "Your work is important."

"The missing girl?" I couldn't remember what case he was referring to.

"The camps," Reeves insisted. His eyes were wide, urgent and it was as if he'd forgotten himself in the moment. "You have to uncover the truth about the camps. If a good man like you tells the world about them, people will believe you."

I snorted at the good man comment, but even so a light

went on in my head. "Right. Right. You're right. Tell me about the camps."

"They were horrible," he said. His mouth hung open as if he was still astonished himself. "Absolute torture mills."

"How did you get out?" I asked.

His response was quick, automatic. "My facility was shut down. Only then was I freed."

It was a strange response and the voice that accompanied it was flat. I didn't realize the significance of this conversation at the time, but God how different things might have been if I had.

"They kept us," he said. "Tortured us physically, mentally, and emotionally. They wanted to know if we could be controlled, used, and if not, duplicated. They cut us open, studied us. When that didn't produce results, they created a breeding program."

"Are you telling me kids were locked up in that place?"

"Yes," he said. "The woman I loved—love—" He stopped.

I was a drunk bastard, so I didn't have the good sense to watch what I said. "Please don't tell me they raped her. I fucking hate rape stories. They're sad as fuck."

"No," he said. "Not raped in the sense you mean anyway. It was mostly the scientists that dealt with us. But a scientist's objectivity can be cruel. Believe me."

"So what happened to her?"

"She had a baby. We had a baby."

I turned and looked at him. After about two glasses of water from Peaches, my drunk edge was softening. My good sense was coming back to me. "What happened to her?"

"I paid someone," he said. "To take her away."

"Where is she now?" I asked.

"Somewhere safe," he said. "I hope."

"The camps are still open?" I asked but it wasn't a real question. It was just acceptance of a sad fucking realization.

"At least one that I know of," he said. "That is why I think it is so important for you to get to the bottom of this. Crack it open and expose them. Not get yourself killed."

I snorted. "What do you expect me to do?"

Reeves sighed like he'd been waiting forever for me to ask that question. "I'll give you everything you need to bring them down."

CHAPTER FORTY-THREE

Two Weeks

I see Jesse coming up the path long before she sees me. I watch her shuffle along, kicking at the dirt as she comes. She is so young. Sure, part of it is the NRD. She'll probably look seventeen forever if she keeps up with the death replacing. Part of it is the childish way she eats a banana with abandon, shoving huge bites into her mouth as if no one has taught her how to eat like a lady. I try to imagine her as an old woman. All grown up with kids maybe, probably still cranky as hell and maybe plump, but alive.

Alive.

The last time I met her in these woods, I'd been with Charlie. I'd called him in to help me figure out why we were being targeted. *Charlie, were you acting on Caldwell's orders even then? Had he already gotten up in your head and messed you around?* God I hoped not. I hope at least in the beginning, he'd come to my aid as my friend.

"Right here," I say. I step forward so she can see me.

"What the hell happened to you?" she says. "Are you sick?"

I shrug and think of Jackson's warning. You should tell

her. How would it sound? *I'm going to die in a couple of weeks. What do you think about that, kid?*

No.

She needs to worry about herself, not me.

"Not all of us heal in a heartbeat," I say. If I pull at her guilt strings, she might shut up. It usually works.

"Where have you been?" she asks and I have my opening.

I am looking for a way to give her information on Caldwell. This secret is not the kind to take to the grave. But I also don't want to get her hopes up and make her think I have answers that I don't.

"Arizona," I lie. "At the old base where Eric Sullivan was last seen. I got this." I open my jacket and pull out the piece of paper I printed neatly for her this morning. I've listened to her bitch about my handwriting enough to know that if I want her to read it carefully, I can't just scribble it down.

She gives me the hard drive I'd sent her to the Lovett's for.

"He's going to know it's gone," she says.

"Of course he'll notice. A computer won't work without a hard drive."

"Oh he'll know long before that," she says. Her cheeks tinge with red.

"Jesse—" I start, my heart speeding up at the idea that she's done something to bring attention to herself.

She wails. "It was the best I could do just to get the drive into Ally's hand and jump in front of that tree."

I try to soothe the hammering in my chest. I am getting too old for this, yet I expected to last longer, didn't I?

"Tree attacks child. That replacement must have made headlines." I hope my voice doesn't betray my unease.

Her eyes widen and she looks up from the paper I gave her. "Is this a medical record? Eric Sullivan, 34," she says. "But he's got to be at least fifty now."

"This is from his file when he was detained in the camps."

"But Caldwell could pass for much younger," she argues. "Almost twenty years younger."

"So he's been dying," I say, testing her with another bit of information. *Tell her everything* a part of me begs. *Tell her everything you can. She's going to have to pick up where you left off.*

"I just don't understand why Caldwell would infiltrate the Church and secure a high position. And how can he do death replacements with all the media attention that's on him? He's watched constantly."

"He could be working off the radar. They might not be replacements, just dying—for other reasons," I say, but I have a very good idea why Caldwell thought securing the topmost position within a powerful organization was the perfect disguise.

I think of all his propaganda, how he is remaking himself as the messiah of this age. I have no doubt that dying and coming back to life is part of that scam.

She puts the picture away. "Caldwell is my father."

"Jesse—" I want to stop her. Don't look at him that way, I think. *Seeing him that way will get you killed, kid.*

"No," she argues. "I need to accept the fact that the guy who wants to kill me is also my dad. If I don't get it through my head he's going to catch me off guard again."

"A father and a dad are not the same thing," I say. Christ, what could I say? I was never meant to have children. Every kid that crossed my path was damned for it. Aziz, Gideon, Jesse. No matter what I do for them, it is never enough.

"This is encrypted," I say, my heart still thrumming in my chest.

"Suckfest," she says, looking up at me from her sneakers. The overwhelming urge to hug her tight washes over me.

"In the meantime, I want you to go see Gloria, all right?" I say before I lose control of myself. "She knows what our next move should be. I'll check back with you once I get the hard drive open." The kid hesitates, looking at the photograph of her father one more time.

"Go on," I tell her. "Go on." *Before I screw up and tell you.*

When she gives me a little salute and turns on her heels, she looks like the perfect child soldier.

I watch her grow smaller as she gets farther and farther away from me. In one desperate moment, I call out after her.

"Jesse!" I say.

She stops and turns. "What?"

I think of all the things I could tell her. All the apologies for my impending death and subsequent abandonment, of my history with her father—any and all of it which is owed to her more than anyone. At the very least, I should tell her about her sister, who Jackson and I are fairly sure is dead.

With an impatient shrug, she asks again. "*What?*"

I raise the hard drive like a coward. "You did good, kid."

Her face breaks open into a beautiful, heart-breaking smile.

CHAPTER FORTY-FOUR

Thursday, April 3, 2003

woke in my own bed, but could not remember how I got there. The first thing I saw after the ceiling came into focus and stopped spinning long enough for me to turn on my side was the brown envelope on the bedside table. I pinched the corner between my fingers as if I wanted to be sure it was real. Bits of memory from the night before came back to me.

I remembered being drunk and stumbling out of the bar. Reeves came up behind me and offered to help. Then when falling into my bed without ceremony, Reeves had been here. I remembered him saying something but couldn't recall his words with any kind of clarity now. Had he given me this? Were there instructions?

I considered the envelope for a moment longer. I knew that if I opened it, there was no going back.

I sat up and placed the brown envelope on the bed in front of me. I stared at the chicken scratch of my name and the way it stretched from one corner to the other across the brown paper. I flipped it over and inched a dirty fingernail under the flap.

The sound of paper ripping and the contents rubbing against the inside of the paper came before a soft thump on the bed. Photographs slipped against one another spreading out over the coverlet. I realized then that I still wore my boots and had smeared mud against the end of the bed.

"Fuck," I grumbled and my headache intensified with the rumble of my voice. I hated to do laundry.

I lifted one photograph and then another, noting the timestamp in the upper corner of each. I wasn't sure by looking at it, as I'm no photography expert, if the timestamp indicated a digital camera was used or if these were taken from a security camera.

The outside of a brick military facility was framed in several photos. I recognized the building, having seen it long before the high fence and razor wire had been erected to enclose the place.

There was also a copy of a document which read: *42 U.S. Code 13724, conversion of military installations into federal prison facility*.

That was how they did it then. False arrests.

You could still actively recruit for your science experiment if you pulled "criminals" off the street. And if only we had a dollar for every time someone was wrongly accused and locked away. So this is what Reeves wanted me to expose? The entire operation: the false imprisonments, the hidden in plain sight facilities, the wrongful detainments, the torture.

I let out a long, laborious exhale. "Fuck." This was no small order.

But it could lead to Sullivan. Not that I'd cared much for finding the man until now. I was more worried about Maisie and Rachel, I knew, but Sullivan was still a problem that had to be solved. After all, either Charlie was right, or Charlie was misinformed.

If he was right then Sullivan had escaped his detainment

and might strike out against us sooner or later. Exposing the torture could placate him or even slow him down. If he felt he'd received even a drop of revenge, it could take the wind out of his sails. That would save innocent lives caught in the crossfire of his retribution and buy me more time to find him and decide if he was really a threat, or just a victim on the run.

Because that was the other side of this coin. If they were hiding the fact that they were running internment camps in the open, they could also be lying about Sullivan. He may not be a terrorist at all, but instead, simply a threat of exposure.

I thumbed through the photographs and my headache grew worse. I recognized the facility because I had trained there. Could Reeves had possibly known that? It was unlikely. If he had, perhaps he was counting on nostalgia or my intimate knowledge of the facility. But I hadn't been there in decades.

According to someone's meticulous notes enclosed along with the photographs, in 1992 Fort Diq was sold to the government, but conversion was delayed beyond the original 1994 projection date. The funding for the project didn't come through until 1996. It would have definitely been up and operational by January 1998 when the under-the-radar detainees were transferred there—and that was what these pictures suggested. *4500 souls inside*, the note said. *At least.*

It was a huge sprawling campus and the level of security around Fort Diq was intimidating. There would be no ridiculous or covert operation to infiltrate the place and march the prisoners to freedom. I wasn't fucking Moses. But maybe there was another way to save them.

I lifted my cell phone from the bedside table and called the number I retrieved from the internet.

A perky woman answered on the second ring.

"The Daily Gazette. How can I direct your call?"

CHAPTER FORTY-FIVE

12 Days

J use a favor to get what I need from the hard drive.

Most of it is junk: church records, finances, and the like. I have to read every document to be sure. I'm in my bed, resting. Today I woke up tired and sore. Old injuries were stiff and my head just wasn't as clear as it could be. What could I say? The machine doesn't work as well as it used to. With the covers pulled over my legs and laptop on, I read the data until my eyes are raw with the effort.

Then I see it.

A list of names nearly 44 pages long. I hit print and the machine on the desk across the room clicks to life, spitting out one page after another.

The list is almost printed when I find a file on a man named Jeremiah. It pops up alongside Alice's name. A growing suspicion in my chest, I throw back the covers and go to the printer. There on the first page is her name, *Alice Gallagher*.

My phone rings and I answer.

"I think I've identified Caldwell's next target," Jackson says. "If we get her first, maybe it will trip him up or slow him down. I've been getting some pictures, but nothing definitive yet."

"Good work," I say, searching the list for more names I recognize. Jesse is there, and Rachel. Jackson is not far down. "Let me know what you need and then you and the kid can go pick her up."

Jackson is quiet.

"Is there a problem?" I ask.

"Why not you?" she asks.

Because all the people I care about, save Gideon, are on this hit list. If Caldwell is hunting them, I have to kill him first.

"I'll tell you when I see you," I say and hang up. Then I call Gideon.

He answers. "You are right. He is hard to kill."

"Gideon," I growl.

"I am being careful," he says. "I am a ghost."

I grit my teeth and let it go. For now. Mostly because I know that no matter what I tell him, he will do as he pleases anyway. "Alice Gallagher. She is Jesse's assistant, best friend, lover, whatever the hell she is. Find out what she is doing. She's done something to piss off Caldwell and I want to know what it is."

"Alice Gallagher," Gideon repeats then he is quiet. I think he's hung up. "You only have twelve days."

"Don't rub it in."

CHAPTER FORTY-SIX

Friday, April 4, 2003

When I arrived at the bar, it was up in flames. I'd seen the black smoke billowing up into the sky blocks before and it had set me off into a jog. My SIG Sauer slapped against my ribs beneath my leather jacket. A firefighter tried to stop me from coming closer as I rounded the large truck blocking off the road. Pedestrians crowded in on the place despite the men trying to push them back to a safer distance.

"Sir, please, you have to move back," the young man said through the visor of his helmet.

"I'm an agent." I flashed my badge even though the FBRD had no jurisdiction over something like this. Why should he know that? "What the hell happened here?"

"Some wacko firebombed the place. The barkeep said a regular patron came in and—"

"That's him. I'm telling you that's him." I heard Peaches' voice over the din—the sound of water splashing against the bricks and flooding through the broken street-front window. I turned toward the sound of his voice and saw him jabbing a finger my way.

"Brinkley," he screamed. "Brinkley."

Thinking that he needed my help to navigate this circus, I started to approach him. But when he took a step back as if afraid, I stopped. Several patrons I recognized and others I didn't, they stepped back too.

"Are you all right?" I asked him.

"That's him!" Peaches yelled again, his paunch jiggling with the ferocity of his words. "Agent Brinkley, right there. He's the crazy motherfucker who burned down my place."

It was as if someone had punched me in the chest. "What?"

"Arrest him," someone said. A roar of assenting murmurs grew louder. I felt the firefighter beside me grab onto my arm and I shook him off.

All of the faces I saw were trained on me with a mix of horror and anger etched into their features. "I just got here."

"Sir, you'll have to come with us," said two uniforms as they pressed in on me. I knocked one back before I had the good sense not to do anything stupid and damning.

With the uniformed officer out of my way, I got a clear look at the sidewalk behind him. There stood Chaplain. A smug grin lit up his face as firelight danced across his dark features.

Run, I thought. *You should run away before they can catch you. Run. Run. Run.*

That was exactly what I did.

I made it all the way to the office before I realized what a moron I was. Fleeing a crime scene was the exact opposite of what I should have done. There was no way I was going to convince the authorities that I'd simply panicked, not a man with my background and training.

"You fucking idiot," I said to myself, busting through the front doors of the FBRD building. Charlie's door was closed and he was on the phone with someone. I slipped past his window without being seen. I'd almost made it to my chair before I realized someone already occupied it.

"Jackson," I said.

She looked relieved. "Good. I'm glad I don't have to hunt you down."

"You're the only one," I said.

Confusion furrowed her brow. "What?"

I told her about the bar, the firebombing, and being accused by Peaches himself. "Not just Peaches," I added. "They all seemed to think I'd done it. Everyone on the street."

"Shit," she said. "We have less time than I thought."

"What are you talking about?"

"Look," she said. She pulled up some videos and showed them too me. Gruesome snuff films. But it was the third one that struck a chord with me.

"I've seen this," I said.

"I know." She pulled from sketches from her bag. "I think you went there looking for Rachel. Right?"

My mind warped around itself. "It's all a show. The girls are paid and they like it there."

Jackson swore. "No. They are taken and forced into this. Listen, I know this is going to sound crazy to you, but hear me out. Even if your brain tries to reject what I say, just hear me out, OK?"

"It can't be weirder than what I've fucking seen tonight."

"I think you followed your contact Fitzgerald to Chaplain's safe house. You saw this—show—and before you could do anything, your mind was changed."

"Changed?"

"Yeah, smudged, rubbed out, altered, whatever you want to call it."

"You're saying I saw an innocent girl get raped and murdered for profit and I did nothing?" My anger rushed to the surface. "Fuck you."

She shook her head. "It's got to be hard for you to see the truth, given what he must've done in there, but think about it. Think about Fizz's death and when you saw him last. Think about tonight and what you know happened and whatever everyone else believes happened."

I saw Chaplain grinning and smug on the sidewalk. "Run," I said. "He told me to run. In my head."

"Exactly," Jackson said. "You would have never fled the scene of a crime. Not in your right mind anyway."

"Shit," I said, the horrible plausibility of it all weighing on me.

"He's moving in on you," she continued. "He must think discrediting you and getting you out of the picture will be neater than killing you himself. We're going to have to bring him down before you get arrested."

"How the hell can we bring someone down who can use mind control?" I asked. "How the hell is he even using mind control?"

"When I entered the remote viewing program, I saw some unbelievable things," Jackson said.

I arched an eyebrow expecting an explanation.

"Another time," she said. "Right now, we have to go. We need to hit Chaplain tonight before he can come up with any more ways to ruin your life."

"We can't take a big team in there. He'll have us all shooting each other."

"No, we've got to keep it small. Me and you."

"How the hell are we going to pull that off?"

"I have a plan," she said. "Just meet me in Beckett Park at 10 P.M."

"I'll be there," I said. When she looked doubtful I added. "If I can I'll be there. I promise."

She gathered up her stuff and left me. I was about to follow her, head back myself and suit up for the night ahead. But I never made it that far, and I never found out what fantastic plan Jackson had for bringing down some kind of psychopathic mutant.

"Jim," Charlie said and I turned to find him standing in his office doorway, his face had lost all its color. "What the hell is going on?"

CHAPTER FORTY-EIGHT

I want to test the kid first. So I lure her out in the middle of the night, knowing she sleeps about as consistently as I do. Part of it is her job. Shadowing replacement clients is a 24-hour affair. After this many years, she's learned how to stay awake.

Also, I know she won't turn down free pancakes. It's after midnight when I see her push through the diner doors. She's wearing a zip-up black hoodie under her boyfriend's jacket. I'm amused by the mismatched shoes peeking out from beneath her dark blue jeans, but when her dog tag catches the harsh fluorescent light above, I stop smiling.

Beneath the canvas green jacket, it looks too military. They are standard FBRD issue now, a way to keep the death replacement agents out of the morgue in the event of a death, but I don't see an agent. I just see the kid looking too much like a soldier.

She plops down across from me.

"What the hell are you wearing?" she asks.

I glance down at my disguise. One of my favorites actually, strawberry-blond beard and mustache, dark shades, and a

Rasta beanie hat are assembled to give me the look of one of my favorite musicians. I'd kept the leather jacket of course and my favorite boots, but the rest of the ensemble was enough to hide the fact I was supposed to be dead to anyone who asked.

I don't answer and she yammers on about her replacements, work and how difficult it can be working with people. It's just good to hear her voice.

The waitress comes to bring our food and I wait until she is out of earshot before I get to business.

"Caldwell's hit list," I say and slide it across the table.

"You want me to read this? It's a million pages long," she groans around the oversized bite of pancakes stuffed into her chipmunk cheeks.

"Look up the word hyperbole," I say.

She squints down at the page and I think of the first time I showed her the FBRD manual, shortly after recruiting her, a scrawny kid who talked too much even then. "Look at how tiny the font is. It must be a hundred names per page."

"Just look at the first page."

She finally quits trying to devour food and accepts the list.

Her cheeks redden. "Why am I the second name?"

"I think it's ranked in order of importance. I would consider anyone on the first couple of pages top priority."

"Is Lane—" she begins, but I'd anticipated her asking about her boyfriend.

"Page 44," I say.

She is visibly relieved. "At least he isn't a priority."

"He isn't the only one," I say and watch her face carefully.

She looks down at the page again, running her finger along the list. I know the minute she sees it. Her finger stops and her mouth comes open slightly.

"She's number eight," she says. "If I'm number two, how the hell is Ally number eight? She's not even a zombie."

She's referring to the fact that Caldwell has been hunting down and murdering Necronites, people with NRD just like him, and killing them off one by one.

"Keep your voice down," I say, but there is no point in trying to keep her quiet.

"They only know about Ally because of me and I'm not even the most important person."

"Cindy is on page 2," I test her, seeing if her surprise is genuine, or if she'll welcome a diversion. "Rachel is on page 14 and I couldn't find my name anywhere."

"Because you're supposed to be dead," she says.

Maybe I think, or maybe Caldwell already has me penciled in for my very own appointment.

Her face pinches again. "I don't understand. How is Ally on this list?"

She is as surprised as I am that Alice is Caldwell's target. Alice is as average as they come. She has no abilities. No power, money, or contacts and from the outside, no means to threaten Caldwell. So what has she done?

And there was the kid herself to consider. I remember Jesse lying in Caldwell's arms. "I want you to take a good long look at your name. Number *two*, Jesse."

Her eyes are fixed on the page but I don't think she is listening to me. She can get as single-minded as I can when working a job. Ally is her job. Lane is her side interest. She might publically declare the opposite to either of them and herself, but this old dog has a good nose.

Why should I care? Because if Alice gets herself killed, I can't count on the kid to keep her head clear. No doubt she would make one stupid mistake after another. I have proof from last year, when Alice was kidnapped. Jesse got herself killed almost instantly.

"I can't save her twice," she says and looks as if she is going to be sick. She is thinking of the basement, where

Charlie delivered me to die a year ago. "If they try to hurt her again—"

"We won't let them get that far," I say. "You're losing color. Look at me."

"Tell me about Liza or something," she says. "And get this freaking plate out of my face before I barf on it."

I reach forward and pull her plate away from her. I see the kid I recruited eight years ago for selfish reasons. I said then, *Give me ten years, and no one will know you burned down the barn and killed a man.* Looks like she was going to get off early for good behavior.

I sigh. "When Jackson finds Liza, the first name on the list, I need you to go get her. She's safer with you and Jackson than alone." By finding the girl, maybe we can disrupt his plans. Maybe we can change something.

"OK, so he is a murderous lunatic who wants to hack up more death replacement agents. Fine," she says, as if I hadn't spoken. "But why Ally? What the hell does Caldwell want with Ally?"

"I don't know," I say. But I intend to find out.

Charlie shut the door behind us as I came into the office. Then he locked it with the turn of his deadbolt.

"What the fuck?" Charlie asked.

"I have something to tell you," I said. Already my mind raced with my options, none of which were ideal. "And it's going to sound crazy."

"Even if it is the truth," Charlie said, letting go of the lock. "This is a fucking mess. Because of what happened in the desert, they'll never believe me, even if I defend you."

His hands went up to his hips, exposing the twin Berettas tucked into his shoulder holster.

I knew he was right, but I decided to tell him the truth anyway. What did I have to lose? "Wright has been recruited —or kidnapped, it isn't clear—by a local drug lord," I began. "Henry Chaplain. He uses NRD-positive girls to make snuff films. Afraid of exposure, he has killed my informant and is now trying to defame me."

Charlie snorted. "The bar?"

"I saw him there," I said. "He was fucking grinning at me

from the sidewalk while the building burned."

He exhaled and ran a hand through his hair.

"You don't believe me."

His mouth fell open. "Of course, I believe you, Jim. Why wouldn't I believe you?"

I had expected him to doubt me. Why wouldn't he? All of it sounded insane to me. But here was my friend, telling me that he believed me despite the odds. Something deep in my chest released.

"Sometimes," Charlie said. "When we try to make things right, we make a big fucking mess. Or we piss off the wrong lunatic. In this case, you've done both."

"No kidding," I said and laughed.

"But you shouldn't have run, Jim. The witness testimony—"

"I know," I said, biting off my own nervous energy. "Chaplain is good at—persuading people. We aren't going to convince anyone I'm innocent."

Charlie considered this. "You need to get out of town."

"You just said I shouldn't run."

"They've called some people in," he said. "I just spoke to them on the phone and they don't sound interested in the truth. I think with the whole Sullivan fuck up—the fact we haven't found him, and the missing girl and now this—they aren't happy. I think it best you become hard to find until I can clear your name."

Charlie's eyes widened then and I looked over my shoulder to see what he saw. There were four men, big guys in dark suits, coming through the front door. I didn't need to ask who they were or what they were here for. It was obvious, wasn't it?

"Sorry, Charlie," I said as several pairs of eyes clamped onto mine through the office window. "But I think it's too late for that."

CHAPTER FIFTY

Friday, April 4, 2003

I'd been sitting in a cold gray room for hours. They hadn't taken my watch because I said I didn't have one. Of course I lied. A common interrogation technique involved removing all clocks and watches so that a person would lose track of time. But I couldn't lose track of time, because I had a 10 P.M. appointment with Jackson and I had every intention of keeping it. No way I was going to let her go to Chaplain's alone.

"We have over twelve witnesses putting you at the—?"

"Why am I being interrogated in a jail cell?" I interrupted. My elbows were on my knees as I sat on the edge of the cot. A toilet and wash basin sat off to my left, and in front of me were two of the suits that had burst into the FBRD office. I let them take me, despite Charlie's insistence that I disappear. I was starting to regret it.

"We are familiar with your service record," the first said. He'd removed his shades and put them in a breast pocket where they bulged. The room had a draft to it, but I had no idea where it was coming from. My view was limited to the cell itself and the partial stretch of hallway that cut across the sliding door to the cell on my right. "You are too dangerous to hold somewhere unsecure."

"Is that so?" I said. "So don't you think that if I wanted to escape, I could have done it at any time?"

"Maybe you thought it best to come quietly?" he offered with a shrug and a thrust of his bottom lip. "Trying to make up for the fact that you ran from the scene of a crime?"

I think Chaplain made me run, I wanted to say, but I'd reached the point where keeping my mouth shut was the better idea.

"If you really think I'm a firebombing maniac, does that make you smart or stupid for sitting this close to me?"

He smirked, but I saw the slightest flicker of concern cross his face. I wondered how long he could refrain from scooting his chair back. It was about a minute before he found an excuse to get up. Wobbly leg, my ass.

"You may have lost control when you burned the bar."

"Do I look like a man incapable of control?" I asked. I hunched my shoulders, enhancing my predatory look and hardened my gaze. It was bullshit posturing, I knew, but it worked on idiots like this, especially when you stared into their eyes without blinking. "You've asked me the same dumb shit over and over, yet your larynx is still in your throat, isn't it?"

"Threatening your investigative officers will not reflect well in your trial," the other one said. He'd been quiet this whole time, leaning against the bars, watching this charade.

"Neither will eyewitness testimony," I said. "It's consistently unreliable. After all, I bet even the eyewitnesses themselves have inconsistent recollections." I was hoping this to be true.

"Actually the testimony was uniformly consistent," the smug one replied. He'd given up sitting altogether and had his hands on the back of the chair, gripping the upper rim, holding it between us like a shield.

"Because the memories were planted," I said. I was speaking to myself. I started laughing. "Of course they were."

Both men looked unnerved. I realized they really did believe I'd lost my mind. And I had access to too many things that go *BOOM*. That'd make me nervous too.

"Where's your partner?" he asked.

"I work alone," I said.

"Not on the Eric Sullivan case," the smug one said.

"Captain Jackson?" I asked. Then I lied. "I have no idea."

"I'm sure you don't," he said.

"What does she have to do with anything?"

"She must be your accomplice," he said.

My anger spiked. "She wasn't even at the bar."

"Then why did we dig your bullet out of her shoulder?"

I froze. "What?"

"It was a bullet from your missing Beretta that was removed from Captain Jackson's shoulder."

I rubbed my face with both hands. I wanted to laugh at the pure lunacy of the situation but I knew this was the wrong time to do so. I was also in the horrible position that if I did not confess Chaplain's involvement, I would likely be indicted myself. On the other hand, if I sent men to Chaplain's door, they might die, or worse, come back even more convinced of my guilt.

"Is she alive?" the quiet one by the bars asked.

"Who?" *Maisie? Rachel?* God I hoped so.

"Captain Jackson," he replied.

"As far as I know," I said. But not for much longer if I didn't get out of this place.

"Because she's your accomplice in the Sullivan case," he said. "You're both working to hide Sullivan."

"I've never seen Sullivan," I said. I was pissed beyond

measure. If it wouldn't have damned me, I would have ripped this bed off the wall and beat them with it.

They looked afraid, which was a small pleasure. "Sergeant James Brinkley, you are suspended until further notice. Your badge and gun will be kept until we see fit to reinstate you, *if* we reinstate you."

I flipped them the bird as they left the cell, closing the door after them.

Their conversation had filled me with doubts. Was this shitshow all Chaplain? He didn't like me in his territory, trying to take his property—as he surely thought of the girls —or fuck with his revenue and so he decided to take me down? Sure, that was one theory. But given the pressure and attention Charlie had fielded over the Sullivan case, I had a feeling otherwise. They'd accused me of working with Sullivan and of putting the bullet in Jackson myself, the day we *claimed* to see Maisie alive.

How big was this? I'd asked Charlie.

I'd gotten my answer. *Big.*

CHAPTER FIFTY-ONE

5 Days

"I don't understand," Jackson says again. "Why aren't you coming?"

"I can't come," I say. I spell it out for her. "First of all, I might spook the girl. If Liza has been running from Caldwell and who knows what else, a big guy with a gun is not what she's going to want to see right now. Second, you and Jesse can move better without me. It's pretty clear that Micah is watching my every move. He's thwarted every assassination attempt I've made this year, and if I go with you guys, he's going to see that. I'm hoping that I'll serve as a distraction so that you and Jesse can slip in, get the girl, and get back here before Caldwell has any idea what's happened."

Jackson looks down at the sketchpad which lays open on her desk. It's Liza, another death replacement agent, and the girl Caldwell wants most to kill—number 1 on his hit list.

"You only have five days," she says. She begins tapping her pencil against the spiral rings that bind the notebook together.

"Don't worry about me," I tell her. I push the drawing Caldwell gave me into her face again. "Keep your eyes open for this. Anything suspicious at all and you get Jesse out of there. Forget Liza if you have to."

Jackson takes the drawing and looks for details I probably can't see. Then she peers over the page. "Liza could be a trap, a way to get Jesse out of our reach."

I have my suspicions it isn't my reach Caldwell is worried about, but until I hear back from Gideon, I can't be sure. "We can't let him kill Liza like he did Chaplain. You know that."

Jackson nods, resigned to what I'm saying.

"Hello?" the kid calls from upstairs.

"Get down here," I tell her, and Jackson quickly folds and tucks the drawing out of sight.

CHAPTER FIFTY-TWO

Friday, April 4, 2003

I'd fallen asleep and when I woke up it was dark in the cell. The silence was deafening and I wondered if I was the only one in the whole building. I'd heard nothing from Charlie or Jackson about what was going on. Jackson. The realization jolted me upright. I remembered our agreement to meet that night and pulled my watch from the secret inner pocket of my leather jacket where I'd hidden it.

10:23 P.M. I was late. If Jackson was still waiting in the cold, dark Beckett Park, I'd be damned. From what I knew about her in the brief time we'd worked together, she'd try to go in on Chaplain alone, maybe even catch him off guard and put a bullet in him before he could fuck with her head.

Nowhere was safe until Chaplain was dead. That was the problem, right? Chaplain could have whatever he wanted from anyone if he was alive. He needed to be dead. As a sniper, I was comfortable with the idea of killing a bad guy. As a man, I wanted revenge against the bastard who was trying to fuck with my life.

11:23

12:02

12:12

Each time I checked my watch my heart sank. Not knowing what had happened to Jackson was rubbing me raw. I imagined the worst. I imagined Chaplain dumping her body off the MLK Bridge into the river with my name carved on her chest. I considered dismantling the bed for screws and shavings that could be used to pop the lock, even if breaking out of jail would make my guilt undeniable.

I heard something in the cell. A strange whoosh sound and then two footsteps. "Brinkley?"

I looked up and saw a man standing in my jail cell. Reeves. Goddamn Reeves.

"What the fuck?"

"We have to go," he said. "You're going to have a bunch of questions, I know, but I'll have to answer them on the way. Chaplain brainwashed your people and you can't stay here."

"Tell me something I don't know."

"Just hang on to me," he said and stepped toward me, arms open as if to embrace me.

Before I could question this, he wrapped his arms around my shoulders and the jail disappeared. There was just a heartbeat in the darkness, and then we were in my bedroom.

"Shit," I said and fell away from him. The back of my knees hit the nightstand and the lamp fell forward. Reeves caught it with both hands.

"Grab your guns or whatever you need and let's go," he said. His voice was barely above a whisper and urgent as he righted the lamp. "We can't stay here. There are cops everywhere."

"They're looking for Jackson," I said and he nodded. "Then they don't have her. Good."

"She's with Chaplain," he said.

"What?" I croaked. He clasped a moist palm over my

mouth and shushed me with a finger to his own lips. He must've thought I was an idiot.

Furious, I moved back the bed and lifted the trapdoor there. Inside was my packed duffle, undisturbed. It was stuffed with money, weapons and all the other shit I thought I might need for any kind of situation like this. They would have swept the apartment and taken everything else for testing. I checked inside the bag to make sure it was all there and when I was satisfied, I zipped it up.

"How did he get ahold of Jackson?" I asked.

"She went to his house and he found her lurking outside."

"How do you know all this?"

"Do you have what you need?"

"From here, yes, but—"

Reeves grabbed onto me and another heartbeat of darkness followed. When we stepped into the world again, we were in Beckett Park, adjacent to Chaplain's house.

"I could never get used to that," I said and tried to quell that dropped feeling in my stomach. I looked around the dark park, the moonlight and shadows shifting across empty benches. The eerie orange glow of streetlamps along the walk were as menacing as any apathetic eye.

"You won't have to," he said. I didn't move. I fixed him with my heavy gaze trying to figure out where the hell to start.

"Why didn't we just pop into Chaplain's house?" I asked.

"I have to be able to see where I am going," he said. "I haven't gotten a good look inside his house yet."

"How did you—"

"We don't really have time for questions." He turned away from me and began to march toward the house. I followed.

If we didn't have time for questions, I'd just accuse him then. "You're Eric Sullivan."

He froze. "How did you know?"

I knew because they'd asked me about him, interrogated me about him and swore I was helping him. But the only person I'd agreed to help was Reeves when I delivered the information to the reporter.

"You used your—whatever the hell you do—to escape a camp that is still open?"

"Yes," he said. "But I can only carry out one person at a time. Sometimes two. I used to be able to only take myself places. I can't just carry everyone out of the camps. I need you to be my whistleblower. Everyone will disregard my testimony. They'll put a bullet in my brain and be done with it. People will take you seriously."

"The wrong people took me seriously," I said.

"You're a decorated soldier. If you uncover a conspiracy, people will believe you."

"When did it start?"

"I don't know," he said. When I looked doubtful, his voice rose. "I wished I could get out of that place every minute of every day for years. One day, that's exactly what happened."

We cut around a tall hedge at the edge of the park and Chaplain's House loomed into view. It looked bigger. The lights coming from the windows illuminated like demonic eyes, daring me to come inside and find out just what kind of horrors Chaplain had in store for me.

"So why are you helping me now?" I asked. "The Wright case has nothing to do with your plan."

"You can't help me if you're dead," he said. "I can't get justice if you're floating face down in a river or behind bars."

"Justice," a voice said from the darkness. "Don't you mean revenge?"

We both whirled and I raised my gun to meet the barrel already pointed at me.

*D*etective Smith stood there wearing black from head to toe, his 9MM pointed at my head. This was a smart idea, given the fact that Sullivan stood there unarmed.

"Whatever you believe or heard about me," I said to Smith. "It isn't true. This will sound crazy but Chaplain—"

"I know," Smith interrupted.

I blinked. "You think you know but—"

"I know what Chaplain can do. The mind shit. He's done it to me."

I took a chance and lowered my gun a few inches from his head to his chest. When he slid his gun down completely, so did I.

"What did he do to you?" I asked.

"We were hunting him in Boston for the same shit he is doing here. My partner got too close and he killed him, after making everyone believe that he'd lost his mind and killed himself, of course."

"How do you know the truth?" I asked.

"That's what he does," he said. "He likes to keep one

person in the loop. Seeing their anguish and isolation is part of the hard-on for him. The real bitch of it is he doesn't have to do it. He has plenty of money and power all on his own. It's like his snuff films. He just enjoys watching the pain. That's what he cares about."

I look back toward the house. "They have my partner in there. We can't stay out here talking."

"She's probably dead," he said.

"Until I see her body go into the ground with my own eyes, I won't believe it," I said and adjusted the ammo in my pockets and made sure I was ready for what would come next.

"Maybe you shouldn't believe it even then," Smith said.

"Good point," I replied and turned to Sullivan. "If you feel him in your head at all, you should just *go*."

"What about you?"

"As soon as you see Jackson, I want you to get her out," I commanded. "Do it or our deal is off."

"I wasn't aware we made a deal," he stiffened.

"Sure we did," I said. "Get Jackson out alive, and I'll be your poster child for the detainee cause."

He disappeared.

"Shit," I said. "I didn't mean *now*."

"Where did he go?" the detective asked.

I jabbed a gun at the house and hoped Smith got the idea. By the way his eyes spread wide, those liquid whites bright with moonlight, I think he did. Without wasting another second, I rushed forward, descending on the dark house that waited.

CHAPTER FIFTY-FOUR

4 Days

I've paced the floor of my apartment until I've worn a path in the carpet. I obsess about what could be happening to my girls. At one point, I even wish that Caldwell would come and talk shit. That would mean he wasn't hurting anyone at least.

My phone goes off and it's Jackson.

"You're late. Talk to me," I demand.

There is a moment of silence before a tentative voice comes through the line. "Brinkley?"

"Alice?" My mind whirls with the possibilities of what has happened and why she could be calling me from Jackson's number. "What's happened?"

"Gloria has been hurt pretty bad and Jesse has been taken."

Fuck. I cover my face with a hand and try to think.

"What's going on?" she asks, angry.

"I'll explain," I tell her. "Can we meet?"

She suggests a donut shop about eight minutes away from my apartment.

"I'll meet you there," I tell her and terminate the call.

I take the highway, knowing it will be less congested this time of night and get off at the 21st Avenue exit.

She is already there when I park and get out of the car. She's standing beside her Prius, fiddling with the buttons on her red coat. I do my best to stay out of sight, and I must've done all right because she jumps when she hears me.

"Why do you have Winston in your car?" I ask, pointing at Jesse's fat pug resting in the front seat.

"It's been a long night," she says. It must have been, because she looks tired and irritable.

"Where is she?" I ask. I mean Jackson.

"We don't know," Alice says, and I can tell she is holding back tears. She recounts what she knows for me. Jackson and Jesse found Liza, but Liza is a traitor. Apparently, she was working with Micah Delaney all along.

"You sent her out-of-state to chase down a girl with NRD. Surely it occurred to you that they might cross paths with Caldwell."

"But—" I begin. Alice doesn't stop.

"After what happened last year, you didn't think this was a trap? Of course it was a trap. Everything to do with Caldwell is a trap. How could you be so predictable and reckless?"

I snort. It's a bitter and offended response. Predictable, me? Really?

"I sent Jackson to protect Jesse," I tell her, trying to recover my wounded pride.

"Gloria almost *died*."

The words strike me as forcibly as any blow. *Gloria almost died. Gloria almost died.*

Jackson cannot view herself. She can't predict her own death. She's told me this. Christ, why didn't it occur to me that her reckless pursuit of Caldwell could get her killed?

Of course it could.

And the more desperate she becomes, the more she pushes herself, the more reckless she'll be.

"You look terrible," Alice says.

"You're more charming than I remember. Has Jesse worn off on you?"

"I am angry and I am tired."

You and me both, I think. Instead, I say: "We need somewhere safe to talk." *Because I need to know what you're doing that is pissing Caldwell off. Because I need to check your story against what Gideon knows, and because I need to know if you can be trusted with the truth.*

"Follow me," she says.

I do.

CHAPTER FIFTY-FIVE

Saturday, April 5, 2003

$\mathcal{C}$oming around the side of the house, I stopped at the first window with light. My sigh was probably audible to the Boston detective as well as myself. Jackson was alive. She wasn't in great shape. She kneeled on the floor at Chaplain's feet without any sign of reverence. Her face was swollen on one side and her bandaged left shoulder was red with blood. But why beat on her? Then I heard Chaplain, loud, angry and at the top of his voice, screaming.

"What are you?" he asked. When she didn't answer, he hit her again. When she looked as equally unmoved, he shoved a blade against her face. "Tell me what you are or I'm going to carve up your fucking face until you don't look like anything."

Then I saw Sullivan. He was just a shadow in the corner of the room, unseen by the others. He didn't stay there long. When he appeared behind Jackson, Chaplain and his buffoons jumped back in surprise. Before they could recover from the shock, Jackson and Sullivan were gone. I blinked, and it was like they hadn't been in the house at all.

Chaplain was howling, turning angrily in a circle as if he expected to see them there and discover the nature of the trick. But he didn't find them. He found us. His gaze fixed on mine through the window.

"Shit," I said and turned toward Smith. "We've got to go."

Smith was frozen, staring through the window like a twelve year old at a titty show.

I shook him. "You know better, pull yourself together detective."

He didn't pull himself together. Instead he raised his gun and pointed it at me.

Shit, I thought, but I never said it. Rough hands grabbed onto the back of my leather jacket, followed by a heartbeat of darkness. Then my feet connected with the brick walkway of the park. The first thing I saw was Jackson sitting in the shadows on a bench, her gun in her hand.

"What took you so long?" she asked me.

"I had to spring him from jail," Sullivan said.

"No time for explanations," I said to her. "Are you OK?"

She stood as if to make her point but her legs were shaky. "I'll live."

"Good. We need to get the detective and the girls."

"I'll take the back and you—"

"No," Sullivan said, interrupting our plans. "I got you out. You can't go back in."

"My reputation won't be worth shit unless Chaplain's head is on a slab. We have to go in, and we have to kill him."

"And save the girls," Jackson added.

"You're both insane."

"Are you going to help or not?" I asked him. He considered this, looking from her to me and back.

He ran a hand through his hair and puffed out his cheeks in frustration. Then stepped forward. "Whatever you do, don't let go."

CHAPTER FIFTY-SIX

3 Days

I pull up at Jackson's house and see the dim light coming through the kitchen window. I knew she wouldn't stay in the hospital unless they shackled her to the bed. I've never known her to follow doctor's orders.

My phone rings, and I decide to take the call in my car before going in to check on Jackson.

"Yeah," I grumble into the receiver.

"Brinkley," Gideon says. "What interesting friends you have."

"I don't have a lot of time," I tell him.

"Three days," he intercedes, the anger is there but not as raw as it was when I first gave him the news. "I'll get to the point then."

"Thank you."

"Alice Gallagher has paired up with Jeremiah Johnson. He is very wealthy through his marriage to a pharmaceutical heiress, Tamara Henderson. Apart from this marriage, it seems he has no real source of income. Yet he could fund the Israeli Army for the rest of his life. The pharmaceutical company, Develacor has investments in everything you can think of: household products, technology, weapons develop- ment, and of course, pharmaceuticals."

"So he uses his wife's money to fund a little, what, operation?"

"Not little at all." Gideon laughs. "He has over 100,000 employees. Nearly as many as Microsoft."

"What the hell is he doing with them?"

"Surveillance and search and rescue mostly. They are watching everything."

"What does Alice have to do with all of this?"

"She is a recent recruit. It seems that she was only picked up late last year to do small search and rescue missions for his local outfit. That outfit is run by his second-in-command and one of his earliest recruits, Nicole Tamsin. Jeremiah appears to have recruited her shortly after her domestic partner was brutally murdered."

"Go back to Alice," I say. "What could she be doing that is pissing Caldwell off?"

"Jeremiah targets many of Caldwell's operations. For example, Caldwell has over fifty people locked in a basement of this farmhouse outside Minooka and is doing some kind of experiment on them. Jeremiah is very close to finding and uncovering this operation."

"How can you possibly know that?" I ask him, but a mention of the farmhouse sends a shiver down my spine. Was it the farmhouse from Jackson's drawing? Well, I guess I'll find out soon enough, won't I?

"Three may keep a secret if two of them are dead," says Gideon. "Everyone talks."

The light through Jackson's window dims and I realize she's just shut a door or gone into another room. "So Alice probably joined Jeremiah hoping to take a proactive approach to the cells that have been hunting and murdering Necronites. I don't blame her. She was stabbed."

"That is what I suspect," Gideon says. "But it would seem he was very happy to have her."

"What do you mean?"

"My informant tells me that Jeremiah sees Alice as a means for recruiting Jesse. If that is true, one must ask the question, what does Jeremiah know about Jesse and what does he want with her?"

"Good fucking questions," I say and at the mention of Jesse, my mind comes alive. "Listen, I want to know more about Alice and Jeremiah, but I need you to work on something else. Jesse has been taken. Find out where Caldwell is hiding her. I want to get her back."

"You only have three days," he says.

My chest clenches. I may not have time to find Jesse. Hell, I may never see the kid again.

"Just do your best."

"Of course," he says, his voice full of tenderness.

I end the call and climb the dark concrete steps into Jackson's house before he can get too sappy on me.

The upstairs is dark and quiet. I move through the shadows of the cool living room into the still kitchen. Pale moonlight filters through the lace curtain, spilling over the sink and oven. I see the light beneath the door and know Jackson is probably down there drawing her ass off.

Sure enough, as I descend the stairs, she doesn't even look up at me.

"Jackson?"

She doesn't turn around.

"Hey," I say and come up behind her. The furious scratch of her pen against the page sounds brutal in this cramped dark space.

I put a hand on her shoulder but she doesn't respond. So I lean around to get a good look at her face.

A thin stream of blood is coming from her left nostril and hitting the page in front of her. She's dragged her lead through it once or twice, giving certain lines a macabre burst of red.

"Shit," I say, and tilt her head back to look into her eyes. They are fully dilated and do not react to the overhead light shining into them. "Damn it."

I yank the notebook away from her and pull the pencil out of her hand. Then I slap her cheeks lightly. "Come on," I say. "Snap out of it."

She reaches for the pencil and paper again but I shove them farther away.

"No." I shake her. "Stop, *stop*."

Her eyes begin to focus. "I need to finish."

"No," I tell her.

"I need to—"

"No." I gesture toward her busted face and wrapped shoulder. "Look at you. How many times have you busted that shoulder?"

She ignores my question.

"I have to find Jesse. He has her. You know that, right? He has her," she says.

"We'll get her back." I'm trying for optimism.

Then I see it, the clump of fabric Jackson clutches in her left hand. It looks like she's been wringing the hell out of it as she drew.

"What is that?"

"Nothing," she says and childishly tries to hide it from me.

I reach down and wrench it from her grip. She cries out as I have obviously hurt some wounded part of her. I feel like a bastard.

"I'm sorry," I say and open up the fabric. I blink once or twice before realizing I'm looking at a shirt with the front blasted open by a gunshot. It's soaked in blood. I know this shirt.

"Jesus Christ," I say.

"He's killed her," she says.

I look away from Jesse's shirt. "How did you get this?"

"Caldwell gave it to me. Told me that for hurting Micah, he's shot her. He says he will kill her again unless I stop looking for her and stop helping you."

"You should stop," I tell her. "He could kill you."

"No," she says, desperately, turning her big eyes up to meet mine. "I have to find her. We're almost out of time."

We.

"Why didn't you tell me?" I ask.

"I didn't know he would take her—" she begins.

"No," I say and crush the fabric in my fist. It isn't until my hand comes away cool and wet that I realize the blood is fresh. He's just killed her, just come and delivered this. Jesse probably hasn't even healed and woken up yet—if she is going to. "Why didn't you tell me?"

Her frown deepens and eyes furrow in a question.

"Don't play dumb," I tell her. "We don't have time for it. Why didn't you tell me you were going to die too?"

"I can't see my own death," she says.

"But you've seen something," I say. "What is it?"

She looks like she might refuse me again, but then her shoulder slumps in its sling. She reaches out for the sketch-book I slid away and flips to the back.

It's a drawing of Micah and Jackson locked arm and arm in the woods. Each one has a gun pressed to the other's temple. Each one looks like they walked through hell to get there. When she moves the drawing aside, I see another nearly identical one laying beneath it. It seems Caldwell lied when he said he wasn't a delivery boy.

"Why didn't you tell me?" I ask her.

"It doesn't matter. We have enough to worry about," she says.

I grab her shoulder and she cries out. I apologize again and loosen my grip. "It matters to me, Jackson. You can't go out there if you're going to get yourself killed."

She shrugs me off, her anger rearing up to its full height. "You're one to talk. I've begged you for months not to go. Just to stay the hell away and live."

"If he has Jesse and is killing her, you know the second we find out where she is, I have to go get her. I brought her into this shit when I recruited her. Everything that happens to her is on my head."

"And everything that Micah does is on mine. I'm going."

What could I say to that?

All of this started with Jackson, Caldwell, and me and I guess it should end that way.

"Fine," I tell her and give her back Jesse's shirt. "Find her."

CHAPTER FIFTY-SEVEN

Saturday, April 5, 2003

*S*ullivan dropped us on the other side of the front door. I recognized the foyer from my first visit to Chaplain's, so I knew what part of the house we'd slipped into. The cracking wooden beams above were dilapidated with neglect. It was a total shit-hole. Or maybe everyone else saw a palace for all I knew. But all I saw were menacing shadows as we inched into the house toward the light ahead.

The folding chairs were in place, along with the velvet ropes. Someone had set the stage for us.

A rock formed in my gut.

The further we moved into the room with our guns at the ready, the more the bed came into view on the other side of the rope. Then I saw the girl.

Rachel Wright. I did what I always do when I find someone at long last. My mind runs through a checklist of features, comparing her to the photograph in my mind that I studied with such intensity. *Is it really her?* Some part of me asks. It didn't help that her makeup was a mess, smeared all over her face in some kind of clown parody. She wore one of those white nightgowns I'd seen on the other girl, and I was starting to think it was some sick part of the performance. The chance to defile something so innocent was part of the appeal.

He doesn't need the money or anything, Smith had said. *He just does this because he enjoys it.* Just as he was enjoying the total destruction of my life and reputation.

Rachel was on her knees, with each of her hands curled into a fist beside her head, all of her straining forward against something that held her back. Her hair was long and uncombed.

She was opening and closing her mouth but no sound came out. Another step, and I realized she had a belt around her throat. The buckle caught the overhead light. Her wrists were also belted to the headboard behind her. I realized now that part of the reason her face was so red wasn't the shitty makeup. She was straining too far forward. She was going to strangle herself if she didn't stop.

"She's the one you wanted," a low voice said. I turned my gun in the direction of the voice and found Chaplain there. Smiling. It was a composed face. I wasn't sure he was capable of such self-mastery, but then again, uncontrolled people do not make it very far in life. I tried to squeeze the trigger but my hand felt weak and useless.

"When I saw you there that night beside Fitzy," he continued, without distress. "I knew what you'd come for. Lucky for me, it wasn't her night, or you would've made a big mess, wouldn't you have? Dead cops are harder to get rid of than hemorrhoids."

"Henry Chaplain, you're under arrest for the—"

"—extensive number of crimes you know nothing about." Chaplain laughed. "I've been in your head. I know what you know. Including what really happened to that little Afghani boy."

My throat and mouth went dry. I realized someone was inching up beside me.

I whirled and saw Detective Smith was almost on Rachel. He had made it all the way to the bed while Chaplain rambled. I'd never been so unfocused before. The way Chaplain could snake eye you—it was dangerous.

"Get away from her, Smith," I said, once I realized he wasn't trying to save her. He had a different look in his eye as he wrapped his fist up in her hair. "Smith."

Two men came through the dark doorway and I put a bullet in each of the guys before they could get close. "Smith!" I yelled again but he was too far gone. Whatever Chaplain was doing to him, it made him forget where he was.

"Goddamnit," I said, and I tackled Smith to the ground. Angry and maybe even afraid, he fought back. He slammed a fist into my cheek and I reeled. I managed to get on top of him and pin him with my knees.

"I'm sorry," I said to Smith, and then I hit him hard in the jaw, a knockout blow. He went limp. I checked his pulse. Of course I didn't kill him, but I wanted to be sure.

Gunfire erupted in the room and I collapsed over Smith, covering my head. When I looked up, four more of Chaplain's men lay dead on the floor beside the first two I shot.

"Who shot them?" I asked as Sullivan stepped into view, helping me off of Smith.

"He can't manipulate her," Sullivan said, nodding toward Jackson. Jackson had a gun pressed to Chaplain's head. The guy was on his knees at her feet, execution style.

"If he bats an eyelash," Sullivan added. "She's going to shoot his ass. And I told him if he thinks he can escape, he is a moron. I'll find him anywhere."

I looked at the bodies on the floor. "If you keep calling your guys in here, they're going to keep getting shot."

Chaplain's smile was tight. "What do you want?"

"I want you to tell me where the girls are. *All* of them. I want to arrest you for the murder of Fizz—Harry Fitzgerald and—" I stopped.

"It doesn't matter what you want," he spat. His curls bounced furiously and his whole body shook. I saw the veins in the side of his neck bulge as he spoke. "This is about what *I* want. It is always about what I want."

The image of the boy, dying in my arms hit me with the force of a tank. My knees hit the floor. I clutched my head screaming. Then I heard the gun fire again and the images stopped. I was shaking, my hands still cradled in front of me as if I was holding Aziz. I wiped at my eyes with the back of my hands and then squeezed my knees. After a breath, I looked over to see Sullivan on his knees too, trying to draw deep lungfuls of air.

Jackson had her gun shoved into the side of Chaplain's neck. "Next time, it'll be your heart. Tell us where the girls are or I'll shoot you again. Then I'll tear this house apart myself."

I saw the blood oozing from a hole in Chaplain's gut. He was going to bleed out, but didn't seem to care one bit. Chaplain was laughing.

Smith had come awake and was pulling himself up onto his feet. "He has NRD," the detective said.

"How do you know?" I asked.

"Because he's killed me once or twice himself, haven't you, Detective?" Chaplain held the oozing hole in his side and chuckled. Well, I'm glad someone was having a good time.

Jackson moved her gun up six inches, repositioning the barrel against Chaplain's temple. He stopped laughing.

"You can mind fuck us all day," I told him. It was hard to look into his eyes. He was so goddamn angry you could almost see twin flames burning in those dark orbs. "But you can't fool her."

"Why?" Smith asked. He had undone the straps around Rachel's throat and wrists. The girl collapsed onto the bed unconscious. "How are you immune?"

"The magnetite in my brain—" she began. She didn't finish. Chaplain twisted her knee and she fell back. Her gun went off blasting a hole in the ceiling. Plaster and dust rained down on top of them as I leapt across the room. Sullivan grabbed Rachel and blinked out. Good. That was what I wanted, and I was glad for once that someone was listening to me.

When I rushed forward to help Jackson, I was hit again with the illusion. The weight of the boy in my arms, the way he rolled limply from one palm to another. He might have thought himself a man. But I knew better. Goddamnit, I knew better when I saw his little mouth part, but not for air. The crooked teeth shining between his dry, cracked lips.

I looked up from the boy in my arms and saw Smith. He was raising his gun to his mouth.

"No," I said and dived forward. But I was having a hard time moving. My mind was flicking back and forth from the desert and Chaplain's stage. I grabbed the gun out of Smith's hand and bent the barrel back away from his face. It fired and shot out one of the cheap lamps by the bed. Sullivan popped up behind Smith.

"Take him," I croaked and Sullivan blinked out. That left just me, Jackson and Chaplain.

But then they disappeared and I was in the desert of my mind again.

The boy had large, beautiful eyes the color of Jackson's. Jackson. I turned in the sand and crawled back the way I came. I saw Chaplain and Jackson in the sand just beyond the boy's dead body. They fought for the gun. Jackson had rolled him and was twisting his arm up behind his back. He cried out and the desert disappeared. My hand burned from sliding it along the wooden floor.

I blinked and something had changed.

Chaplain was fighting Jackson for her gun. He had her on her back and he was slowly pushing the muzzle up toward her face. It was almost at her chin when I descended on him. The same moment Sullivan reappeared.

I stomped on Chaplain's leg and Sullivan grabbed ahold of his arm. One moment I saw Chaplain howling about his leg, the next, I saw those fiery dark eyes turned up toward mine.

The world fell away.

"No," Sullivan yelled. I realized I had the gun in my hand and I'd pointed it at Jackson. Her eyes went wide. "No."

I see a flashing red light. Goddamnit, are you going to wait until he gets to the fucking door? I lifted the gun a little higher, because this time I could see it, a flashing red light on the front of Aziz's vest.

Chaplain elbowed Sullivan hard in the face, knocking his head back. In that stolen moment, Chaplain stabbed him. Where had the knife come from? I didn't know. Maybe he had it on him the whole time. Maybe he took it from Jackson. Furious, Sullivan ripped the knife from between his ribs and shoved it into Chaplain's eye. Blood poured out of one man onto another and something happened.

My mind cleared. Jackson was no longer in the desert, wearing a flashing vest. The relief on her face when I lowered the gun was clear, but before I could apologize for scaring the hell out of her, someone screamed.

Someone screamed bloody murder.

Sullivan and Chaplain erupted in blue fire. I stumbled back away from the white hot heat of it, but wasn't quick enough. Blisters formed along the back of my hand where I'd tried to shield my face from the light, and I knew part of my left cheek and ear had been exposed from the burning fire blooming there.

Hissing with pain, I tried to touch my seared flesh, but that only made it worse.

Sullivan clutched the side of his head and wailed. He stumbled back away from Chaplain who was clearly dead, his corpse charred to a husk. Sullivan disappeared. Then reappeared, still screaming and writhing. He took a couple of steps away from me and I saw his backside.

It was the first time I could ever remember seeing him from behind—his shoulders, jeans, head and that sandy blond hair. Something inside me clicked. But before I could get to him, grab ahold of him and see if he was all right, he was gone again. This time, he stayed gone.

Jackson, panting on the floor, looked up at me over the charred corpse. She had blisters along her right side, the side that had been too close to the blaze that had consumed Chaplain. She took a deep breath. "How do you feel now?"

CHAPTER FIFTY-EIGHT

Sunday, May 4th, 2003

I was sitting in Charlie's office when he played the tape for me. It was like a badly choreographed play. It has been confiscated during the raid on Chaplain's house. In the film, we appeared to be trying to kill ourselves more than Chaplain.

Charlie looked up from his computer screen. "What the fuck is this?"

It was my first day back at work. After a brief stint in the hospital, I was still suspended until they'd allowed me to come back. Since I didn't have the heart to go by Peaches' place, I'd almost quit drinking.

"What the fuck is this?" He rewound the tape so I could see the last part again, the part where Chaplain and Sullivan appear to ignite in flames spontaneously.

"Accelerant?" I asked. I tried to explain in a way my friend would understand. Charlie didn't believe in anything he couldn't see, smell, or touch, which probably explained why he believed so much in women and booze. To tell him that Chaplain was good at hypnosis and the old house had simply been too damn flammable to handle all the gunfire—all these nonsensical excuses were more convincing than saying he was some kind of freak with telepathic powers.

"And there's this," he said and threw the paper on top of the desk for me to see. I'd already read it several times. The reporter had been kind enough to send me a copy when the story broke and every story thereafter. I humored Charlie anyway by opening the paper and pretending to read: *Torture Camps Revealed.*

Beneath that were the pictures, one of the prison and another of men and women marching out of it. Their possessions were slung over their shoulders. Some of them even waved amicably at the crowds of supporters lined along the fences, holding signs to celebrate their release.

I read the article aloud to Charlie: "Last month The President ordered the suspension of such detainment camps as the one pictured above at Fort Diq. Thousands of detainees were released yesterday morning, greeted by the cheers of supporters and their families. Twenty-two individuals were still held under the Congressional compromise, awaiting a trial for their alleged crimes."

"I've read it," he said. "I loved your interview. Very moving. But that part where you discovered the camps while investigating a missing person, total bullshit. I like how they paint you as a hero though."

I just smiled. "Someone will probably put a bullet in my head any day now."

He arched an eyebrow. "Maybe not. I haven't gotten any shit for this." He shook the paper at me. "Which is pretty surprising."

I considered that. Why hadn't anyone paid me a visit for speaking up about the camps? Were they afraid of making a martyr of me? I doubted it. There were always freak accidents after all.

"I just wonder if you've put two and two together," Charlie said, pulling me back from my thoughts.

"Hmm?" I asked and lowered the paper.

"Our missing person cases have plummeted. A drastic restructuring of the departments have been ordered and they are pushing the death replacement project to the forefront. You've been reassigned."

"Come again?" I asked.

"How are you getting along with the Wright girl?"

I was surprised by his question. "Good."

It was the truth. I'd seen Rachel every other day since her release. She was bouncing back quickly now that the drugs were out of her system. It turned out that Chaplain couldn't control people with NRD as well as he could everyone else. Jackson believed the magnetite in her brain protected her, and she was probably right. Chaplain had relied on drugs to keep the girls complacent. Without the drugs, Rachel was proving to be a spunky, sweet kid. She was a chatterbox, but charismatic. I liked her.

"I'm glad to hear it. You've been reassigned as her handler."

"Excuse me?" I said and sat forward in my seat. I tossed the paper onto the desk.

"Finding missing people is no longer the FBRD's primary mode of operation. The death replacement industry has moved from beta into full blown functionality. I either fire you, or I give you a job. I thought you'd prefer to keep working. Was I wrong?"

"No, but—"

"Good," Charlie said. "I'm sending you to Atlanta to get some training. You'll do fine. It's just more bureaucratic bullshit that you'll have to memorize. But I think you'll make an excellent handler."

"Why me?" I asked him. "What makes you think I'm qualified for this?"

Charlie grinned at me then, but it was a little sad.

"You'll do what's in their best interest and keep them safe," he said, clamping a large hand on my shoulder. "And you'll be good at the politics. You're charming. Your liaisons will love you."

I stood and accepted the new badge Charlie offered me. Mostly, I was just happy to have my Beretta back. It wasn't until he'd put it in my hand and I felt my fingers squeeze around it affectionately that I realized how much I'd missed her.

I must've looked doubtful, because Charlie slapped my shoulder again. "I believe in you, Jim. I always have."

When I came back from Atlanta with folders full of shit to memorize, federal regulations, protocols, forms, papers and procedures, I really wanted a beer. But the first thing I'd done was check on Rachel. I helped her get a cute apartment downtown. It was one of those artsy places with exposed beams overhead and a brick accent wall to compliment the painted ones.

She'd filled it with bright furniture. A lime green chair that looked like a bubble. A hot pink couch with fluffy blue throw pillows. A white rug with thick purple swirls and abstract whirls that could've been a toddler's handiwork.

I'd slipped into her apartment with a box of donuts I'd promised to bring back from a café in Atlanta. Part of me scoffed at the idea of Federal Agent turned delivery boy, but another part secretly loved it. The way she would smile when I would fulfill her requests, mostly small trivial things, it made me feel like less of a bastard.

I closed the front door behind me and was unnerved by the quietness of her apartment.

"Rachel?" I called out.

No answer. I drew my gun, as my heart hammered.

I felt like a fool when I found her in her bed sleeping. She was lying there, pink cheeked and dreaming with two huge headphones over her ears. She'd cut her hair into a bob and it suited her. She was wearing magenta pajamas, and her bed sheets were black satin with red pillows. I had no doubt that the bright colors were a way of putting that white cotton gown behind her.

Bold, outrageous and in charge. That was Rachel. She was sweet too, especially that afternoon when I tucked her in, pulling the covers up over her sleeping body. Moving the couture magazines and basket of nail polish to the bedside table, I watched her sleep with a small smile on her face and felt at peace for the first time in a long time.

After a couple of replacements, Rachel and I had settled into a nice rhythm. And after I would get her out of the hospital and put her to bed, I'd walk down to the riverfront. I'd sit on a bench not a quarter mile from where they'd pulled Fizz out of the water. It was a morbid habit I'd taken up in the wake of the shitstorm that was this past spring.

It wasn't just how weird it had all been—the teleporting, the mindfucking—after all, I'd become handler to a young woman who died so others didn't have to. I'd been the partner of a woman who could see the future and draw it.

I'd left normal town a long fucking time ago.

I was on the bench when I saw Sullivan.

He just appeared, his back to me as he watched the water. The wind was rippling the surface and the high noon sun made everything shine, even the dingy iron of the bridge.

"I was wondering if I'd ever see you again," I said. I set my back against the bench and felt the heat from the wooden planks through my leather jacket.

"I wanted to say thank you," he said, turning around. He

faced me and I got a good look at him. He squinted against the sun in his eyes, his freckles scrunching up. I knew immediately that he'd changed. Somehow. "The camps are actually closed and that's thanks to you."

"I should thank *you*," I said. "Jackson still has her brains in her head."

He came and sat beside me on the bench. "How've you been? Do you like your new job?"

Yes, I thought and he nodded as if I answered. That should've been my first clue. But already my mind was turning away from the chitchat, from the small talk to the important matters. Sullivan and I had unfinished business.

"I know," he said aloud. "You have questions about Maisie. She's safe. Happy."

"You're her father," I said. I sat forward and rested my elbows on my knees. "Her biological dad."

"I wasn't lying when I said I met her mother in the camp," he began. "It's amazing how much a man's feelings can intensify in a place like that. We avoided sex for months. We were scared of exactly that kind of thing happening. Georgia— Maisie's mother— knew having something happen to her baby would kill her. And it almost did. I didn't take Maisie for me. I took her hoping it would heal some broken part of her mother."

Yes, because if you were a man who needed his children, you would've taken Jesse, right?

"Did it?" I asked.

Sullivan nodded. "It's helping. Georgia is a little more herself every day."

I laughed. "What are the chances that I'd get Maisie's and your case on my desk at the same time?"

Sullivan gave me a lopsided grin. "I asked someone I trusted—"

"Memphis," I interjected. "No need to be shy with the details now."

"If you had the file, then it wouldn't be in the hands of another detective. I didn't want anyone else looking for her. I knew they would send someone after me when they realized I wouldn't come back this time. Worse, they might've sent someone after Maisie, looking for another way to control me."

"They know what you can do?" I asked.

"They know and they've used it to their advantage. They trained me to do things I'd never believe I'd do in a million years."

I thought of the boy I killed in the desert. Definitely something I never thought I'd do.

"I tried to refuse them once, and they hurt Georgia. They —" He stopped speaking.

"You are the one that took Maisie out of the camp."

He ran a hand through his hair. "She was so small. It never worked with Georgia, but you don't know how many times I wrapped my arms around her wishing we'd disappear, only to find that I couldn't take us both. When I found out where Maisie was placed, I visited her all the time. I would go and check on her and then come and tell Georgia how she was. I think it was the only thing that sustained her in those years. It was better for Maisie to be with the Michaelsons than in that place. I don't regret giving her to the placement agency, but now, she belongs with us. We're together again, and that's what matters. Georgia needs her."

I looked out over the water. "There's only one problem."

"I know," he said.

"A couple lost their only kid and then their lives," I said. *Did you make them suffer?* I thought of the charred, decapitated bodies in the burning house. I didn't need to ask how he'd gotten Maisie's teeth.

"No," he said and looked honestly offended. "They didn't suffer. I snapped their necks. I was as gentle as I could be."

It was a clean shot, they had said. *The boy didn't even know what hit him.*

"I know it doesn't make it better and I don't expect you to let me go for that. I'm a monster, and I always will be," he said. He stood up and moved away from me. "I just wanted to thank you for all that you've done and to give you a gift. You can call it a token of gratitude."

"What gift?"

"Go to the bar," he said. "You'll know it when you see it."

I couldn't bring him in if he didn't want to be captured. No cuffs would hold him. I could try to put a bullet in his head, but he wasn't going to stick around long enough for me to do that.

"You won't see me again," Sullivan said with a small little smile. "Or maybe you will."

Then he was gone, leaving only the wide open river coursing before me.

CHAPTER SIXTY-ONE

Sunday, June 29, 2003

It took me a few days to get up the nerve to see just what Sullivan's "gift" was. But when Sunday rolled around and Rachel told me to quit hovering long enough for her to have a date with some boy from a band, I went down there. I walked the cobblestone street leading me to Blackberry Hill with slow steps. When I looked up, I saw the sign had been redone. The wooden board no longer showed black smears left from the firebombing. Instead, a neon square stood in its place with a swirly *Blackberry Hill* sparkling in the late afternoon light. Two mugs clinked together and spread apart as the fluorescent tubes flicked on and off in time.

"B?" a voice called.

I looked down from the sign and saw Peaches. He stood on the sidewalk with a cigarette hanging out of the corner of his mouth. His shirt and pants were covered in paint, a light industrial gray. It splattered across his clothes and his forearms, matting the grey-white fur there. I couldn't tell with that damn cigarette hanging out of his mouth whether or not he was scared to see me. The last time he thought he saw me, I'd firebombed the place he loved most in the world.

I didn't take a step closer. I stood where I was with my hands in the pockets of my leather jacket, unsure of what to do with myself. Peaches also stood and stared. He took a long drag on the cigarette and exhale the smoke into the warm air around us. Then he smiled.

"Where the hell you been, brother?"

My heart broke. I hadn't realized until that moment I'd been afraid of what he might say.

I came up to the curb and offered him my hand. He laughed at me and pulled me into a hug. "How's your new job?"

How do you know about my transfer? I thought.

"It better be the best thing since sliced Wonderbread if it's keeping you away from me."

Sullivan was right. I did know my gift when I saw it. Nothing in Peaches betrayed confusion, anger, or regret.

"How've you been?" I asked. "I'm sorry I haven't come by to check on you sooner."

"That's life, man," he said. "We come. We go. But I'm good. Get in here and see what I've done with the place."

I held open the heavy wooden door while Peaches smashed out his butt on the sidewalk before putting it into the ashtray out front. With the smell of cigarette smoke clinging to his hair, I followed him in.

Plastic had been brought in and laid over the floors.

"We had to gut the whole place," Peaches said. "And let me tell you, insurance companies take their sweet fucking time giving you your money. But it's fine. The furniture is going to be delivered Friday, and I hope to have us stocked by then."

"4th of July?" I asked.

"That's right." He grinned. "4th of July Bonanza and grand reopening. There's even a dart tourney if you're interested."

A warm feeling spread over my chest. I didn't have the

heart to tell Peaches I'd quit drinking. "I wouldn't miss it for the world."

His grin widened and he bent to pick up the paint roller that sat waiting in the drip pan. He rolled it a few times through the industrial grey pool before pressing the sponge to the wall for the second coat. The place would look real nice when he was done. I had no doubt.

"I'm sorry," I told him. My chest grew heavy as I watched him roll the thick goop onto the wall.

"For what?"

"If it wasn't for me, your place would've never been firebombed."

His mouth came open and he paused, holding the roller against the wall. "That's not your fault. He was a maniac. Maniacs do whatever the hell they want."

So he did know something of Chaplain and of what really happened.

"I'm just glad you were here," he said. "No one got hurt and that was thanks to you."

He knows something, yes, I thought. *But not everything.*

The jukebox sprang alive then of its own accord and began to play *I Want It That Way*.

"Besides," he added, grinning at me as he lifted the brush again. "The jukebox didn't get hurt and that is all that matters."

I looked over his shoulder at the beast against the far wall. It was as large and cumbersome as always, with one long black char mark along its side. It was plugged in too, with its face lit up expectantly.

"Thank God," I said sarcastically. "That'd be a real tragedy."

CHAPTER SIXTY-TWO

1 Day

I've put the last box on a tall stack. Then I look around the storage unit and out across the parking lot. When I am convinced no one is here but me and Gideon, I pull down a small wooden box and open it. The wood is cool to the touch, having rested for years in this locked room. When I lift the lid, it resists, the hinges creaking and dust coating my fingertips.

"That's your Python?" Gideon asks. He is leaning against the far wall, arms crossed in discontent. He's trying to show me how mad he is with my decision, but the gun piques his interest nonetheless.

"Yeah, it was my father's gun," I say and lift it from the velvet indentation.

"In my country," Gideon says. "Fathers give their sons goats and wives."

"Welcome to America," I tell him and smile because he's being grumpy enough for the both of us.

I turn the gun over in my hand and feel the metal barrel warming with my body heat.

"My dad believed that this gun was lucky," I say.

"Who did he shoot?"

"No one," I say. "He didn't have to. That is why it's lucky."

"Have you shot anyone with it?"

I shake my head. Not yet.

He pushes himself off the far wall and his shoes scuff along the concrete floor. He puts one hand over mine.

"Don't go tomorrow."

I look up at the kid, and he is a kid in so many ways. He has a nice beard now, but still so much to learn. And I don't have the time to teach it to him.

"If someone had you, I'd be there. You, Jesse, Rachel and Jackson. You're all I've got. I would die for any of you."

Gideon looks down and I can see the red in his cheeks. I don't know if he's sad or angry or both. I reach out and pull him into a hug.

"I wasn't going to tell you where she was," he says into my leather jacket before prying himself away. "I don't want to be responsible for your death."

Now you know how I feel, I think, but I don't burden him with that. "Let me explain something."

I close the box and hand him the Python. He marvels over the gun while I speak.

"Jesse is in this because of me. You are in this because of me. I took her from her family and I took you from yours. The only difference is, I've lied to her every step of the way. I didn't tell her I knew her father or what he is capable of. I didn't tell her about her sister, who is probably dead by now because neither Jackson nor I have found a single trace of her in ten years. I didn't even tell her about the angels or powers or give her advice about what she should do to be safe and stay alive. I recruited her because she tied me to Sullivan, and I knew if I kept her close I'd get another shot at him. I needed things to get dangerous for her so I'd have another chance to make things right.

The least I can do is save her life after gambling with it, don't you think?"

"You owe her more than you owe me," he says. "So you will go to her even though I ask you not to."

Gideon traces the barrel opening with a long slender finger His dark eyes remain on the gun.

"You have to understand," I tell him. "I am responsible for all this. I made Caldwell what he is. I led him to Chaplain. I'm the reason he can do the shit he does. I should've been the one to plunge a knife in Chaplain's eye, but I didn't. This is all on me."

Gideon looks up at long last. "Let me come with you."

"No," I tell him. "I should've never put a gun in your hand and taught you to shoot it."

"It is what I wanted."

"It doesn't matter if you wanted it," I say. "It was wrong. I only took you out of the desert because of Aziz. I felt so damn guilty over what I did to your brother, that I did exactly what your family asked me to do. Only I should've sent you to medical school, or law school, or hell—anything respectable."

"My family does not blame you for Aziz," he says and gives me back the gun. "I do not blame you for my brother."

The Python is cold and heavy in my hand. It isn't alive, not yet.

"I can't take you," I say again.

He tries to talk over me. "But I—"

"And," I intercede. "They're going to need you after I'm gone."

His mouth falls open. "Me?"

"You're smart. You can find out things that others cannot. You have skills that I didn't have time to teach the kid. Teach her like I taught you. And don't lie to her like I did. You'll take good care of my girls when I'm gone."

He looks ashamed and I realize it may not be shame at all. It may simply be that I've put a terrible burden on him. I've asked him to sacrifice himself for three women he barely knows.

"I know it is a lot to ask—" I begin.

"No," he says, shaking his head. "I am honored. I will do my best."

I place my hand on his shoulder and he sags under the weight of it.

"You have to tell me what you know," I say. "Where is this farmhouse?"

Gideon's face crumples as a cool October breeze blows into the storage unit. "He knows you are coming. He wants you there."

"I know," I tell him. "I have to go, Gid."

You show up when no one else does, Charlie had said. It's as true now as ever.

His face softens and his shoulders slump. "You would find out even if I did not tell you. Jeremiah has found her. I am sure even now he is informing Alice and preparing the counterattack."

"Why would he inform Alice?" I ask him.

"He wants her to trust him," he says. "He knows that if he wins her trust, he will win Jesse."

"Why does he want Jesse?" My heart races at the possibility of a threat. Threats that I cannot fight because I just don't have enough time.

"This is the only answer I have for you," he says, and I can tell he is trying not to be angry with me on the last day of my life. "You asked me for a way to stop Caldwell. Then do not die. Do not go."

"Alice and Jackson will go," I remind him. "I won't let them go alone."

Gideon hands over the envelope he has been holding out

on me. I already know what is in it. Jesse's location, which is no doubt connected to that farmhouse from Jackson's drawing. He found the kid and all the information I asked for on Jeremiah.

"It does not seem he means her harm," Gideon says when I dump the contents of the envelope onto the stack of boxes beside me. "But there are whispers about the angels amongst his crew."

"What do you think about all that? Are they really angels? Jackson doesn't think so."

"Men have built and destroyed nations believing they were instructed to do so by God," he said. "It doesn't matter if the angels are real or not. The outcome will be the same."

Gideon walks to his car and I wonder if he is simply going to drive away without saying goodbye. I suppose I deserve it. But after he leans into the front seat and grabs something, he heads back.

He hands me another envelope.

"What's this?" I rip the flap while opening it. Inside is a single, large photograph. The girl in the picture is fourteen maybe fifteen with a blue backpack slung over her shoulder. She's talking to a woman on her right, a woman who looks just like her—same blond hair, full pouty lips and big bright eyes. Caldwell is walking beside them, his hands in his pockets and a small smile on his lips.

Despite the fact she's all grown up, I'd recognize those big blue eyes anywhere.

"Maisie?" I ask.

Gideon smiles. "Yes, she's alive."

After I put Jackson's luggage in the trunk of the Impala, I drove her out to Lambert airport. I parked in the unloading zone outside of the terminal and walked her to the sliding glass doors. We stood in the awkward place where the doors opened for us, and then affronted by our disinterest, closed again, only to open a moment later.

"You're going to look for him?" I asked her.

She shook her head. "Micah won't be found until he wants to be. I know he's changed his name so that there's no paper trail. Whatever he's going to do next, he doesn't want me to know about it. Not yet anyway."

"You don't need paper," I teased her. "You've got plenty."

It was just the kind of corny joke that made Jackson smile. She looked down at the rolled sketches protruding from beneath her arm, the beginnings of her next case.

"Thank you for not shooting me in the head," she said, over the whoosh of the opening doors.

"Thanks for not shooting me when it looked like that was exactly what I was going to do."

She shrugged. "I didn't think you'd make the same mistake twice."

"You have more faith in me than I do."

"Yes," she said. "I do."

"I'll see you around?"

"You will," she said with the certainty that only Jackson could pull off.

I helped her adjust her rucksack onto her back, while the doors dutifully stood open. She grimaced, but it's what she got for leaving the hospital early not once, but twice.

"You need a bag that doesn't hang off your shoulders," I lectured for the twelfth time.

"Do I look like the rolling luggage type?" she asked.

I grinned. "No, you don't."

"Why do you think they took us off the Sullivan case?" she asked, her face pinched and serious. "If he really was such a serious threat, why do that?"

I didn't have an answer.

"Maybe someone made them *forget* to look for Sullivan," she said and adjusted the weight of the pack, favoring her good shoulder.

Made them forget. Like Peaches.

"You know it is my fault he is the way he is," Jackson said, watching my face for some kind of reaction. "When Micah and I were children, we were kidnapped by our father. Our mother had just left him and he didn't like it. He killed her and took us to Florida. When the police found us, we were placed in foster care. My aunt took me back, but she did not want my brother, who reminded her too much of our daddy."

"That's a shit thing to do," I said.

Jackson shrugged. "I should have protected him. I could have insisted that we remain in foster care together. Or we could have run away. Anything. I feel like if I had, Micah would've turned out differently."

She started toward the terminal and I expected her to leave without saying goodbye. The doors opened again and she walked through. Before it closed she looked back at me over her wounded shoulder and said: "Those things we're most ashamed of make us who we are, don't they? I wonder if this will always be true."

CHAPTER SIXTY-FOUR

12:01 A.M.

I could die now. Any minute.

I cannot sleep. I know I should so that my mind will be clear and my body rested. *Rested.* I laugh. There will be plenty of time for that when I'm dead.

It is late, too late for phone calls when my phone rings anyway. I'm expecting a call from Jackson or Alice, the gunshot that starts my last race.

"Hello?"

"I'd tell you not to go," Rachel says, softly. "But you've never been one to follow orders."

"Oh if that were true," I tell her. "I'd probably have fewer regrets."

Her breath is heavy in the phone. "Are you scared?"

"No."

"You never could lie to me," she says.

I change the subject. "How are you up so late? Aren't you locked in your room at a certain time?"

"I'm practicing for tomorrow," she says. "I may have to take a little trip all by my lonesome, remember?"

"Are you packed?"

"Unfortunately, but I'm still hoping that you're going to call me in exactly 24 hours and tell me to go back to sleep."

You and me both, I think and I realize for the first time it's true.

I don't want to die. Not now in the middle of things, with still so much to do.

"Go get our girl," Rachel says finally, and I think she's hung up on me. But then I hear her voice, cracking. "Thank you. Thank you for everything you've done for me."

"I should've done more," I tell her, rubbing at the ache in my chest with an open palm as I lay on my back in the darkness.

"Shut up," she says. "You were perfect."

I have to laugh at that one and she laughs too, even though the sound is choked with her sobs. Then silence stretches across the line between us and I start to wonder if she really has hung up.

Finally, she says: "I love you."

Of course I say it back.

CHAPTER SIXTY-FIVE

I'm standing in Jackson's hideous yellow kitchen, eating what I am pretty sure is my last meal: A Hawaiian Handful, condiments oozing out one side and a pile of oversalted fries waiting on the wrapper. I don't go easy on the ketchup or anything else. Heart disease and bikini season are no longer my problems.

It would've been perfect if they hadn't shorted me the extra pickle I asked for. But what can I do? It isn't like I have time to go back for a refund.

I listen to Jackson pack a bag in the other room. She's shoving whatever she thinks she needs into the same canvas bag from long ago. It is one of the many reasons I feel like we've come full circle—2003 to now. Every so often, she'll stop stuffing the bag and I'll hear her flipping pages in her sketchbook the way an attorney might review their notes before a big case.

We don't talk. We're both rehearsing the possibilities over and over in our heads. How many times have we drawn our guns this morning? Executed this or that strike? Countless.

The back door swings open and someone's heels scrub at

the carpet. Alice appears, eyes sharp and assessing. To avoid speaking first, I shove my burger into my mouth and take a big bite. She flinches.

As if finally remembering what she came here for, she says, "I want you to meet someone."

A tall man with a close-cropped beard steps into the room. He pushes his glasses up on the bridge of his nose and puts his hands in his pockets. Before he does, I notice he is not wearing a wedding ring. I wonder if Alice or anyone else knows about the rich wife or where the money for their oper-ation comes from.

It hits me then that I'm not supposed to know who Jere-miah is. I straighten my back and scowl. "Who the hell is this?"

"You asked me what I've been doing to piss off Caldwell," Alice says. She points at the man beside her. Jeremiah manages to look like a refined English professor.

"You've been doing this guy?" I'm trying to keep the mood light until I can get a better read on Jeremiah. It hasn't escaped my notice that he's holding his cards close. After all, he must know who I am.

"Don't be idiotic," Alice bristles. She tucks her hair behind her ears and a light blush fills her cheeks. I've prob-ably pissed her off, embarrassed her at least, insinuating that she would sleep with a man. She falls back on her profession-alism as always. "This is Jeremiah. He is leading a resistance against Caldwell. And I can see your face, Brinkley, so before you say anything insulting, let me warn you that it isn't a small operation. He has more connections than you do. Play nice."

She was right about that. I didn't have as many friends as the billionaire, or as many toys. But I'd learned long ago that the bigger you are, the harder it can be to get into tight places where most of the work gets done. I had no doubt that Jeremiah found managing his *resistance* exhausting.

I wipe my mouth and smile. "James T. Brinkley."

We shake.

"Yes, I know," he says, reflexively. When I arch an eyebrow he adds, "You were Jesse's handler and liaison for the FBRD."

I almost laugh. I've never heard such a succinct and underdeveloped assessment of my skills. I break his gaze before Alice's dark eyes can burn a hole in the side of my head. What the hell is she expecting me to do? Hit him? Tell him to shove his resistance up his ass?

Maybe I should have, because who the hell wants to spend the last hours of their life playing nice to a privileged prick in a sweater vest?

I replay my conversation with Jackson. Just this morning she showed me the pictures of the farm, of Jeremiah and Alice and someone who I haven't met yet—the second in command, Nicole Tamsin. Add these scenes to Gideon's legwork and I know this is my ride to the farmhouse. My job may only be to distract Caldwell long enough for this motley crew to get our girl back, but I'm taking the job seriously.

"So what's the plan?" I ask.

Alice goes off immediately about Minooka, Illinois, how we will all take an SUV like one big happy family. I try to convince them to take the Impala, but I am overruled. It hits me then, that I may have driven her for the last time. My stomach drops as I look out the little kitchen window above the sink and see the beautiful sleek black body in the drive-way. *This is goodbye, baby*.

Reluctantly, I turn my attention back to the conversation and realize I've missed something.

"We do not want to go up against him without Jesse," Jackson says. I hadn't seen her enter the kitchen. I steal a glance at Jeremiah.

He looks thoughtful. Maybe it's the sweater vest, or

maybe he knows more about what Caldwell is capable of than I gave him credit for.

The Python settles against my lower back. "I have my own gun."

"We have our own equipment too," he says and tries to soften his words with a tight smile, as if to say *I'm not better than you just because I'm a filthy rich bastard.* Has he ever killed anyone himself? I wonder.

Just as Jeremiah walks out, Lane walks in. Tall with a slight stoop to his shoulders, blue eyes and dark hair, he looks like a Labrador ready for a car ride.

"No," I say, before I think my reaction through.

Alice folds her arms across her chest. "He can handle himself."

I snort. "As well as you can."

"No more solo missions," she squeals. Her face ripens with her anger and she dares me to argue with her. "Get this commando crap out of your head. It's done. We are all together now."

I snort but bite my tongue. Is that how they'll handle it when I'm gone? All together?

When I am gone.

Tomorrow.

I wish with everything I've got that they will be OK, but another small voice is disappointed by the idea that they don't need me as much as I've needed them.

I breathe and refocus. I try to accept the idea of Lane. He cares about the kid. There's that. Even if he is about as experienced as the wart on my ass. He thinks he is strong and in control and it's a joke. The arrogance of youth is dangerous. I told him so in the letter I wrote yesterday, the one I just gave to Jackson not two hours ago and asked her to deliver after I'm gone.

Gone.

Tomorrow.

The realization keeps winding me.

When we nearly died in the basement last year, I asked Lane to look after Jesse. He'd been too eager, too desperate to prove he could. Caldwell would break him like fine china, with relish and delight at the little sounds he'd make while he did it. I know firsthand how he'll get in that pathetic head of his and make Lane hunt Jesse like a dog.

Just looking at him standing there, his big blue eyes beaming at Alice. I can see the making of their uneasy truce.

Alice I like.

I admire someone who can stay on her game despite her own emotions. I've no doubt she wants to kick Lane's balls in, but she is willing to stomach that desire for the sake of getting Jesse back. She will always put Jesse first. I've seen it too many times to believe otherwise.

I take a page from her book and shove my own feelings down, deep. I remind myself that only one thing matters. At the end of the day, Jesse will be safe from Caldwell.

But even as my mind clears, I can't help but wonder: *Why do you scare him?* I search those defiant brown eyes—defiant and determined. *What about you makes Caldwell count his steps, Alice?*

I don't have much time to find out.

CHAPTER SIXTY-SIX

We have just turned off I-55 when Jackson screams. "Stop the car. You need to park, now."

I swerve onto the shoulder, but then the car dies. It coasts toward the ditch and I have to slam on the brake to make it stop rolling. It doesn't help that Alice is screaming in my ear.

"Brake!"

The car hangs off the edge of the ditch, tilting forward, but the emergency brake is in place. We aren't going anywhere.

"We'll have to walk from here." Jackson flips through her sketchbook. She stops on a page. It's not a picture she is looking at, but notes along the margin. "It's almost a mile."

She scribbles a note for only me to see, *this is Jesse's doing. She's blasting everything. Like Rachel?* Then closes the sketchbook.

My heart knocks against my ribs. It is a warning. If Jesse's power is getting out of control, she could be like Rachel when I found her that first time. She could be as much a danger to us as Caldwell himself.

"That's consistent with the map," Jeremiah says. Jeremiah is the first to climb out. A blast of cool October air rushes into the car before he closes the door behind him.

"What the hell is she doing out here?" Alice asks. "What did they do? Lock her in an outhouse?"

I haven't failed to notice the way her eyes keep sliding right toward the blonde beside her. She hasn't formally introduced herself, but she has to be Nicole Tamsin, the one whose partner was murdered brutally. She looks tough, but not as vicious as Gideon implied. He described her to a T though, athletic body and dangerous gaze included.

"She is in the ground," Jackson says and her face pinches in pain.

"They buried her?" Lane kicks his door open and jumps down onto the street.

"Now I know why you brought the damn shovel," I grumble to Jackson and we climb out as well.

We pull all our gear out of the back of the black SUV and suit up. As soon as possible, we get off the road and into the trees. Alice is to my left, wearing the orange hunter cap I put on her head when she refused to take a gun. We walk for a while, long enough that my muscles warm and my breath is heavier. I shrug my shoulders to adjust the weight of my pack when Jackson leans toward me and says something about the sound of water. I raise a hand, hoping everyone will stop.

"Shhh, shhh," I urge when it is pretty obvious that only Jackson understands hand signals.

No one moves and I strain to hear better. There is something in the trees. Branches creak and sway, though I can't detect a breeze on my face. From the sound of it, it's much bigger than a squirrel.

"There." Jackson points at the tree. It's a beast with a multitude of fat branches. "She's right there."

Jackson darts forward and I don't grab her in time. "Shit,"

I say and think of the drawing she showed me: her and Micah locked in battle, their own fight to the death.

"Jackson, hold," I yell, abandoning any element of surprise. If someone is in the trees, they already know we are here.

Jackson is halfway across the clearing when her knees buckle and she goes down. Alice jerks forward and I grab ahold of her jacket and force her down as Lane falls on top of her. A bit excessive considering we aren't being shot at but at least the little twat is making himself useful.

"Did she get shot?" Alice asks, spitting the grass out of her mouth. I remain crouched beside them looking for any movement, but I don't see anything. Jeremiah and Nicole have gone absolutely still beside me, guns up and ready.

Come on Jackson. Don't be dead.

"What's happening?" Alice begs.

I charge out into the clearing, but keep low. I make it to Jackson. Alice follows me and I have just a moment to worry about her before I realize she is doing a better job of keeping low than I am, given our height difference.

We kneel beside Jackson, rolling her over and checking for a wound. Nothing. No blood. I look into the trees and see someone. He or she is wearing camo and blending with the treetop surrounding them. If it wasn't for the black gun or small movements, I may not have seen them at all.

"What is this?" Alice asks and shows me a small metal dart about an inch long. I recognize it.

"A sedative. Military grade."

"Why would they sedate us if they want us dead?" she asks. "Torture?"

"They didn't want her dead, but I'm not willing to bet they feel the same way about me," I say. After all, hadn't Micah asked Caldwell for Jackson? I'm assuming he wanted her without a bullet in her head. I don't think Caldwell is as sentimental, but he probably isn't stupid enough to piss off his Magic 8 Ball. In my case, I figure we're close enough to the actual death, he'll take my head whatever way it comes.

Lane finally makes it to us. "Is she OK?"

Alice fills him in.

I turn and see that Nicole and Jeremiah have fallen back. Good. That makes it easier for me to follow my plan.

I grin and give Alice my gun. I can see the panic and rejection screwing up her face before I even have a chance to let go. "Just hold on to it for a minute. Keep your eyes open, and if you see anything, point and shoot."

I tear open Jackson's canvas bag and pull out the masks I asked her to pack.

"Put this on," I say and give Alice a mask. I give one to the boy too before fitting one over Jackson's face.

Then I grab a couple of tear gas canisters from the canvas bag and hurl them into the woods. The canister whistles through the air before thrashing the branches on its way down. Hissing sounds emit from the undergrowth and smoke begins to seep out of the dense tree line. I yank my own mask down over my face and lift my assault rifle. The Python shifts against my lower back as if anxious to see battle.

Not yet, I tell the gun. *Not yet.*

"You're a jerk," Alice says looking back toward the friends I left unguarded. If Jeremiah really is so badass, let him prove it.

"We are going to have to run," I say, as they look up at me with wide, fearful eyes. I don't wait for them to panic or argue with me. They wanted to be here, and if they're going to be here, it's my way or the highway. For the next few hours anyway.

"Ready. In 3...2..." The boy's hand tightens on Alice's pack. "Run."

I scream and hurl another tear gas canister into the trees. It whips through the branches, then crashes to the ground. I stay low in the clearing, while Jeremiah and Nicole wait crouched to the right where we came in, and Lane and Ally make it safely to the large tree on my left, where Jesse is supposed to be buried.

I let out a battle cry, a little showmanship if you will. If this is my last hurrah, you better believe I'm going out in style. My second scream is swallowed by the sound of gunfire in front of me.

I crouch down and wait, but I don't have to wait long. My first target tumbles from the tree line a little to my right, coughing and hacking. I prop the rifle against my bent knee and blast three rounds through the front of his chest.

The sound of gunfire turns my head 180, to the tree line on the opposite side of the clearing. Bullets hit the trunk of the front most trees, spitting bark into the air, but none of the bullets are hitting the second target stumbling toward me. This one has managed to pull his black shirt up over his nose. Before he lifts the gun, I put a bullet in his head and he falls back, disappearing into the dense smoke covering the ground.

I look to see who fired the shots and find Alice, coat open, chest heaving, and gun raised. She must have seen the man creeping up behind me and shot at him.

Her eyes are wide with surprise and I laugh, knowing full well she just shot a gun for the first time in her life.

I see movement and glance up. Two men in the tree above Lane and Ally are turning their guns down, taking aim at the top of their heads. I put bullets in both of them and they fall from the trees, slamming the ground in front of Alice and Lane.

The gunfire stops, and I decide to make a round before the smoke gets too thick. I even double back to see if Jeremiah and Nicole are clear and can't find them. I can hear his voice though, barking orders at someone.

"We're on the east side," he says, his voice one with the white smoke. "Send Evan and Kirby with the ATVs. We will regroup at the main house."

The main house, I wonder, thinking of the elusive farmhouse from Jackson's drawing.

"Ally needs—" Nicole begins but Jeremiah doesn't let her get too far.

"Keep your head clear," he says, chastising her like a child. "Whatever happens, I expect you to do your job."

I don't know what the girl says to this, maybe nothing. I only hear Jeremiah. "We *need* to move back. The gas is getting too close."

Convinced I'm not going to hear anything more, I go to the tree where I left Jackson, Alice and Lane.

"Nikki?" she asks and I hesitate, both because it takes me a minute to realize she's shortened Nicole's name and because I'm not sure how honest to be.

"They probably fell back to escape the smoke."

"You should've given them masks," she hisses.

"I didn't have enough," I say and it's true. In fact, I realize I don't even have one for the kid, once we dig her up.

We inspect the ground for a possible grave and find a rectangle of disturbed earth. Alice is about to remove her mask, maybe to get a better view, but I put my hand on top of her head so she can't lift it.

"Keep it on," I warn her and we start digging.

I think of Charlie and Smith, so recently unburied from my own plot at Mt. Olivet's. A sick feeling slides through my muscles as we push deeper and deeper into the earth.

I can't help but feel like I am digging my grave, pushing myself closer to my own death.

We dig Jesse up and pull her out. It helps that the grave wasn't very deep and there are three of us. But when I see the kid in the coffin, I feel murderous. The world tilts and I know that if Caldwell appeared before me at this moment, every cell in my body would be bent on destroying the son of a bitch.

Alice is crying and begging us to pull Jesse out of the hole.

We lift her body, and she's covered in her own shit. In her death, Jesse's body expels all that is unnecessary. We stretch her out on the dirt beside the hole and I don't even know where to start.

"Turn around," Alice commands. "Both of you, while I clean her up."

After handing her the backpack, I obey, ashamed of my own relief. I lift my gun a little higher and survey the area. Lane is still beside me, looking at the trees as if waiting for orders himself. Neither of us say anything as Jesse is stripped and cleaned behind our backs.

My pride in Alice grows more than I ever thought possible. She knew what to do when I didn't. She isn't afraid of getting her hands dirty or doing the work. I suddenly feel intense gratitude that Jesse has her.

"The farther we get from the grave the better," I say. I look back the way we came, toward the car, in the direction where I know there is no farmhouse. We have Jackson, we have Jesse, and we are all alive. If we can just get to the car and leave, then I might live to see another day.

"We can't drive out of here," Alice says. "The car is shot."

"We'll have to walk the three or four miles into town," Lane adds. He's sweaty from digging and has a smudge of dirt across his right cheek.

"Just walking will take an hour or so," I say. "Dragging Jesse and Jackson will take longer."

"It's the best plan we've got," she says and I have to agree.

Yes, says the old bastard in my head. *Just go. Get as far away from here as you can.* I lift Jackson up and throw her over my shoulder. It isn't the first time I've had to carry her like this.

We don't get very far.

"What's wrong?" I ask when I see Alice and Lane struggling with the kid's body.

"She's breathing," Alice says. She puts the back of her hand beneath the kid's nose and I see for myself her chest rising and falling in a slow, steady rhythm. "She's waking up."

They each take one of her hands, looking like a choreographed scene from a soap opera, as Jackson grows heavy on my shoulder. When her fist tightens on theirs, I should feel relieved. But for some reason, my limbs go limp.

The kid's eyes fly open and she leaps to her feet, knocking both Alice and Lane to the side.

For just a minute, I see that wild, uncaged energy I saw coursing through Rachel so long ago. I try to maneuver Jackson off my shoulder, feeling for one instinctive moment that I should grab ahold of my gun. I'm too slow. Before I can even put Jackson down, the kid is running, blasting past us in the opposite direction.

I watch her run full speed toward what I know must be the farmhouse.

She shouldn't be able to move that fast, but I'd been through this with Rachel. *Shouldn't be able to* no longer applied. When Rachel first went *live*, was first *possessed* by her angel as she describes it, she'd lost it. She had hurt herself and tried to hurt Jesse.

Before I can warn them to proceed with caution, Lane and Alice run after her. I try to reposition Jackson across my back, leaning in such a way that the majority of her weight is distributed across my hips and quads instead of my back alone.

The three of them disappear and I've no choice but to follow slowly and deliberately. I won't leave Jackson alone in these woods.

"Well, we *almost* made it out alive," I tell my unconscious friend.

When the trees break and I finally see it, my heart throbs. I feel like I've come to the edge of a great precipice and I'm looking out over the vast valley below, knowing that the only thing left is to leap.

The white paint has peeled away in places showing a gray, dull wood beneath, and the windows are completely covered with dust. The cornstalks surrounding the house have been bent back in places, and the front door stands open. I put two and two together and figure that the three of them went into the house.

"Did no one teach you kids not to go into strange houses?"

Jackson moans and I turn and gently set her down. Her eyes flutter open and focus on me. I point at the stalks around us, silent spectators come to watch our final performance. "We made it."

"The corn," she says. She reaches up and squeezes my hand, wincing as she pulls herself up. She looks around, shifting her weight on unsteady feet. "I don't want to die here."

"If he has the nerve to show his face, you'll beat him," I tell her. I put a steady hand on each of her shoulders. "I've no doubt you'll win."

I go into the goddamn farmhouse. No one looks hurt and Jesse isn't trying to kill anyone. Good. Maybe she has got herself under control. Relief washes over me. She spares me a smile and I move forward to squeeze her neck, maybe even ruffle her hair, but bump into Alice who is holding a child in her arms.

"Brinkley." She exhales my name. "Where is Gloria?"

"Here," Jackson groans, coming up behind me.

"We need to carry out these bodies," Lane says and leads me down to the belly of the house. I take one precarious step after another into the dark. There I see all the bodies lined up and remember something that Gideon said. *He is trying to use them like some kind of experiment. He is trying to get power from them, like he got from Chaplain.*

I lift the first person I see from the floor and climb the stairs. We form a line, the five of us, bringing one body at a time out of the basement and into the cornfield, where we lay them down. Around us the evening bleeds into twilight.

I slide a big guy off my aching shoulder and think I hear voices again. I creep further out into the field, trying not to brush the cornstalks as I approach. I come up on Jeremiah, whose back is to me. He speaks into a handset, a big, ugly device, maybe a CDMA450.

"No, hold your position until Caldwell shows himself."

"Are you sure you want to leave Jesse uncovered like that?" his second in command asks. I recognize her voice even over the gargle of the speakers.

"She's more than enough for him now," he says.

"Are you sure?" she asks and the way his muscle tenses says a lot about how much this guy likes to be questioned.

"I can feel her."

I can feel her.

"What the fuck does that mean?" I say and step out into plain view. The sun is dangerously low in the sky now and the air is more purple than gold.

Jeremiah turns and lowers the walkie-talkie. I look him over again and realize he isn't wearing any protective gear. Nicole did.

"You've got NRD," I tell him.

"You're going to die soon."

I lift the Python from its secret hiding place and Jeremiah goes very still. I point it at his forehead.

"I'm not going to hurt her," he says, slowly lifting his hands.

"Are you like them?" I don't elaborate. After all, if he doesn't know what I'm talking about, I'm sure as hell not going to spill it.

"I'm not going to hurt Jesse," he says, his eyes narrow behind his glasses.

I cock the revolver. "That's not what I asked you. You have NRD, but are you also like them?"

"No," he says. "I'm something else."

"I don't have time to talk bullshit with you. Tell me who you are and what you want or I'm going to put a bullet in your brain. I may do it anyway, because really, what have I got to lose?"

Jeremiah must see the pointlessness in arguing with a dead man. "You are correct. I have NRD, just like my sister and father. I understand that Caldwell is hunting and murdering a select number of people who he has referred to as *the partis* or sometimes *the called*. He kills them and absorbs their special abilities. I think you witnessed this yourself with Chaplain, did you not?"

I don't answer. "What's your power?"

"I don't have one," he says and I don't believe him, but before I can hurt him, I hear someone cry out. I have a terrible moment of indecision as to whether I should kill Jeremiah or not. He doesn't give me a chance. I glance at the house for one second and when I look back, he's disappeared.

"Damn it," I mumble and run toward the house.

I've made it all the way back, climbing the steps when I realize it wasn't a real scream. Someone was just fumbling with a body. Just inside the door I look up and see the kid, her mismatched shoes clearing the top landing as she creeps up the stairs. I don't know why, but I hesitate to follow her.

Jackson puts a hand on my arm.

"Jeremiah has NRD," I say and pull her away from the staircase into the hallway. I see Lane pass with a body, but if he has seen us, he doesn't show any sign.

"What do you mean?" she asks, keeping her voice low.

I repeat what I heard.

"You think he's like Rachel and Jesse. Like Sullivan," she says because she never really did get the hang of calling him Caldwell.

"It would explain his interest in all of this," I say. I'm about to say more when I feel that familiar buzz in my brain.

"Shit. He's here." I whirl around and Jackson does the same, but we don't see him.

We both glance at the staircase toward Jesse, and at the same moment, dart forward. We don't make it up the stairs before an explosion rocks the house. A great boom rattles its frame and I hear the crack of splintering wood.

Lane unceremoniously drops the body he's carrying and Jackson and I pick up the slack, all of us filing out of the house away from the blast. As we come into the yard, I see Alice, running up to us, blond hair flying like a banner behind her.

"Where is Jesse?" she asks.

"Upstairs," I say as Jackson and I lower the body down.

"Upstairs?" she repeats as if it is unbelievable. And maybe it is. Thick black fumes funnel into the sky, and the entire upper level is on fire.

Somehow, I know the kid did it. She blew up the whole fucking room. *She's more than enough for him now*, that's what Jeremiah had said. A rush of relief and pride washes over me. God, I hope it's true.

Alice is screaming Jesse's name and it is all I can do to hold her in place and keep her from running head-first into the fire.

The pressure between my ears builds to an uncomfortable degree. Jackson too turns toward the darkness just outside of the fire's dancing shadows and looks at the cornfield expectantly.

I hear his voice before I see him. I wonder if that is why he waited until full dark, simply for the sake of his entrance.

Brinkley, he whispers in my head like we are the oldest of friends. *I'm so glad you came.*

CHAPTER SEVENTY

7:15 P.M.

Jesse emerges from the smoldering house. I move to grab ahold of her and keep her close but I'm not quick enough. Jesse passes me, walking out into the yard toward the corn swaying in the firelight.

She just stares at it, as if waiting for something to happen. Then I realize she must be able to hear Caldwell in her head as well as I can—if not better.

Caldwell slips between the stalks into full view, meeting her in the yard. He's the perfect polished politician, with one exception. He's dragging a burned body.

She did this, he tells me, squeezing himself into the small space between my temples. Even twenty feet away, I can see his lips aren't moving.

She's becoming quite the little monster, Brinkley. I'm so sad you won't live to see her in her full glory. Or maybe you don't want to see it. Isn't that why you've been so hard on her all these years? Aren't you afraid of what will happen the moment you loosen that collar? Don't want her to be like me, do you?

Alice sees Caldwell and charges forward, no doubt with

the intention of putting herself between him and Jesse. I grab her arm with my left hand.

"No, no, wait," I say when she starts to struggle. "Look."

Caldwell's men emerge from the darkness, guns drawn. How did he get them all here? I'd heard no helicopters or engines. If he'd carried them, the way he'd carried Maisie back to Georgia, his gift must've grown in the last ten years.

He speaks aloud, for whose benefit I'm not sure. "He was supposed to guard this house." He drops the charred body without ceremony. "But he was too afraid to confront you. He hid upstairs, cowering like a dog. I only gave him two jobs: sedate and annihilate any unwanted guests. It was hardly too much to ask for, now was it?"

Were we unwanted? I think. *I thought you'd been counting down to this day.*

Caldwell turns his gaze to me and grins.

"You look well, Alice," Caldwell says. I feel her tense in my grip and I let go of her, but stay close.

"He can read your mind," Jesse says. So she does know. Good. She isn't as in the dark about this part of him as I feared.

She's going to tear you apart, I think at him.

You really think so? I would love a challenge.

"You are a smart, smart girl," he says to Alice.

I've missed something. Perhaps because he is having conversations with everyone. Alice, Jesse, me and maybe even his men. "If only you hadn't caused me so much grief, I'd have liked to get to know you better."

What is it about Alice? I ask him. *She's got you on your toes.*

Why would I tell you that? He laughs.

I don't give up that easily. *What can she do to you?*

Jesse makes the smallest of movements and then I see the pale purple shimmer envelope her.

Caldwell must see it too because he lifts his hands. Alice moves forward to stop him from touching Jesse, and I have to grab her again and hold her back. She's safer here near the porch with me. Lane seems to understand this already. He stands quiet and ready on my right.

"Look," Lane whispers.

Caldwell touches the pale purple light. Like water, it ripples and glides around Jesse.

His grin widens as he presses harder, his fingers flattening against a hard surface that wasn't there before. He can't get through it. It's some kind of force field.

"You do not disappoint," Caldwell says to Jesse. "Oh what I could do with your gifts."

He slides his hand admiringly over the barrier, and I see Jackson slip away and disappear around the side of the house. If only one of us can survive tonight, let it be Jackson.

Micah is waiting for her.

I put my hand on the Python, thinking for one panicked moment I should rush after her. I don't get the chance.

Caldwell appears in front of us, and I feel like a fool for not expecting it. I jerk forward to put myself between Caldwell and Alice, but the purple shimmer returns. This time it isn't around Jesse, who stands behind Caldwell. The field is enveloping Alice.

Caldwell can't touch her.

"Get away from her," Jesse says. Her warm breath rolls like smoke from between her lips into the cold night. The house is still burning, and I can feel the heat through the leather on my back.

You'll never use Jesse the way you want, I warn him.

Ah, but you aren't sure are you? Caldwell says, eyes meeting mine. He turns to Lane, standing unprotected beside me. *You've always wondered just when she might turn.*

She'll beat you, I bluff, but his words have shaken me. Every muscle in my body twitches for what will come next. *And Jackson will kill your AMP. After tonight, you'll have nothing.*

Let's find out, shall we?

Shots fire and I jump.

I tuck and roll but it is far from graceful. I'm sore from carrying Jackson and the sleeping victims. I think I may have even sprained something while running around in the trees. When I look up, Caldwell has Alice by the back of her coat. I lift my gun to shoot him, but Jeremiah and Nicole burst around the side of the house blasting their own firearms. Caldwell disappears.

Jeremiah speaks to Alice for the briefest of moments before she takes off into the corn.

Then he sees me and this time doesn't act like a deer caught in headlights. He covers me from the gunfire erupting all around us. Jeremiah's men, I realize, are in a full blown gunfight with Caldwell's men. All I care about is Jesse, who kneels nearby, pressing her hands over Lane's bleeding throat. Not a headshot. Good. Lane will live—well, after he dies.

Tucked safely into a corner of the porch I see Jeremiah look at Jesse as well. I shove my gun under his chin.

"When you're gone, who is going to give Jesse the support she needs to defeat him?" he asks, trying to meet my gaze but unable to, given the tilt of his chin.

"Jackson."

"Alone?" Jeremiah says. When I don't answer he adds, "She is going to need me. They all are."

Jesse leaps up from Lane's dying body and takes off into the corn after Alice. An intense desire to go after her seizes me. I shove the barrel harder into Jeremiah's jaw before shoving him away and taking chase.

When I look back, Jeremiah is just watching me go, his expression unreadable.

I don't see the kid. I go in the direction I thought she went, but she isn't there. I hear the guttural moans of fighting, the thuds of flesh colliding with flesh.

I break through the side of the corn and find myself on the edge of the woods, just in time to see Jackson deliver a strong front kick to Micah's gut. Micah hits the dirt on his hands and knees, winded.

I point the Python at Micah's head and pull back the trigger.

"No," Jackson screams. "No."

She knocks my hand down. "He's my brother. He's my baby brother, Jim."

I look at the man kneeling in the dirt. The sack of shit is responsible for delivering Jesse to Caldwell not once, but twice, and he didn't give a damn if it got the girl killed. And that was just Jesse. How many other sketches had he rendered for Caldwell that cost someone their life?

"I'll do it," she begs, pulling on my arm. "I'll do it, I swear to god."

"If he lives, Jesse—"

"I know," she says, her face crumpling. "I know. I'll do it."

I hear a child crying and turn toward the sound.

"Go," Jackson says, terror taking ahold of her face. "Hurry."

I look at Jackson one last time and run.

*E*verything slows down. I can't seem to move through the cornrows fast enough, or escape the sounds of Jackson struggling. Hearing cries slightly to my left, I adjust my position, cutting across several rows as cornsilk brushes my face.

I squeeze between two tall stalks and see them.

Caldwell is choking Alice. He strikes her twice across the face with his free hand and it occurs to me he isn't using tricks on her. *Why?*

Why not use your tricks on Alice?

I see the three of them there, and in a moment of brilliant clarity, I know why he can't just kill her. If he kills Alice, it will forever turn Jesse against him, giving her the conviction she needs to destroy him once and for all. And yet, he can't let Alice live either. To let her live means Jesse can never be corrupted. She will always work against him, to protect the one she loves. Alice, too, will protect her in turn.

So here he sits, in a precarious balance, searching for a way to master her, subdue her, and take what he needs from his oldest daughter.

A child, the one Alice held onto earlier, clings to the back of her legs, screaming her head off.

The swell of fire to my left makes me glance at the blazing house, the smoke funneling into the sky. This is it. This is the place and moment I die.

This is my last chance to save myself.

No, I think. *It could never have ended any other way.*

It occurs to me now, I started my journal in the wrong place. I began with the moment Memphis walked into the office and sat down in front of me. But we began before that, the moment a boy in a bomber vest stumbled through my rifle's scope.

If I hadn't shot Aziz, I wouldn't have come back to America and joined the FBRD. Raising my gun that once had caused me to raise my gun a thousand times. Out of guilt, out of necessity—it didn't matter.

So here I am.

Jesse bursts into view and slams her fist into his jaw. She gets in two more hits, and I can tell by the wild, angry expression on her father's face, he is both surprised and furious. He hits her back, and the world speeds up, pulling itself into sharp focus.

I dart forward, drawing the Python as I move.

Jesse hits the dirt, her knees giving underneath her while Alice staggers at her side, protected by Jesse's own force field.

Protect yourself. Why won't you protect yourself?

Because I don't deserve to be saved.

Hadn't I said this? But I see the kid in the dirt, giving all she's got for the sake of someone she loves.

She does deserve to be saved. I regret that I never told her so. I regret that I'll never have a chance to explain why I was so hard on her, why I was so scared that if I didn't ride her ass she'd become like him, that she would let her power twist her into something darker. I'd called her *kid*, *his* kid, never seeing her for herself.

I was no better than Caldwell.

I lift my gun and shoot.

Only I do not see the bullet hit him. In the darkness stretching out endlessly in front of me, I see Charlie.

He comes forward, places a hand on each side of my neck and smiles.

Jim. Am I glad to see you—

Did you enjoy this book? You can make a BIG difference.

I don't have the same power as big New York publishers who can buy full spread ads in magazines and you won't see my covers on the side of a bus anytime soon, but what I *do* have are wonderful readers like you.

And honest reviews from readers garner more attention for my books and help my career more than anything else I could possibly do—and I can't get a review without **you!**

So if you would be so kind, I'd be very grateful if you would post a review for this book. It only takes a minute or so of your time and yet you can't imagine how much it helps me.

It can be as short as you like and yes, I cherish every. single. one.

So please go to your preferred retailer and leave a review for this book today.

Eternally grateful,

Kory

Get Your Three Free Stories Today

Thank you so much for reading *Dying for Her*. I hope you're enjoying Jesse's story. If you'd like more, I have a free, exclusive Jesse Sullivan story for you. See Ally survive her first death replacement gig, during her first week as Jesse's assistant. You'll also see how the lovable Winston came to be Jesse's loyal companion.

You can only read this story for free by signing up for my newsletter. If you would like this story, you can get your copy by visiting **www.korymshrum.com/jessenewsletteroffer**

I will also send you free stories from the other series that I write. If you've signed up for my newsletter already, no need to sign up again. You should have already received this story from me. Check your email! Can't find it? ➜ Email me at **kory@korymshrum.com** and I'll take care of it.

As to the newsletter itself, I send out 2-3 a month and host a monthly giveaway exclusive to my subscribers. The prizes are usually signed books or other freebies that I think you'll enjoy. I also share information about my current projects, and personal anecdotes.

If you want these free stories and access to the giveaways, you can sign up for the newsletter at ➜ **www.korymshrum.com/jessenewsletteroffer**

If this is not your cup of tea (I love tea), you can follow me on Facebook at **www.facebook.com/korymshrum** in order to be notified of my new releases.

You just finished *Dying for Her: A Companion Novel* the third book in the Dying for a Living series. Keep reading for a special preview of *Dying Light*, the fourth novel in the Dying for a Living series.

Jesse

"Come on," I wail. "Jumping out of a burning building is not the craziest thing we've ever done!"

"If you hadn't panicked, the building wouldn't be on fire," Ally snaps back. She tucks the bundled laptop under her arm and starts yanking open desk drawers. Post-it notes of every color fly through the air, followed by pens, a stapler, paper-clips and a Kleenex box.

I search the open office space for another door. Nada. Only one way in and out.

"I had to do something." I thought firebombing the bad guy was my one good idea on this mission to retrieve a laptop for Jeremiah. "If I hadn't, we'd still be stuck with *him*."

We both turn our gaze to the locked door twenty feet

away. A row of unoccupied desks rests between us and where we entered. The office is spacious, with rows of silver table-tops running the length of the room. Spacious—but not spacious enough with a homicidal maniac just on the other side of the door.

Something large slams into the locked office door, rattling the walls. Ominous black smoke seeps through the cracks and the smell of campfire wafts in. That smell is surely going to cling to my hair until I wash it.

"Just because we've been reckless before doesn't excuse it now." Ally slams a desk drawer shut and yanks another open. Her disheveled blonde hair hides most of her face, revealing only terrified eyes. She gives up trying to find a weapon in the desk drawer and hurries to the window. Her gaze falls on the street below. "God, Jesse. *No*. We'll never survive a fall from this height."

I shrug and pucker my lips. "It's fine. I've fallen from higher. We'll be fine."

She blinks at me.

"You're forgetting about my shield thingy." I'm talking out of my ass here, but there is no way I'm letting him come in here and hurt her. He can trade punches with me all day if he wants, but not with Ally. I'll have to find a way to break the window, jump out, and shield her on the way down.

The door shakes for the fourth time and a thick crack appears to the left of the jamb. A thicker plume of black smoke rolls through the crack and floats to the ceiling. The white popcorn tiles disappear beneath the black fog.

I go to the window and look through the glass beside her. The glass is cold under my palms and my breath fogs on the surface despite the growing heat of the room. Down below, tiny cars cut corners around buildings. One could easily be mistaken for a child's toy.

Shit, it really *is* far down.

I meet Ally's eyes and shrug. "We don't have a lot of options."

Sweat forms at my hairline and in the folds where my coat sits snug against my body. Chicago shines brightly around us, each pinpoint of light from the buildings and streets illuminating the dark sky.

My gaze flits from building to building, from illuminated window to illuminated window, but I don't see salvation. We aren't close enough to another skyscraper to signal for help. No scaffolding or window-washer platform is available to carry us to the safety of solid ground or to the roof above, where we were supposed to meet Jeremiah.

The coms in our ears buzz incoherently for the billionth time. Ally sighs in irritation. As the coms stop crackling she mashes the speak button flat with her thumb. "For the thousandth time, we can't understand you. Something is wrong with our signal. If you can hear us, we are on the 34th floor of the Jensen building and we're trapped. Send help." A look of resolution solidifies on Ally's face. "Jason's going to kill us."

"No." I squeeze her arm. "So what if he's like a hell-bent terminator with unlimited healing ability." I snort, trying to hide my panic. "I've got this."

She cocks her head. "It's great you have firebombs and shields but we have to be careful. We don't know the repercussions of your powers yet."

"And getting ourselves locked in burning buildings with raging madmen is playing it *so* safe."

"You know what I mean." She steps away from the window and shifts the laptop in her arms. She yanks open more office drawers.

I arch an eyebrow. "A paper cut isn't going to hurt him."

"Paper cuts hurt." She forces a smile. "But we need something to slow him down. And you're not helping."

I throw my hands up and pick an aisle of desks. After

uselessly searching two drawers, I lift one of the office chairs and immediately know this flimsy, ergonomic piece of crap won't be able to break a window. I throw it anyway. It bounces off the glass and comes back at me with a vengeance, clipping my knee.

"Fuckity fuck! Ow. *Ow*."

Ally looks up from the drawer and scowls at me. "Injuring yourself before he even breaks into the room is not what I had in mind."

I give her a hard stare, rubbing my throbbing knee and stumbling to another desk.

I have half a mind to remind her that it wasn't *my* idea to come to Chicago. I was happy in Nashville. Sure, my boyfriend Lane—ex-boyfriend—wasn't talking to me, but everything else was okay. The first time Jason, the insta-healing terminator tried to rip my head off, Ally had a fit. Jeremiah capitalized on it, of course.

Come to Chicago where it's safer. We have more people and more power there. And Caldwell is up to something in the city. We could really use the extra hands.

I just wanted to stay in bed and mourn Brinkley, the man who'd given his life trying to kill Caldwell. Everyone else keeps acting like I'm supposed to be working here.

The crack in the door widens and I see an angry eye fix on me. Jason screams as if the very sight of me enrages him.

Gabriel appears at a desk two rows up from the one I'm searching. He flickers in and out, unable to hold his form with another partis—a weirdo with powers like me—nearby. He's crystal clear when I'm alone, but when there's two or more partis, I'm lucky if Gabriel can materialize at all. This is real inconvenient given that I need him most when the others show up looking for a fight.

"Here." Gabriel points at a giant rock sitting on top of one of the desks. "Use this."

No, not a rock, I realize. I place my hands on the massive stone. It's an amethyst the size of a grapefruit. Beside it sits a little note: *Don't touch me. Please. You'll change my energy.*

I look up, but Gabriel's gone.

I lift the rock off the desktop. It sinks into my palms like dead weight, the purple spikes poking my flesh. "Sorry, but I need your energy to club this fucker."

I meet eyes with Jason again as he inches his fingers through the crack and starts swiping at the locking mechanism we latched behind us.

"Get over here," I shout to Ally.

Ally makes it halfway across the room before the door explodes. Splinters the size of my leg fly at my face. I duck behind the desk, clutching the gigantic stone to my chest.

I peek over the tabletop and see Jason standing in the flames. His body smolders. His blistered arm melts from burnt to scabby to pink. He spots me behind the desk and we lock eyes. His face twists into a murderous grin.

"Stop hiding," he calls out. "Let's do this."

In my peripheral vision, Ally darts to another desk, staying low.

Jason takes a step toward me. "Just think, this power could be yours if you'd challenge me already."

"Fighting is such a commitment." I stand slowly, but keep the desk between us. I'm hoping it buys me time if he does anything crazy like lunge for my throat. "You have to get close. You have to touch people. Sometimes, like you, they *smell*. No, thank you."

Jason's face goes perfectly smooth. Was it something I said?

A flash of black wings catches my eye. Gabriel's still here, even if he can't materialize. The scent of rain overtakes me as Gabriel dials up my power. My muscles contract and my body warms. My skin starts to itch around the collar of my shirt and across my belly. I feel like I have to pee.

I try not to squirm. "You know who else is in the city? Caldwell. Why don't you kill him instead?"

Jason's face twists up in fury again. "After I'm finished with you."

"Why does everyone keep saying that?" I would put my hands on my hip if not for the giant amethyst. "Don't you think I'm a badass?"

"You're smaller."

My temper flares. "You're trying to kill me because I'm *short?*"

Ally coughs on the smoke filling the room and I jerk my head toward the sound. Jason doesn't hesitate.

"Jesse!" Gabriel's voice booms in my head.

My soul rips open, power exploding from my center in all directions. It's like someone is yanking my intestines out of my belly button. I'm so overwhelmed but I can't stop the power from flooding out of me or even slow it down.

Fire and smoke whoosh away from me as if blown by a great wind. The air around me shimmers like pavement on a hot day. Blue flames roll over the surface of my body, suspended about three inches above my skin before erupting outward toward Jason, the office around us and anything else in its path. The only object that is safe is the amethyst cradled in my hands.

The walls and ceiling shudder under the force of my firebomb, raining dust and plaster down on our heads. One minute the windows shatter, and glass spills out into the night air. The next minute cold winter air is sucked into the room.

I open my eyes and find Jason sprawled on the floor, unconscious. My power blast knocked him out, burned his skin, but didn't kill him. Damn.

I come around the desk, or what is left of it, and peer closer. His flesh is already healing.

I try to use my breath to slow my heart rate. I need to calm down, but my head is throbbing.

"Ally?"

No answer.

"Ally!"

"Here." She pulls herself to standing in the middle of a cluster of desks that had obviously been pushed together in the blast.

She shakes glass out of her hair and checks the laptop in her arms for damage.

"Kill him," Gabriel says in my ear. The weight of the amethyst doubles in my hands. "*Kill* him."

The idea of killing Jason and taking his healing powers appeals to me. Instead of having to die in order to heal myself, I could simply stay alive, and after a few breaths, be as good as new again. Wasn't that a hell of a prospect? Less pain. Less wasted time. Less danger for myself and the people around me.

I lift the amethyst, my eyes fixed on his skull.

"Jesse."

I lift the rock a little higher as a strange calm washes over me. No, more than calm. Peace tinged with excitement. Oh god, I *want* to kill him. I don't think I've ever wanted to kill anyone.

"*Jesse.*"

Ally's face appears in front of mine. Eye to eye, she blocks my view of Jason. "Baby." She's whispering. "We need to get out of here."

Her voice. Something about Ally's voice seeps into my mind and untangles my thoughts. The cold hand inside me, the one delighting at the idea of peeling Jason open and stealing his ability to heal, grows warm. Its hold on me slackens as her brown eyes come into focus. I can't murder someone in front of Ally. What the hell am I thinking?

My muscles relax and I let the amethyst slip from my fingers to the floor.

"Come on." Ally squeezes my shoulders. "Maybe we can crawl down the hall a little bit and find the stairs."

"No we can't go that way—" I don't finish my thought. The smallest movement steals my attention and I turn just as Jason snatches up the amethyst and throws it at Ally.

"No!" I scream as the rock sails through the air. "Gabriel!"

My shield goes up around Ally. The shimmery purple light envelops her from head to toe. The rock ricochets off the force field, shoots through the broken window and out into the night. Jason screams and runs at me, head down as if he might tackle me like some football player.

"Fuck this." I sidestep Jason and grab hold of Ally. Her shield falters just long enough for me to wrap her in my arms and yank her forward. Before she can process what is about to happen, I shove her out the big window and don't let go.

Her shriek is muffled by the wind whipping around us, tearing at our hair and clothes.

I suppose this is a perfectly natural reaction to your friend shoving you out of a high-rise building.

"It's okay." I squeeze her against my chest. "The shield will hold."

"Right?" I ask Gabriel.

"What about you? What about you?" Ally screams.

"You will not survive the fall." He plummets with us, his wings folding back to embrace the drop. "You must shield yourself."

"Ally lives, not me. We have a deal."

"You must shield yourself also."

"I don't know how. You have to help me."

"Envision it." Gabriel's wings open, lifting him up into the air. "See it grow larger."

The field shines about an inch or so above Ally's skin, it touches parts of me, but it sure as hell doesn't cover anything important.

"Hurry," Gabriel says. "See it around you."

I close my eyes and see us falling in my head. The building rushes past us. The freezing air tears at our clothes and hair relentlessly. Lights shine from windows in a blur as we pass. I picture my shield bigger. I picture it around me and Ally, covering us both from head to toe.

"Good. Do not stop now," Gabriel says.

I peek my eyes open to see purple has crept over my arms and shoulder, the shield half devouring my body—until pain erupts through my legs, my back, and the whole world goes black.

Did you enjoy this excerpt from *Dying Light*? You can find and purchase the book at your favorite retailer or learn more at www.korymshrum.com.

ACKNOWLEDGMENTS

I would like to gratefully acknowledge my Horsemen of the Bookocalyspe: Kathrine Pendleton, Angela Roquet, and Monica La Porta. Thanks also to Mike Billington and J. Richie for their expertise on all things military. And a shout-out to Michelle Pike for last minute edits. You guys were indispensable. All mistakes are my own.

Many thanks to family, friends, bloggers, and Twitter-ers who first showed love for *Dying for a Living* and no less enthusiasm for this third book. There are too many to name, but I adore every single one of you.

Thanks to Tim O' Brien for writing a great and inspiring book *The Things They Carried* (Mariner Books; 1st edition October 13, 2009), which I shamelessly used as Gloria's bible.

Thanks to John K. Addis for his help with the cover and author photo. And for you horror fans, I highly recommend his awesome book, The Eaton.

And thank you, Kimberly Benedicto, my love and biggest fan. I hope you like this ending better.

Kory M. Shrum is author of the bestselling *Shadows in the Water* and *Dying for a Living* series, as well as several other novels. She has loved books and words all her life. She reads almost every genre you can think of, but when she writes, she writes science fiction, fantasy, and thrillers, or often something that's all of the above.

In 2020, she launched a true crime podcast "Who Killed My Mother?" sharing the true story of her mother's tragic death. You can listen for free on YouTube or your favorite podcast app.

When not writing or producing her show, she can usually be found under thick blankets with snacks. The kettle is almost always on. When she's not eating, reading, writing, or indulging in her true calling as a stay-at-home dog mom, she loves to plan her next adventure. (Travel.)

She lives in Michigan with her equally bookish wife, Kim, and their rescue pug, Charley.

She'd love to hear from you!
www.korymshrum.com

ALSO BY KORY M. SHRUM

Dying for a Living series

Dying for a Living

Dying by the Hour

Dying for Her: A Companion Novel

Dying Light

Worth Dying For

Dying Breath

Dying Day

Shadows in the Water: Lou Thorne Thrillers

Shadows in the Water

Under the Bones

Danse Macabre

Carnival

Devil's Luck

Design Your Destiny Castle Cove series

Welcome to Castle Cove

Night Tide

The City: the 2603 novels

The City Below

The City Within

Learn more about Kory's work at: www.korymshrum.com